Margaret Dashwood and the Enchanted Atlas

Beth Deitchman

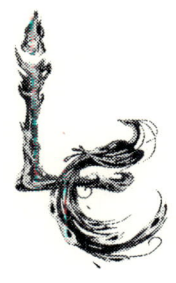

Luminous Creatures Press Books

Secret Room
By Emily June Street

The Velocipede Races
By Emily June Street

Mary Bennet and the Bloomsbury Coven
By Beth Deitchman

The Painted Dog and Other Stories
By Beth Deitchman & Emily June Street

Ungodly Hungers
By Beth Deitchman & Emily June Street

Coming Soon:
The Gantean
By Emily June Street

CHAPTER I

*M*argaret Dashwood gazed out the carriage window, eagerly taking in the passing scenery. At any moment she expected to see Norland Park's beloved shape rising above the gentle landscape of Sussex. She pressed her forehead against the glass and sighed. As the post-chaise rounded the bend and the familiar lane unrolled in front of her, Margaret could no longer contain her impatience. She opened the window, letting in a rush of cool air, and leaned out for a better view.

"Margaret, do sit down," said Mrs. Dashwood, her voice trembling with emotion. "I worry for your safety."

"But Mama! How can I be still when at any moment our dear, dear Norland will appear? The last place we ever saw Papa alive?"

Mrs. Dashwood remained silent, dabbing at the corners of her eyes with a handkerchief. Margaret, not wishing to upset her mother further, resumed her seat but left the window open.

"There it is! Dearest Norland!" Margaret cried. "Oh, see how the sun catches the stone! It is still the most beautiful building in all of England."

Mrs. Dashwood smiled. "I believe you exaggerate at least a little, my dearest." She leaned against Margaret for a better view. Mrs. Dashwood's breath caught. "But it certainly is a handsome house."

"Do you miss it, Mama?" Margaret asked as her mother settled back into her seat.

"From time to time, my dear, although I am so fond of our cottage in Devonshire." She patted Margaret's hand. "Besides, who knows what alterations we shall find after six years' absence."

"Indeed" was Margaret's only reply as she resumed staring out the window and willed the carriage to greater speed.

Soon enough they swept up the broad drive. A lone figure stood outside, dwarfed by Norland Manor's grandeur. Margaret assumed her sister-in-law Fanny, or more likely her brother John, had sent a servant to greet them.

"Is that John?" came Mrs. Dashwood's incredulous query.

"I believe it is," Margaret replied. "I did not expect to see my brother so immediately upon our arrival."

"Nor did I," said Mrs. Dashwood. "What do you suppose it signifies?"

But Margaret had no chance to voice her opinion, for the coachman had opened the door to assist the ladies. Margaret took his hand, stepped from the coach, and then waited for her mother to alight. Together they turned toward Mr. John Dashwood.

"Welcome to Norland," John said. He took a step forward as though to embrace Mrs. Dashwood, but stopped. "I must apologize for Fanny's absence. She feels rather ill and regrets terribly not being here to welcome you to *our* home."

"Indeed." Mrs. Dashwood's tone contained a rare chill.

An awkward moment passed in which Mrs. Dashwood fixed her eyes on John, who stared at the ground.

"Shall we go inside?" Margaret suggested.

"Yes, splendid!" replied John. "Follow me. We have made two rooms ready for your stay. Margaret, you shall be in your former chamber. I suppose you would like to wash away the dirt of travel and then take some refreshment?"

"Thank you, John. We would," Mrs. Dashwood replied, relief coloring her voice.

"Very well. I shall see that your things are brought up to your rooms. In half an hour tea will be served in the salon. It is down—"

"I do remember where the salon is, John," said Mrs. Dashwood.

"Oh, yes, of course." Color rose in John's normally pale cheeks. "Well, then, I shall leave you to it." He made a hasty bow and hurried off.

Mother and daughter watched his progress down the hall and then exchanged glances filled with meaning. They climbed the stairs in silence, Margaret reflecting upon the bitter-sweetness of their return. At last they had arrived at the house that had so long been their home, the location of such happy memories, only to be reminded so forcibly that they were mere visitors, not even afforded the hospitality ordinarily bestowed upon strangers.

Margaret's thoughts were interrupted by their

arrival at her chamber. "Will you be all right, my dear?" enquired Mrs. Dashwood.

Margaret turned a bright face to her mother to allay the concern in Mrs. Dashwood's voice. "Of course, Mama. All will be well." She kissed her mother on the cheek. "I shall see you at tea. Perhaps you could have a little rest?"

Mrs. Dashwood clasped Margaret's hand briefly and then continued down the hallway. Margaret watched her go before reaching for the doorknob with a shaking hand. She took a deep breath and stepped inside. Almost nothing remained as it had been. She sighed. "What did I expect? I brought all of my effects to Devonshire. Why would Fanny not choose to change everything else?"

Margaret stood by the window and stared out at the grounds, resuming her earlier reflections. She had been only thirteen when her brother and sister-in-law had taken possession of the manor, a child too young to understand the whims of her great uncle's will, in which Norland would pass from Mr. Dashwood to his son John and to John's son, Harry, then just a baby of two or three. In the depths of their mourning, Margaret, her mother, and her two sisters had found themselves at the mercy of John and Fanny, who had made their desire to be sole residents of Norland Park abundantly clear.

She left the window and settled in the chair by the cold hearth, still deep in memories. Her mother and sisters had not known that she nourished a secret grief during the months after they left Norland; not only had Margaret lost her home and her father, but she had also been deprived of her only friend in the magical world. With this thought a sudden fear gripped Margaret, bringing her back to the present. She clasped her hands to her mouth. What if Fanny, in her zeal to make Norland Park her own, had discovered the books and other magical items hidden throughout her father's study? What might her sister-in-law have done?

Margaret giggled nervously as she imagined the dreaded event. "Oh, dear," she said to herself. "I should think Fanny would have run screaming from the house. She could barely abide the idea of Elinor marrying Edward. How would she feel knowing that *she* had married a sorcerer's son?" That thought gave Margaret comfort. "No, neither of them could have discovered the books and remained civil, which means I shall find what I have come for."

She reached into her pocket and pulled out a wrinkled paper. Until she had received the letter from her father's solicitor, Margaret had had no idea that anything of her father's had remained behind in Sussex. Before the Dashwood ladies' departure, Margaret had collected all the books she could find with hopes of continuing her magical education by herself. For five years those books had been her sole connection to her father and the magical world to which he had introduced her. But then this letter had arrived six months before on her eighteenth birthday, surprising and delighting Margaret, who again opened it and read:

Dear Miss Dashwood,

I write on the occasion of your eighteenth birthday to inform you of an inheritance awaiting you at Norland. Your father insists that you will understand and will know where to find the items in question.

Although I must confess that I cannot fathom his meaning, should you have any questions, you may direct them to me at the address provided.

I wish you the best of luck and felicitations for your birthday.

Sincerely,

Mr. Frederick More, Esquire

Margaret's excitement had given way to despair as she considered the difficulty that faced her. She had long since learned spells for revealing items hidden by magic, but convincing Fanny and John to receive her and Mrs. Dashwood had seemed an insurmountable task. And yet, here she sat, in her former chamber, mere hours away from searching her father's study. She had only to survive a few hours' conversation with John and Fanny. Sighing at the prospect, she glanced at the little clock above the hearth, which reminded her that she had only a little while to prepare. Margaret rose and poured water into the basin on the table near the door and splashed a little on her face. Once refreshed, she braced herself to return downstairs for tea.

When Margaret arrived in the salon, she was surprised to find Fanny seated across from John, the picture of good health. Margaret glanced over to her mother with raised eyebrows, but said only, "Hello, Fanny. I am glad you are well after all."

"Thank you, Margaret. But I can assure you my health is precarious."

"Should you be sitting with us?" Mrs. Dashwood said.

"Propriety demands that the *mistress* of the house be present to receive her guests."

"Indeed."

Silence fell.

"I hope you find your rooms comfortable," John ventured at length.

"Yes, John, thank you," replied Mrs. Dashwood.

"I imagine you shall discover a number of changes have been made to Norland," Fanny said. "It is only fitting that the house should reflect the taste of its mistress."

"Oh, yes," agreed John, all eagerness. "The alterations we have made demonstrate only the finest taste."

"Oh?" Mrs. Dashwood hid her feelings more effectively than Margaret would have thought possible, indeed more effectively than Margaret herself managed. How proud her oldest sister Elinor would be of their mother's conduct!

As the tea was served, silence descended again upon the occupants of the salon, broken only by the sound of spoons clinking against porcelain. John cleared his throat as though to speak, but at a frown from Fanny, turned his attention to the cake on his plate. Mrs. Dashwood sipped her tea and said, "The tea is lovely, Fanny."

"Thank you," Fanny replied.

Margaret tasted her tea, casting surreptitious glances at Fanny's alterations to the room. So much that had reflected the simple elegance of Norland's former inhabitants had been replaced with ostentatious arrangements of *objets d'art*, which proclaimed their worth if not their owners' taste. Margaret's eyes alighted on a figurine of a shepherdess in brightly colored Grecian garb situated on the mantel between two plaster angels complete with little wings. Next to them, as though standing guard, was a bronze Foxhound. A bust of Shakespeare completed the strange tableaux. Margaret was sorely tempted to cause the dog to bark and the little angels to fly, but she restrained herself. She could not afford to alienate Fanny, not until she had managed to retrieve the books she knew awaited her.

"Margaret," came Mrs. Dashwood's voice, interrupting Margaret's reverie, "John has asked you a question."

"I beg your pardon, John. I must have gotten lost in thought. The room has been altered, and I was attempting to see it as it was before we left. Pray, what would you like to know?"

"I was wondering how you occupy your time in Devonshire?"

Margaret sipped her tea. Of course, if she were to tell him the truth, John would turn her out of his house. Instead she said, "Oh, in the usual ways that young ladies occupy their time. I walk if the weather is fine. I read when it is not. From time to time I attend a ball if I am inclined to dance. And I practice the *pianoforte*."

"I suppose as the only daughter left at home you are a comfort to your mother," John said amiably.

"She is indeed!" Mrs. Dashwood said with enthusiasm.

As no one wished to contradict this statement,

silence again settled over the salon, only to be relieved by the chiming of the mantel clock and the entrance of the maid to set the fire.

Mrs. Dashwood cleared her throat and asked, "Where is Harry? I should think he would be old enough to join us for tea without his nurse."

Fanny brightened at the mention of her son. "Harry is away at school. All the reports indicate that he is *thriving*, as I knew he would."

Margaret strongly suspected that her sister-in-law embellished tales of Harry's success, but held her tongue, concentrating instead on her tea and glancing from time to time at the mantel clock. She let her mind wander as Fanny prattled on, regaling them with tales of Harry's schoolboy antics. After what seemed an age, the dreadful hour ended, and Margaret was released from her brother and sister-in-law's company until dinner. Everyone breathed a sigh of relief.

Much to Margaret's dismay, dinner proved even more tedious than tea, with the company already having exhausted all topics of conversation. But at long last the day came to a close, and Margaret returned to her chambers to prepare for her evening's excursion. While she waited for signs that the household had settled into sleep, Margaret retrieved *Magic for Stealth*, the little book full of spells for concealment and revealing that she had found in a market in London when visiting her sister Marianne and Colonel Brandon. She turned to the page detailing the True Vision Spell, useful for revealing traces of magic and hidden objects, and reviewed the directions:

To enact the True Vision spell, the sorcerer must first close his eyes and clear his mind. With eyes closed and mind cleared, begin chanting the incantation: "With no veil let me see all that lies in front of me." On the third time through the incantation, open the eyes. If the spell has been performed correctly, the sorcerer will see both what is visible to the naked eye and anything that is concealed by magic, including treasures and traps.

The spell had proven easy enough to master, even after she made her usual adjustment of translating the incantation into French, Margaret's language of preference for spell casting.

As the hour was still early, Margaret indulged her curiosity and enacted the spell in her chamber. She closed her eyes and quieted her mind, a difficult task given her excited state. But soon enough she felt the calm of meditation settle over her, and she whispered, "*Que le voile se retire; que la vérité soit révélée,*" three times. She opened her eyes, but saw nothing out of the ordinary. "Ah, well. I had not the skill to hide anything with magic when I last called this room my own. Had I found something, I would have been surprised indeed!"

She returned her book to its hiding place in her trunk and then crept to the door. Stillness filled the hallway, and Margaret felt certain everyone had settled into sleep. She steadied herself against her growing excitement. Grasping the muslin bag she had retrieved from her trunk, she entered the hallway, where she stood, waiting for her eyes to adjust to the darkness. Then Margaret headed down the hall toward the stairs.

A momentary panic overtook her when one of the stairs creaked, and Margaret paused, fearing that she would soon be discovered. A few minutes of stillness proved that no one had heard. With breath held, she slipped carefully down the rest of the stairs, exhaling in relief when she reached the landing. Margaret hurried to her father's study.

"How peculiar," she whispered when she found the door locked. Then she fixed her attention on the lock and commanded, "*Laissez-moi entrer!*" After a moment of silence, she heard the satisfying click of the lock opening. A second, indecipherable sound accompanied that of the lock, but Margaret paid it no mind. When she gained the safety of the room, she leaned against the closed door, thankful to have arrived without discovery. From her vantage point, she could already tell that the study had remained untouched, her father's things still as she had left them, except now covered in a thick layer of dust.

As she wandered through the oddly unchanged room, taking in the details, Margaret recalled the night six years before when she had undertaken the same task. That evening she had left her father's study, she thought for the last time, her small arms laden with as many of his books and papers as she could find. Time had effected several changes between that night and her return visit. Though she still nurtured a gentle sorrow, her eyes were not clouded with tears for a recently departed father, and she had five more years of magical education, as improvised as it had been using only her father's rescued books.

"Nothing seems to have been touched in years," Margaret marveled, picking up a dry quill from the desk. It crumbled in her fingers. "How is it possible

Fanny has not subjected this room to her taste?" With a burst of pride in her father's skill, she concluded that the lock had proven impenetrable to Norland's current inhabitants. Otherwise how could she explain the study's untouched state? It was a good room, spacious, well furnished, with a big hearth. Thick rugs adorned the floors. Moreover, the placement of the enormous walnut desk afforded a view out the large windows that included the woodlands. Margaret sighed, grateful that something of her former life remained intact.

Once Margaret was certain that nothing of any value to her had been left lying about, she closed her eyes and cleared her mind. In the silence of her father's study, she found this task even easier. She performed the True Vision Spell and then opened her eyes, gasping at the sight in front of her. Nearly everywhere she looked she saw secret compartments filled with her father's belongings. "Goodness, Papa! What a treasure you have left behind!"

The first compartment was in the desk and required her to pull out the big drawer on the left side. She felt around inside the empty space for a latch, her fingers finding it almost immediately. When the latch clicked, a little door sprang open. Margaret knelt in front of the desk and reached into the compartment. By the light of the moon streaming through the windows, she made a quick examination of each item she pulled from the desk. There were four volumes of text written in her father's hand. "He must have kept records," Margaret supposed. A glimpse inside the first book confirmed her assumption. One by one she placed the books into her bag.

After Margaret emptied the desk of its treasure, she turned her gaze to the first set of compartments hidden in the bookshelves lining the walls. The True Vision Spell revealed that more books awaited her once she managed to open the compartment. "Now how do I open this one?" Margaret murmured, considering the shelves. "Oh, Papa!" She smiled, reaching for a book midway through the second shelf. "You made this one too simple." As she pulled *Sermons to Young Women* from the shelf, she heard a grinding of gears and stepped back, still grasping the book. The entire shelf rotated, disappearing into the wall, while another shelf came forward with a little lurch.

"Goodness!" Margaret exclaimed at the sight of so many books. She looked into her sack, which was nearly full, and realized that she would require more than one night's efforts to recover all that her father had stored in his study. She began tucking more books into the bag, glad that she had made room in her trunk to accommodate her inheritance. "As it is, I am still not certain I shall be able to take everything."

Once she emptied the shelf, she heard the gears grind again, returning the original row of books to its place. "Ingenious," she whispered, and then, her bag full, she turned to leave. "Oh!" Margaret cried, frozen in her spot, rendered incapable of movement by what she faced. In front of her stood two ghostly forms, flanking the door. Both wore full armor and carried enormous battleaxes. Trembling, Margaret backed away until she was pressed against the bookshelves, unable to tear her eyes from this sight.

The two ghosts watched her with what Margaret could only imagine was curiosity and then slowly they bowed. With raised eyebrows, she dropped a little curtsy in reply. Nothing happened. Margaret studied the apparitions, an idea taking shape.

"Are you Ghostly Guards?" she asked, trying to keep her voice steady.

Both of the shadowy forms nodded.

"What an honor to meet you! I have read of the Ghostly Guard, of course. Did my father place you here to protect his study?"

The ghosts glanced at each other before the one on the right gave a curt nod.

"And have you kept everyone out until now?"

Again came a curt nod, accompanied by the faintest jingling of armor.

"Yet you allowed me in. Did my father instruct you to do that?"

Another nod.

Tears flooded Margaret's eyes, her tender feelings for her father as fresh as they were the day he exhaled his last breath. "Ah, Papa! How many times I have regretted your passing from this life! I only hope that with the help of your last effects I may grow to be as accomplished a sorceress as you were a sorcerer!"

The Ghostly Guards stood, unbothered by Margaret's outburst. Her tears lasted for another moment before she took hold of herself, thinking of her oldest sister Elinor's calm in the face of such emotional storms. A sudden wave of fatigue covered her. The effort of maintaining the True Vision Spell after a long day of travel was taking its toll.

"I shall have to return another time," she announced. "I have no more room in my bag."

As Margaret approached, the Guards moved aside, one of them holding the door for her. She curtsied to them before leaving. As soon as she had passed the threshold, the door closed behind her. The lock clicked softly, and she heard the same strange sound she had heard earlier. This time she recognized it as the clink and hiss of crossing axes.

Returning to her chamber, careful to make very little noise, Margaret reflected on the ease with which she had accomplished her task. Surely her father would have left traps? But perhaps, she reasoned, the Ghostly Guards were trap enough. With a shudder she wondered if their ghostly battleaxes could do as much damage as material ones.

Safely back in her room, Margaret unpacked her bag and stowed her father's belongings in the secret compartment she had devised for her trunk. Then she collapsed onto her bed and fell into a deep sleep.

CHAPTER II

*T*he following morning Margaret arose early enough to peruse one of her father's books before going downstairs to break her fast. She recovered it from its hiding place and settled herself by the window. Margaret noticed immediately that Mr. Dashwood had used the diaries to catalogue his magical discoveries, record interesting spells, and explore his ideas. "Papa," she whispered as she turned a page to study yet another diagram of a complex spell, "how I wish I had had more time with you. My esteem for you grows ever more ardent with each page!" A tear coursed down her cheek at this proclamation.

When she had recovered herself, Margaret turned to the next page and gasped. There was her name! She read with alacrity:

May the Eleventh, Norland Park.

It gives me great joy to have discovered in my youngest daughter an aptitude for magic. This morning I observed Margaret playing with a doll. When the doll rolled away from her, she held out her hand, and the doll jumped into it. Fortunately, no one else witnessed this event. I shall continue to watch her progress.

Margaret paused. She had no memory of this incident, though a hazy vision of dolls dancing in her nursery took form in her mind. "It is a miracle no one else discovered me!" she said. Warmed by her father's obvious pride in her ability, she resumed reading, hoping to learn more about her earliest attempts at magic. But she found instead that his thoughts had shifted.

My own work proceeds apace. I believe I have found the spell that will help me to complete the next stage of my current endeavor. It is a little known spell, very difficult to perform, but I expect that under the correct circumstances, it should not affect my vitality too seriously. I cannot afford to cause my dear wife any more worry, or she will never leave me alone with my work. She frets so over the smallest sign of fatigue or illness.

Margaret laughed. How often he had made the same observation aloud to her! Margaret remembered with fondness her father's words when he sent her to rest after a magic lesson: "So that your mother will not worry about you, my dear. The less attention she pays to what you do, the easier it will be to do it."

The clock on her mantel announced the hour,

informing Margaret that she would soon be expected in the breakfast parlor. Reluctantly, she closed her father's book and hid it with the others. Before leaving her room, she gave herself a quick glance in the mirror and then proceeded downstairs.

The rest of her family had already gathered around the table when she arrived in the breakfast parlor. Ignoring a chilly look from Fanny, Margaret sat next to her mother and poured herself a cup of tea.

"I hope you found everything accommodating?" Fanny said.

"I did, thank you, Fanny."

"Indeed? I thought perhaps your lateness indicated some difficulty in sleeping."

"None at all, but I thank you for your concern." Margaret did her best to remain cordial. Elinor had written at length about the subject, entreating her to remember her manners "no matter how Fanny behaves."

As usual, however, Fanny seemed inclined to test both Margaret and her mother's promises to Elinor. "I imagine you do not use half of the china and linens that you brought from Norland to Devonshire, do you Mrs. Dashwood?"

"As a matter of daily use, no I suppose I do not." Mrs. Dashwood kept her eyes on the slice of toast she was covering with marmalade. "But it is comforting to know that they are there for the guests who visit us at the cottage."

"Indeed," Fanny said. She pursed her lips.

"I say," John began, unaware of his wife's displeasure, "I thought I heard someone wandering the house last night, but when I looked out of my room, I found I was quite wrong."

"Are you certain?" Fanny asked. "Who would be wandering about in the middle of the night? Should I gather the servants and question them?"

Margaret turned her full attention to her breakfast, hoping no one noticed the color rising in her cheeks.

"No, no, I do not think that will be necessary," John said. "Perhaps I was dreaming."

"Perhaps," Fanny replied, sounding unconvinced.

"Fanny," Margaret said, anxious to steer the conversation away from this dangerous territory. "I would like to take a tour of the park today. What improvements should I anticipate?"

Fanny turned an animated countenance toward Margaret. "I am pleased you asked, Margaret! We spent a good deal of time and funds on our improvements to the park. I imagine *you* may not appreciate it, but the park was in quite a sad state when we took possession. Now, however—"

Margaret nodded absently as Fanny spoke, only half listening. Instead she combed her memory for a spell she might employ to muffle the sounds of her movement through the house that evening. At last she decided to consult *Magic for Stealth* when she returned to her room.

"What do you think?" John said to Margaret.

Margaret turned to her brother, eyes wide. "About what?" she said.

John's face fell. "About the changes to Norland that Fanny has effected?"

"Oh, I am sure that they are marvelous!" Margaret pretended to an enthusiasm she did not feel.

Fanny and John smirked at each other, their satisfaction in her words obvious. Margaret exchanged a pained glance with her mother.

Soon enough Margaret was released from the excruciating breakfast and prepared to wander the grounds. The day was fine, and she required only a shawl and her bonnet for protection against the breeze's slight chill. Margaret set out on the path that would take her to the walnut grove. But as she approached the grove's location, her stomach dropped. Where once magnificent trees had reached toward the sky, now stood a monstrosity of glass and timber, packed, Margaret could see even from her vantage, with plants. "But why?" Margaret lamented. "When the gardens produce such beautiful flowers, why would Fanny allow this *horror* to replace my trees?"

Disheartened, Margaret turned her back to the greenhouse and surveyed the landscape. With relief she saw that the estate's rich woodland still rambled across the property. She set out at once to take refuge in its cool depths.

The air, redolent of trees and undergrowth, seemed charged in the woodland, and Margaret followed her favorite path to the clearing where she and her father had spent many happy afternoons. It was here that her father had begun to teach her simple spells. Margaret stood in the center of the clearing and closed her eyes.

"Margaret, my dear," Mr. Dashwood said, "I have been watching you."

"Have you, Papa? Why?" Margaret replied, worried.

"No need to fret, Margaret. I have a secret to tell you if you can promise not to tell anyone."

Margaret adored secrets, but she sensed the weight of her father's charge. "Must I, Papa?"

"Yes, Margaret, I am afraid you must. It is terribly important."

Margaret's curiosity overwhelmed her and she promised, rather rashly, that she could keep the secret. "What is it, Papa?"

"I am a sorcerer."

"Oh, Papa, you are just being silly. There is no such thing as a sorcerer. They're just in fairy stories."

"You are wrong, my dear. Observe."

Margaret followed his gaze, intrigued by this odd turn of events. From her mother or Marianne, she expected strange declarations and beliefs, but not from her father. He appeared much steadier, like Elinor. Then Margaret gasped. She did not know how, but there was a leaf dancing toward her. Yet there was no wind.

"Hold out your hand," Mr. Dashwood instructed.

Margaret did as she was asked, and the leaf floated toward her, landed, twirled several times, and then settled on her palm. "How did you do that?" she whispered.

"Magic, my dear."

"And why did you show me?"

"Because you have magic in you, too. It is time for me to teach you to use it."

Margaret opened her eyes and dabbed at her cheeks with her handkerchief. "I must put a stop to this sentimental nonsense," she instructed herself with a firm voice. "What would John and Fanny think if they saw me indulging in such feelings? I would be subject to no end of disagreeable commentary." She tucked her handkerchief away and strode off to complete her examination of the grounds.

Her heart heavy with disappointment in the changes to Norland, Margaret returned to the house in time for tea. She stood outside the drawing room composing herself. Once certain that she could be civil, she entered. The room was empty but for her mother seated near the fire with her needlework.

"Ah, Margaret! I am relieved it is you. I thought perhaps—"

Margaret went to her mother's side. "I understand." She checked the door before continuing. "Time has not improved either of them. Nor has it been particularly kind to Norland."

"Oh?" said Mrs. Dashwood.

But before Margaret could enumerate the many insults suffered by the estate at Fanny's hands, the mistress herself entered the drawing room, John just behind her.

"Ah, you have already arrived," Fanny said. "Well,

I suppose I should ring for tea. I had not expected you to be so prompt."

"I did not wish to keep anyone waiting," Margaret replied as amiably as she could manage.

"How was your walk?" John asked.

"Lovely," Margaret replied. Then seeing a possibility for escape, she continued, "I am afraid I have overexerted myself." She punctuated her statement with a yawn.

"You should go to your room and rest, my dear," said Mrs. Dashwood with concern.

"But I do not wish to be unsociable."

"I insist, Margaret," said Mrs. Dashwood pointedly. "I could accompany you—"

Though it pained her to deny her mother refuge from Fanny and John, Margaret said, "Oh no, Mama. I shall be fine. I simply require a little rest, as you suggested."

"Of course, my dear. But if you need anything at all, you may call on me."

Margaret kissed her mother. "I shall, Mama. Fanny, John, please excuse me," she added before leaving. She could not help but overhear Fanny's comment as she exited the drawing room.

"Such a delicate constitution. How will she ever manage to take care of a husband and children, never mind a household?"

Margaret did not wait for her mother's reply, instead racing up the stairs and down the hall to her chamber. Once safely tucked away, Margaret passed an agreeable afternoon consulting *Magic for Stealth*. The shadows had begun lengthening by the time Margaret's search for a useful spell proved fruitful:

> *The Darkness Falls spell is a favorite amongst sorcerers who engage in clandestine activities. It casts a shadow around the sorcerer that both muffles any sound he may make and cloaks him in darkness. Only cats can see through the shadows around a sorcerer employing this spell, but as they seldom care what humans do, they pose no threat to the sorcerer's safety. The incantation is relatively simple for the complexity of the spell: "Darkness falls."*

"That will do," Margaret said, excited. "Once I make an adjustment, of course." She stood in front of her mirror and said, "*Que l'obscurité soit.*" With a little gasp she watched her form disappear behind a shadow. She gave silent thanks to Elinor for persisting in her French lessons even when Margaret had complained vehemently. "Nothing makes a spell sound prettier than translating it to French. Now to lift the shadow. How would that go? Ah, yes, *que l'obscurité se dissipe!*" She reappeared in the mirror, beaming at her success.

When Margaret arrived in the drawing room before dinner, she was surprised by the presence of a handsome stranger. She watched the stranger standing by the fire for a moment, taking in the details of his appearance—his tall stature, black curls, and graceful form. Before she could move further into the room, the gentleman turned and favored her with a smile. Margaret's knees weakened, and she struggled for composure. The stranger took a step toward her.

"My dear sister, I would like to present my friend Mr. Weston Ellsworth. Mr. Ellsworth, this is my youngest sister, Miss Margaret Dashwood.'

Margaret blinked at John, for she had not noticed him standing by the door. But recovering herself quickly, she held out her hand, which Mr. Ellsworth took. "Miss Dashwood," he said. He bowed gracefully to her, still clasping her hand in his. "How lovely to meet you. John has spoken so highly of his sisters. I must admit that I never believed his tales of their beauty. Yet here you stand before me, and I understand how wrong I was to doubt him!"

Margaret looked at John, barely able to conceal her astonishment.

"Yes, well, perhaps you have embellished my words a bit, Ellsworth," John said, turning away from Fanny's angry countenance.

"Not at all. In fact, I believe you were not liberal enough in your praise," said Mr. Ellsworth.

"I am pleased to meet you, Mr. Ellsworth. Will you be staying at Norland long?" Margaret said, eager to change the topic.

"Alas, no. I am on my way west and thought it would be a crime to avoid seeing Dashwood and his marvelous home." Ellsworth turned to Fanny. "Its mistress has taken such care of it." He bowed again. "But I am meant to stay only for dinner."

Fanny astonished Margaret with the warmth of her reply. "Such high praise from the master of Ellsworth Hall! I am quite overcome by the compliment!" She extended her hand for him.

Mr. Ellsworth brought Fanny's hand to his lips, the picture of charm. He turned to Margaret. "I am not sure I would characterize myself quite that way. My uncle was lord of the manor, but produced only one heir. My cousin inherited the title, but showed no interest in maintaining the family home, so it fell to me. It is not much, truly. Nothing like Norland."

"Mr. Ellsworth, you must not be so modest! Margaret, Mr. Ellsworth has the finest home in all of Yorkshire. Everyone believes so," Fanny said. "Do you not agree, John?"

"Of course!" John replied, perhaps more heartily than was necessary. "Ah, and here is Mrs. Dashwood," John added. "Mr. Ellsworth, I would like to present Margaret's mother, my father's second wife."

"Mrs. Dashwood," said Mr. Ellsworth with a bow.

Before Mrs. Dashwood could reply, Fanny raised her eyebrows meaningfully at John who said, "I suppose we should go in to dinner." Fanny took his arm and led him out of the drawing room.

Mrs. Dashwood smiled at Margaret and Mr. Ellsworth and then followed Fanny and John.

"May I, Miss Dashwood?" Mr. Ellsworth offered his arm.

"Thank you, Mr. Ellsworth."

"I count it a great honor, Miss Dashwood." Together they entered the dining room where Mr. Ellsworth pulled back Margaret's chair with a show of civility.

"Thank you, Mr. Ellsworth."

"Of course, Miss Dashwood." He took his seat directly across from her.

Fanny sniffed audibly, and Margaret glanced down the table in time to see her sister-in-law purse her lips at John. Margaret turned her attention to the floral arrangement on the table.

"What brings you to Norland Park, Miss Dashwood?" Mr. Ellsworth asked, breaking the silence.

"My mother and I are on our way to London to visit my sister and her husband. We have not seen Norland in many years, and I had a desire to stop at my childhood home. Fanny and John were kind enough to indulge me."

"Ah, so you will not be here long, either?"

"No, we leave the day after tomorrow."

"Then I need not feel it such a pity that I am to leave Sussex so soon after making your charming acquaintance."

She blushed but met his blue eyes nonetheless. "You are flattering me, Mr. Ellsworth."

"Not a bit, Miss Dashwood. If I wished to flatter you, I might claim upon meeting you that 'I ne'er saw true beauty 'til this night!'"

"How fortunate for us you managed to refrain!" snapped Fanny.

Margaret ignored the outburst, saying instead, "Are you a devotee of poetry, Mr. Ellsworth?"

"How could I not be? Poetry is the language of love and passion, and what is a life without love and passion, Miss Dashwood?"

"Exactly! I do not think I could bear to live without the sublime beauty of poetry."

Fanny gave a sharp laugh.

"Do you disagree, Fanny?" Margaret said, struggling to contain her anger.

"There is certainly more to life than poetry, Margaret. One does not eat poetry or shelter oneself with poetry. No, there are far more important considerations than words on a page."

"My dear Mrs. Dashwood, I must respectfully disagree. Certainly poetry cannot feed the body or protect it from the elements. But it nourishes the soul and in the end is that not the most important consideration we have?" Mr. Ellsworth said.

"I have never understood what use talk about the soul is," Fanny rejoined. "What do you think, John?"

"About what, my dear?" said John, who had been enjoying his supper with gusto.

"About poetry being food for the soul, my dear," Fanny said, her voice growing ever more clipped.

John paused, his fork halfway to his mouth, brow furrowed in thought. "I suppose something has to feed one's soul, although I do not care for poetry. I do not understand why poets cannot be more straightforward with their meaning. Get right to the point, as it were." He returned to his meal while Fanny glared at him.

Margaret observed their exchange with growing mirth. The glimmer of merriment in Mr. Ellsworth's eyes told Margaret that he shared her amusement. For the first time since arriving at Norland, she was truly happy to be there.

After dinner the company retired to the salon. John buried himself behind a paper while Mrs. Dashwood and Fanny sat by the fire, intent on their needlework. Mr. Ellsworth took a seat next to Margaret who had settled herself on the sofa. Margaret pretended to ignore her mother's attempt at a surreptitious glance.

"Perhaps you would favor the company with a reading, Miss Dashwood?" Mr. Ellsworth said, handing her a book.

She glanced at the title and looked up at him, delighted. "How did you know?"

"I judge you to be a young woman of sublime taste. What poet, aside from Shakespeare, could satisfy that taste but Cowper?"

"I could not be more in agreement, Mr. Ellsworth! Have you any favorite poem for me to read?"

"I prefer whichever poem you choose, Miss Dashwood. I bow to you in the matter."

Margaret thumbed through the book before choosing. With a steady voice, she read a favorite she shared with her sister Marianne, looking up every now and then to find Mr. Ellsworth's gaze trained on her. She reserved her most dramatic voice for the final stanza:

> No voice divine the storm allayed,
> No light propitious shone,
> When, snatched from all effectual aid,
> We perished, each alone;

She paused before continuing, conscious of the room's stillness:

> But I beneath a rougher sea,
> And whelmed in deeper gulfs than he.

At length the others stirred. Mrs. Dashwood wiped away a tear, John unfurrowed his brow and returned to his paper, and Fanny sighed, for what reason Margaret could not fathom. But it was Mr. Ellsworth whose opinion she most craved, and in that quarter she was soon satisfied.

"Miss Dashwood," he said quietly. "You read with such sensitivity, such passion. I cannot imagine anyone not being moved by your interpretation of

Mr. Cowper. Why, the poet himself must have stirred in his grave, so thrilled to hear his words read with such grace, such passion, such accomplishment."

Margaret blushed under the desired praise. "I thank you for your kind words, Mr. Ellsworth. But surely you adorn the truth."

"Indeed, he does," snapped Fanny, without looking up from her work.

"No, Mrs. Dashwood, I exaggerate nothing. From now until my last breath I shall always hear Miss Dashwood's voice whenever I sit down to read this poem. And I shall cherish the memory of this evening." Mr. Ellsworth glanced at the clock and then looked back at Margaret, his brow creased in thought. At last he took a deep breath and said, "Dashwood, I shall accept your offer to stay the night after all. If you do not mind the late notice, Mrs. Dashwood." He turned his blue eyes beseechingly on Fanny.

"Of course, Mr. Ellsworth," she said, although her tone proved less than welcoming. "I shall see to the arrangements."

"Excellent!" said John. "What changed your mind?"

Again Mr. Ellsworth fixed his gaze upon Margaret. "The lateness of the hour," he said.

Margaret returned his smile, conscious of her mother's interested attention, though pointedly refusing to meet her eyes.

A servant entered the room, seeking John. A moment later John dismissed the servant and announced, "Unfortunately Fanny has taken a bit of a turn and sends her apologies. She has decided to retire for the evening. I think I will follow suit. Ellsworth, if you will follow me, I shall show you to your room."

Ellsworth rose and bowed to Margaret and Mrs. Dashwood. "Until tomorrow, then, ladies. I look forward to it." The gentlemen strode off, leaving Margaret and her mother alone.

Mrs. Dashwood turned to Margaret, her eyes wide. "My word," she said. "What an interesting turn of events!"

"What do you mean, Mama?" Margaret said.

"I never would have thought that John could have such a charming friend. It almost raises my opinion of him."

Margaret did not reply, though she did agree with her mother. She never would have imagined a man like Mr. Ellsworth would have any reason to call John a friend. Perhaps there was more to her brother than she suspected. At length, Margaret rose and accompanied her mother to their chambers.

"Good night, Mama," Margaret said before heading into her room.

"Good night, dearest," Mrs. Dashwood replied. "Sleep well."

While Margaret waited for the household to quiet before beginning her evening's work, she wondered which room held Mr. Ellsworth. His appearance at dinner had provided a welcome distraction from the general unease she felt in Fanny and John's company. She thought again about the pleasant sensations his praise and proximity inspired in her.

"Goodness," she whispered, "I must stop this. I have work to do. I can think about Mr. Ellsworth later." And with that enticement, she whispered the words of the Darkness Falls spell, "*Que l'obscurité soit*," and left her room.

Margaret had almost reached her father's study when she heard footsteps. Forgetting that she was already hidden by her spell, she ducked behind a curtain and peered out, surprised by the sight that met her: Mr. Ellsworth striding down the hallway. Such was her curiosity about his appearance there that she nearly stepped from behind the curtain to address him. Only as she started to pull the curtain back did she realize that she would also have to explain *her* presence in the hallway. As she did not wish to lie to Mr. Ellsworth, she chose to follow him at a discreet distance to see what he was doing.

When Mr. Ellsworth approached the study, Margaret began to worry. What if he should somehow manage to get inside? What might the Ghostly Guards do to him? Though she did not wish to reveal herself, she decided she had better intervene. She cast around for an excuse for being about in the middle of the night. The library! Yes, of course. She could say that she had risen to get a book.

She ducked into the library and whispered, "*Que l'obscurité se dissipe.*" Then she searched the shelves for something suitable, landing on a second volume of Cowper's poems. Clutching the book, she hurried back to find Mr. Ellsworth.

"Mr. Ellsworth?" she said quietly, feigning surprise.

He whipped around. "Oh, it is you, Miss Dashwood. You startled me." He took a step forward into the moonlight that streamed through the windows. "What brings you out of your bed so late?"

Margaret held up the book. "I confess that I had a sudden desire to read another volume of Cowper. I knew that my father had one in his library." She indicated the room she had just left.

"Ah, so that is where the library is located! I do not know how I missed it. I have heard your father possessed a remarkable collection of books, and I wished to see it for myself. I hoped to find another volume of Cowper."

Margaret held out the book. "Would you like this one, Mr. Ellsworth?" she said, struggling to keep her voice even.

He took the book and examined it. A shadow passed across his face, replaced immediately by a smile. "This is precisely the volume I had in mind. But you had it first, Miss Dashwood," he protested, handing it back to her.

"Oh no, Mr. Ellsworth. I have read it so many times. You should take it this evening. I can find something else."

"Thank you, Miss Dashwood. I shall read late into the night with the design of discussing these remarkable works with you over tea and toast. Sleep well, Miss Dashwood." With a small bow, he took his leave.

Margaret stood staring after him for a few minutes, her errand in her father's study forgotten. At length, she returned to her room, convinced that she would never get to sleep for anticipating the next day and another chance to talk to Mr. Ellsworth.

CHAPTER III

*M*argaret took extra care in dressing before breakfast the next morning, glad that no one was there to watch her. "I am being silly," she said as she examined herself in the mirror. "He leaves today, and I doubt I shall ever see him again." That thought pained her more than she cared to admit, however, so she banished it.

"Ah, Miss Dashwood," said Mr. Ellsworth as Margaret entered the breakfast parlor. He stood and held out the chair next to his.

"Good morning, Mr. Ellsworth," Margaret said, taking the proffered chair. "I hope you slept well."

He laughed. "Not as well as I would have liked, for I was occupied by Cowper's exalted poetry." From down the table, Fanny sniffed. "If there are better ways to pass one's evening, I cannot think of them," Mr. Ellsworth continued.

"I am certain that I can think of several," Fanny said, though she did not supply any examples.

"Perhaps we should continue our discussion about

poetry after breakfast, Miss Dashwood?" Mr. Ellsworth cast a dark look toward Fanny and then turned back to Margaret. "Although I have business in town that requires my presence this evening, I may be persuaded to stay a little while this morning if you would consent to show me Norland's celebrated grounds."

"Of course!" Margaret replied. "I thought that your business would be taking you to the west," she added.

"I have had a sudden change of plans." Mr. Ellsworth paused and looked at the table. "I hope that I shall be allowed to call on you in London, Miss Dashwood."

Margaret's heart soared. Mr. Ellsworth would be in London! And he wished to call on her!

"We would be delighted to receive you, Mr. Ellsworth," said Mrs. Dashwood. "We arrive in London the day after tomorrow." Margaret beamed at her mother and nodded her agreement.

"I look forward to paying a call soon after your arrival," Mr. Ellsworth said.

"Pity you wish to leave today, Ellsworth. I am planning a hunting party in a few days' time. You would be most welcome," John said. "Ah, but I forgot. You have no taste for hunting." John shook his head in amazement.

"You do not care for hunting, Mr. Ellsworth?" Margaret asked.

"I confess I do not. So much noise. I prefer the quiet."

"As do I, Mr. Ellsworth."

"I suppose you do, Margaret," Fanny said. "Being such a reader of *poetry*." Fanny's expression was cold. "And with so few people of any substance with whom to occupy your time."

Margaret took a breath and was about to answer her when Mr. Ellsworth interjected. "What better way could a young woman occupy herself, Mrs. Dashwood? Indeed, it is for her skill as a reader of poetry that I have such respect for Miss Dashwood. One may read a person's worth in how she entertains herself."

"I believe we have different measures of worth, Mr. Ellsworth," Fanny retorted.

"That is quite apparent, Mrs. Dashwood." Mr. Ellsworth's manner was all politeness, but his eyes, which held contempt for Fanny, communicated his meaning quite clearly. In that moment Margaret did not think she could hold him any higher in her estimation.

Fanny turned her attention to her tea. To see Fanny silenced provided more gratification than Margaret could have anticipated. That Mr. Ellsworth had risen to her defense left Margaret in no doubt of his regard, and now she was to spend the morning showing him the grounds. She thought she had reached the limit of her felicity until she remembered that he was to call on her shortly after she and her mother arrived in London. Margaret pictured herself the happiest of young women.

The day was fine and warm as Margaret and Mr. Ellsworth set off to explore Norland. Their path took them first toward the hill crowned by the greenhouse. Mr. Ellsworth stood looking at the hill before sighing sadly.

"I know greenhouses are thought fashionable, but I never understood their attraction. Look at that hill. How much better would it appear adorned by nature—a grove of trees, for example—or left alone to rise, solitary, above the manor?"

"The most beautiful grove of walnut trees once stood here. Before my father died and John took the house."

"Ah. I can only imagine who made the decision to pull down the majestic trees and order this greenhouse erected.' He turned toward Margaret with a look of mortification. "Forgive me if I have overstepped my bounds. I have spoken poorly of a member of your family. I—I simply cannot believe that anyone could prefer the work of man to that of Nature."

"You need not apologize, Mr. Ellsworth," Margaret said. "I share your sentiments completely."

Mr. Ellsworth's countenance brightened, his worry vanishing. Margaret met his eyes. They stood in that attitude until Margaret's prudence overcame her desire, and she broke their gaze.

"Shall I show you more, Mr. Ellsworth?" she said.

"Of course! I shall follow wherever you lead." Mr. Ellsworth held out his arm, and Margaret took it. Together they made their way toward the little copse of old trees that Fanny, in an unintentional act of mercy, had left untouched.

Margaret heard Mr. Ellsworth's rapid intake of breath upon entering the wilderness. She was glad that he understood its beauty. Margaret could not abide a person who did not feel the splendor of Nature's more wild places. They strolled down the path, taking their time to breathe in the cool air and the scent of trees and earth.

At length Margaret brought Mr. Ellsworth to a little bench situated near a babbling brook.

"This is one of my favorite places in all the world, Mr. Ellsworth."

Mr. Ellsworth listened to the brook, the wind in the trees, and the birds singing from their hiding places among the branches. "I understand why you would count it so. It is certainly a beautiful place."

"Of course, I imagine that there are more beautiful places," Margaret said. "But I have seen so little of the world that I must content myself with the natural wonder of England."

"Would you like to see more of the world, Miss Dashwood?"

"Oh yes, Mr. Ellsworth. It is my dearest wish!"

"A commendable wish, Miss Dashwood, one that contributes to my growing admiration of you."

"It does, Mr. Ellsworth? And why is that?" Margaret held her breath as she awaited his reply.

"For two reasons: first of all, I share that desire. But your wish also speaks of a curious mind, which I find appealing. Many young women long only for a husband and a home of their own—not a bad aspiration, I suppose. Yet to me it demonstrates a lack of imagination."

Margaret had nothing to say to this astounding proclamation.

"I hope I have not shocked you, Miss Dashwood!"

"Not at all. Well, perhaps a little, but only because you seem to understand me better than anyone else of my acquaintance." Torn between boldness and propriety, Margaret could not look at Mr. Ellsworth as she spoke, afraid of her words' forwardness.

"I cannot claim a complete understanding, Miss Dashwood." His voice was light, inviting Margaret's glance. "I imagine a few surprises await me as our acquaintance grows."

Margaret returned his smile, too happy to speak.

They enjoyed the morning in one another's company for a little while longer before Mr. Ellsworth said, "I am afraid, Miss Dashwood, that I have lingered far too long. I must leave for London. But I will not fret long over our parting, for I know that I shall see you soon."

"Nor will I, Mr. Ellsworth."

He studied her. "You are an enchanting young woman, Miss Dashwood."

"Thank you, Mr. Ellsworth," Margaret replied softly.

They returned to the house in silence, having spoken everything that needed saying for the time being.

Margaret watched from the wide windows of the drawing room as Mr. Ellsworth galloped down the drive and off to London. Her contentment was only a little marred by the thought that at some time she would have to tell him of her sorcery. She pushed the idea away. "I shall know when the time is right," she whispered.

The day dragged by in the absence of Mr. Ellsworth, but at last midnight arrived. Margaret cast the Darkness Falls spell and then made her way to her father's study. She found it as she had left it, with the Ghostly Guards flanking the door. They bowed to her with a faint clanking of armor.

Margaret curtsied before turning her attention to her task. "*Que le voile se retire; que la vérité soit révélée,*" she whispered. A quick search of the room revealed that only two secret compartments remained to be emptied of their treasure. The first one, located in a panel behind a painting of a landscape, proved simple to open. Though heavy, the painting came away from the wall with no trouble. Margaret found two ancient books and a small pouch filled with a powdery substance inside the hidden compartment. Despite the promptings of her romantic nature, Margaret knew enough about sorcery to leave the powdery substance alone until she could identify it. She laid the books in her sack with care and tucked the pouch into her pocket. Then she slid the compartment's door shut and attempted to wrestle the painting back onto the wall.

Her efforts, though earnest, amounted to nothing. A cold hand on her back interrupted her. Startled, she whipped around. One of the Ghostly Guards stood behind her gesturing for her to step aside. "Goodness me," she whispered as she complied. "Your hands are cold!"

The Guard examined his hands. Then he bent over, picked up the painting, and slid it back into its place on the wall.

"Thank you," Margaret said. "I do not know how I would have gotten that back in place!"

The Guard acknowledged her thanks with a bow of his head and returned to his post. Margaret turned her attention to the final cache of relics from her father's secret life as a sorcerer, hidden in the bookshelf next to the window. Although she could detect the secret compartment's outline in the back wall of the bookshelf with the True Vision spell, she could find no way inside it. After a moment of contemplation, she removed the books, thinking those blocked her view, but still she could not solve the puzzle. She ran her fingers over and over the back wall of the bookshelf. She could detect no irregularities in the wood.

"Well, this is bothersome indeed! I cannot think what my father felt was worth such strong protection." She turned to the Guards. "Do you know how to open this?"

The Guards looked at each other and then back to Margaret, both shaking their heads.

"No, why would you?" she mused to herself, staring hopelessly ahead. A slight clank and creak from the Guards caused Margaret to remember herself. "I must apologize!" she cried. "That was terribly rude of me. I know you are doing your best." She was relieved to receive a slight nod from both of the Guards.

Margaret resumed her attack on the panel. She tried a simple unlocking spell that her father had taught her, but still the compartment guarded its secrets. Next she attempted a more complicated spell, to no avail. She was just short of blasting a hole in the bookshelf when she thought she heard her father's voice say, "A simple 'please' will suffice."

Nonplussed, she looked around the room. Aside from the Ghostly Guards, she was alone. What had happened? Had her father paid her a visit from beyond his grave? Margaret's skin prickled at the thought. Then she realized he had often said the same thing to her when she was learning a new spell. Laughing nervously, she steadied herself, fixed her gaze upon the back of the bookshelf, and said, "*S'il vous plaît.*" A little panel slid back to reveal a small box sitting on a shelf behind the wall. She picked up the box, surprised by its weight, and watched the panel slide shut. Setting the box on her father's desk, she returned the books to their places.

Despite the late hour, Margaret studied the box sitting on her father's desk. She could find neither hinges nor a clasp. "Curious," she said. She picked it up again, feeling its weight. "This will take some work." Resolving to have a closer look at the box in her chamber, she tucked it under her arm, picked up her bag, and turned to say goodbye to the Ghostly Guards.

But the room was empty. Margaret blinked several times, thinking perhaps a trick of the moonlight prevented her from seeing the shadowy figures. She took one step forward and then another. "I suppose when I found the last of my father's belongings, guardianship transferred to me and the Guards were discharged of their duty." Margaret felt a pang of regret at their absence. She had grown fond of the silent specters. They represented a lingering piece of her father, guarding the safety of his study, allowing it to remain untouched, undefiled by Fanny's taste, until such time as Margaret could retrieve his effects. Margaret sighed. "I did not even have a chance to thank them." Hitching the box under her arm, she tiptoed out of the room and snuck back upstairs.

Once in the safety of her room, she said, "*Que l'obscurité se dissipe*," banishing the Darkness Falls spell, and set about opening the mysterious box. A closer examination under candlelight revealed neither a clasp nor a hinge. "How puzzling," Margaret whispered, yawning. "I imagine it will prove easier to open in daylight." She hid the box in her wardrobe and climbed into bed, the efforts of the evening allowing sleep to take her without a struggle.

CHAPTER IV

*D*uring the night the good weather gave way to rain and bitter cold. A ferocious wind howled, rattling the windows and awakening Margaret. Torrents of rain beat against the glass. The storm's violence prevented Margaret from returning to her peaceful sleep, so she rose, lit a candle, and rifled through the various items hidden in her trunk. She found a sheaf of letters, which she brought back to her bed. Tucked into her covers, Margaret found the letter with the earliest date and began reading.

Longbourn 18 May, 17—

Dashwood,

I thank you for letter of Monday last with the clever advice concerning protection charms. The hyssop proved a powerful ward indeed. I am relieved to report that everyone escaped without harm, so the next steps in our scheme may move forward according to plan.

As for your query regarding language and translation spells, I have always had fine luck with Langlois's Compendium for unusual solutions to many such problems. If I am not mistaken, Langlois was himself something of a linguist and included an entire section devoted to work in that area. His emphasis may be a bit heavy on French sorcery, but we must forgive him his patriotism. The fifth edition is currently in print and contains references to little known Indian spells as well. I do wish I could be of more material assistance in your work, but as you well know, my specialties lie elsewhere.

The next meeting has been scheduled for the thirtieth of June; I expect everyone will be in attendance, including, I am sure you will be pleased to know, the Bristlethwaites. I shall be hosting at Longbourn as my wife and two daughters are expected at her sister's house in town. I must say, old chap, I envy you your situation. Alas, the promises of Matrimony's Holy State have not yet been fulfilled, nor, I am beginning to suspect, will they ever be. Moreover, neither of my girls has demonstrated any aptitude for magic. Perhaps in time one of my progeny will, but with such a mother as Mrs. Bennet I am not sure there is much hope.

And so I come to the end of my paper. Until the thirtieth, I remain as ever

Your friend,

J. Bennet

Margaret had never heard her father speak of this Mr. J. Bennet, nor had he ever mentioned anyone called Bristlethwaite. She felt certain that she would have remembered such a name. From the letter's content, she deduced that these people were fellow sorcerers. In its tone she could feel the warmth that attends deep friendship. "Papa never told me of his friends," she said with a pang of loneliness.

Pushing the feeling aside, she turned back to the letter, which had raised more questions than it had answered. What was the scheme of which Mr. Bennet had written? She could determine only that it was dangerous from the necessity of protection charms and Mr. Bennet's relief that no one had been harmed. But what were they trying to do? And why was her father interested in language spells? The book that Mr. Bennet had mentioned intrigued her enough that she once again left the comfort of her bed to search through her trunk.

She examined book after book before finally finding the one she sought. "Here it is," she murmured. A quick perusal through *A Compendium of Magical Spells by Henri Langlois* revealed its impressive scope. She considered abandoning the letters in favor of this fascinating book, but decided against it. She returned it to its hiding place and resumed her bed to continue reading, hoping the letters would answer her questions.

By the time the household had begun to stir, Margaret had read letters from a variety of different sorcerers, yet her questions remained unanswered. The letters only provided more evidence that her father had secrets about which even she had known nothing. Margaret sighed. Discovering this new side of her father left her feeling forlorn. She longed more than ever to talk to him.

"Is everything all right, my dear?" asked Mrs. Dashwood.

Margaret looked up from her breakfast. "I am a little tired; the storm kept me awake."

"My poor dear. Perhaps you should return to your room after breakfast and rest," said Mrs. Dashwood.

Margaret leapt at the opportunity. Containing her excitement as best as she could, she said, "I suppose that would be best, though I fear it is rather rude of me."

"Indeed—" Fanny began.

"Not at all my dear," Mrs. Dashwood insisted. "You must be well for our journey tomorrow. I am sure that Fanny and John agree."

Neither Fanny nor John spoke, the one glaring at her tea, the other hiding behind his newspaper.

"Well, then, I shall retire and rest," Margaret announced.

Back in her room, Margaret could not believe her good fortune. She could finish the letters and examine the impenetrable box that lay cloaked on her wardrobe's floor! Wrapped in a blanket against the cold wind still battering her windows, Margaret resumed reading. A letter dated only a month before her father's death left her breathless:

March 20, 17—

Mayfair

Dearest Dashwood,

I must confess that your last letter broke my poor heart. My dear man, are you entirely certain of your impending demise? I know that your efforts with the atlas have exhausted you, but surely there is something you can do? Ah, but I know you of old, Henry, and you will do nothing to save yourself when there are more discoveries to be made, more work to do.

Therefore I have taken the liberty of contacting Miss Cottlebury, who has sent along one of her healing elixirs. You are to put a teaspoon of the powder in tea three times a day. Promise me you will do so, Henry. I cannot bear the loss of so dear a friend so soon after that of my beloved husband. I shall look for a letter confirming your receipt of the powder and attesting to its power of restoration.

Yours,

Eugenia Bristlethwaite

Margaret let the letter fall into her lap and stared into the fire. Was it true that her father need not have died? She remembered the white powder she had found in her father's study; at least now she knew what it was. Why had he put it away? Why had he not taken it? She could not believe that her father would have been so irresponsible. But then she remembered the last few weeks of her father's life and thought that perhaps he did not have the strength to do what Mrs.

Bristlethwaite asked of him. If only he had confided in her. "I was old enough to help," Margaret whispered through a tight throat. She took a deep breath and pushed that thought from her mind.

Margaret's eyes strayed back to the letter. Something else had caught her attention. *Your efforts with the atlas.* Memories tugged at Margaret. She sat on the floor of her father's study, a book in her lap. She could open the book and scents reminiscent of places would waft toward her. Salty oceans, crowded markets. Strange spices she could not identify. In her mind's eye her father smiled indulgently as she played with the book. Then he reached for it, saying, "It is not yet finished, my dear. But when it is, I shall take you on a journey. Would you like that?"

Her father's atlas. She had never thought that it differed from other fathers' atlases. But now she understood that it was special, and she guessed what was in the box at the bottom of her wardrobe. She retrieved the box and set it on the table next to her chair where she sat staring at it. Although she willed it to reveal its secrets, nothing happened.

"*Révélez-moi ce que vous cachez!*" she demanded.

The box remained stubbornly sealed. She repeated her command, but again nothing happened. Then she remembered hearing the voice telling her to use a simple "please" in her father's study. "*S'il vous plaît,*" she said, but to no avail. She searched for a more specific instruction. "Ah, yes! *Ouvrez!*" Margaret held her breath, afraid she had failed again, but then the box melted away, leaving behind a surprisingly compact book with an embossed cover. Margaret recognized it as the atlas she had played with as a child, although it had seemed much bigger then. Or maybe she only remembered it that way.

Before she could begin to explore the atlas's pages, a knock sounded at the door. From the hallway a servant called, "Miss Dashwood? You are wanted downstairs for tea."

"Thank you!" Margaret called. "I shall be right down." With a pang she returned the atlas to the wardrobe.

"I say," John began after the tea had been served. "The strangest thing has happened; this morning I tried the door to Father's study, and it opened!"

Margaret stopped stirring her tea and sat very still.

"Why is that strange, John?" said Mrs. Dashwood.

"It has been impenetrable since his death. But now, as if by some miracle, the door opens with ease!"

Fanny looked from Margaret to Mrs. Dashwood, suspicion narrowing her eyes. "How odd that such a miracle should occur so soon after your arrival."

"What are you suggesting, Fanny?" replied Mrs. Dashwood.

"I think I am being quite clear." She pointed a reproachful finger at Mrs. Dashwood. "You took the key and now you have returned to liberate something—no doubt of great value—from the study!"

"I can assure you, Fanny, that nothing could be further from the truth." Mrs. Dashwood kept her voice even, though the color rising in her cheeks betrayed her anger.

Margaret studied her hands, which were clasped in her lap. Her mother had no way of knowing the veracity of Fanny's accusations. Nevertheless, Fanny's incivility angered Margaret, founded as it was upon Fanny's ill opinion of John's family.

"Now, now," said John, attempting to placate his wife by patting her hand. "I am certain we can find a suitable explanation."

"Maybe age wore down the lock," offered Margaret, hoping that no one would recognize the silliness of her suggestion.

"Is such a thing possible?" Mrs. Dashwood asked.

"I should think so," John replied. "It seems as reasonable an explanation as any other."

Fanny sniffed but said nothing.

"Then again, perhaps it was magic," John said. Margaret held her breath, terrified she would be discovered, but then he laughed, and Margaret exhaled.

"Do not be ridiculous!" Fanny exclaimed, all indignation. "You know as well as I do that there is no such thing as *magic*. You should not jest about such things."

Chastened, John sipped at his tea. For once Margaret agreed with Fanny on one count: the less spoken about the subject, the better. Fanny would be horrified, and possibly terrified, to know that she was connected—even simply by marriage—to a sorceress. Whether that mortification would lead her to hide or to report Margaret's magic, Margaret could not tell. But she remembered her father's exhortations and chose caution, for as he had often reminded her, "The practice of magic has been outlawed and the penalties for discovery are severe."

Margaret's thoughts were interrupted by the sensation of being watched. She looked up from her tea, into which she had been staring.

"My dear, did you rest this morning? You are so pale." Mrs. Dashwood wore an expression of concern.

"Am I? I must confess I am still a bit fatigued." Margaret replied.

"Oh, my poor dear!" said Mrs. Dashwood. "Back to bed with you. I am sure that we can spare you."

Margaret rose, needing no further exhortation. "I believe you are right, Mama. Rest would be the best thing for me."

Gaining the privacy of her room, Margaret at once liberated the atlas from its hiding place. Gently, almost reverentially, she cradled the book in her hands. Power radiated from the beautiful book, almost overwhelming her. "Gracious," she whispered. Then with shaking hands, Margaret opened the atlas. Written on the inside was an inscription in her father's hand:

To Margaret,

"I have done nothing but in care of thee—

Of thee my dear one, thee my daughter—"

Love,

Papa

At the familiar words, Margaret's eyes brimmed with tears. "Ah, Papa, you knew me so well."

Before settling in to read the atlas, she thumbed through its pages, stopping now and again to marvel at what she found. The book was filled with maps and drawings, some so lifelike that Margaret thought they moved. Scents rose from the pages, too—smoky wood, loamy earth, briny air—just as they had when she was younger and played with the book in her father's study.

Some of the pages contained text, but elsewhere, detailed maps sprang off the page so that Margaret could pass her hand through them, tracing streets with her fingers. She stopped on a page labeled "Paris" and read the note:

> *The center of French sorcery, Paris is a city of great beauty and marvelous but sometimes dark power. It is crucial for the sorcerer venturing to the French capital to speak impeccable French. See the languages section of this chapter for added notes about employing the Many Tongues Spell in conjunction with holding the Atlas. Meanwhile, the major attractions and main Parisian thoroughfares are highlighted in the maps on the following pages.*

Astonished, Margaret turned the page and examined the map of Paris. The River Seine wound its way through the city. She ran her finger along it and saw the noble Notre Dame and the lovely Louvre Palace, so life-like in their detail. She stared longingly at the map, wishing she could see the city for herself. "Perhaps some day," she whispered and resumed her exploration.

In the middle of the atlas, Margaret found a letter addressed in her father's unmistakable hand and dated just a few days before his death.

Dearest Margaret,

It gives me great pain to know that I have finished this gift for you and will not be here to witness your joy upon receiving it. Nor will I be able to teach you to use it, which is why I have secreted it away in my study, under the watchful eyes of two members of the Ghostly Guard. If you are reading this letter, you have developed sufficient skill as a sorceress to command the atlas, making me the proudest of fathers. I have no doubt that such a time will come.

I take comfort in the knowledge that my final gift will allow you to pursue your dreams of travel. But take care; you must heed all the instructions that I have laid out in the atlas's pages. And beware of letting it fall into anyone else's hands. It contains immense power that when unleashed could wreak severe destruction. Not everyone you meet will have the best intentions, my dear, trusting Margaret.

Once you have liberated the atlas from its hiding place, I urge you to contact my old friend, Mrs. Eugenia Bristlethwaite. She is an accomplished sorceress and can help you learn to navigate the atlas's intricacies. She is one of a few sorcerers whom I have entrusted with knowledge of the atlas's existence. She will also prove a wonderful travel companion.

I bid you bon voyage my dearest daughter. Perhaps we shall meet again in the next life.

Your loving father

Margaret's eyes widened when she saw the addresses contained in the postscript. The first one she recognized from a letter in her father's collection, but the second she knew from her years in Devonshire. "Barbary Hall?" Margaret could not believe her good fortune. She had heard the residence spoken of before, its exotic name piquing her curiosity, and now she was to write to its mistress! Margaret gathered what she required to compose her letter, and after a few moments' consideration, she set her pen to paper.

Dear Mrs. Bristlethwaite,

I hope you will forgive the forwardness of my writing to you without our first having been formally introduced, but circumstances have prevented an earlier acquaintance. I have only recently discovered your friendship with my father, Mr. Henry Dashwood, at whose posthumous urging I write to you. It is my hope that I shall be able to meet you in the very near future either in London or at your house in Devonshire. We have much to discuss, Mrs. Bristlethwaite, not least a gift from my father, which I have just received.

I look forward to hearing from you at your earliest convenience. My mother and I will be in London the day after tomorrow at the address below.

With hopes of friendship,

Margaret Dashwood

Satisfied with what she had written, Margaret copied it to another sheet of paper and then addressed both letters, one to Mayfair and one to

Devonshire. She set them aside and once again took up the atlas. Settling into her chair, she turned to the first page and began reading.

How to Use The Atlas:

I have enchanted this atlas to provide everything you need in order to embark on successful journeys around the world. In addition to detailed maps, you will find extensive information about local customs as well as a complete lexicon of local languages. To operate the lexicon, you must always keep the atlas on your person, which is why I have made it so small. I cannot stress that instruction enough. But there will be more on that in the warnings section of this introduction.

Before embarking on a journey, familiarize yourself with the local customs of the place you plan to visit. Many unnecessary conflicts have arisen from a simple misunderstanding of customs.

Several spells requiring mastery on their own become much simpler in the presence of the atlas. To move from country to country, one must employ the difficult Folding Spell. But the power contained within the atlas aids the sorcerer who ordinarily finds this spell too demanding. To travel, simply turn to the page featuring your desired destination, hold the book open to that page, and utter the words of the Folding Spell, "Fold x into y." (Replacing, of course, the x and y with names of locations.) You need not attempt to imagine the place to which you travel; the atlas performs that task for you.

Margaret giggled at these instructions; her father remembered how literally she had taken everything as a child. With a smile, she returned to the atlas.

I have devised the Many Tongues spell to provide access to the atlas's extensive language lexicon. Immediately upon arrival in your destination, utter the spell's incantation, "Sounds become words, words become sounds." You will be prepared for any encounters with local residents. The presence of the atlas on your person will ensure the proper working of the spell and prevent any unfortunate misunderstandings or mispronunciations.

And now I must enumerate my warnings: Never let the atlas out of your possession. I cannot lay enough emphasis on this point. You may be stranded in a foreign land with no understanding of the language. Moreover, the book is imbued with a great deal of power. Should it fall into the wrong hands, this power could be employed to the detriment of the entire world. My warnings sound hyperbolic, but they are nonetheless sound. I urge you to heed them.

Before you travel, consult the list of safe arrival and departure points identified in the maps. While common sense should guide you in these choices, many sorcerers have no common sense and therefore must be reminded. England has comparatively lax laws against the practice of our craft. In other countries you may not even receive a trial before you are beheaded. Should you be seen arriving in such a country, you will place yourself in grave danger. It has taken years of dedicated research for me to find these many safe locations. I implore you, make use of them.

Margaret closed the atlas, her desire to test it somewhat diminished by the strength of her father's warnings. Still clutching the atlas, she went to her window and looked out at the gathering darkness, her imagination alive with the possibility of travel.

CHAPTER V

*T*he morning of Margaret and her mother's departure dawned grey but dry. Though a cool wind stirred the leaves, it lacked the violence of the previous day. Margaret, anxious to leave for London, managed to dress and pack her trunk before the feeble sun's rays peeked through her windows. Before heading downstairs, she made sure that she had left nothing behind. Satisfied that everything was prepared for her journey, Margaret set off for the breakfast parlor.

Fanny sat at the table alone. Margaret hesitated in the doorway before taking a small step backward, intent on leaving unnoticed. But Fanny called her name. With a quiet sigh, Margaret entered and took her seat.

"I am glad that I have the opportunity to speak to you alone, Margaret," said Fanny.

"Oh?" Margaret raised her eyebrows.

"Yes. It concerns Mr. Ellsworth. I know that he wishes to see you again, and I must caution you against it."

"And why is that, Fanny?" Margaret asked.

"Because it is not seemly for you to throw yourself at a man so soon upon meeting him, although perhaps I caution you too late," Fanny said, her tone brisk. "Your lack of propriety is one thing when witnessed only by members of your family. But should the rest of society see you behave with such wanton disregard for your reputation—"

"I have no idea of what you speak, Fanny," Margaret asserted, her cheeks burning with indignation. "But I see no reason my behavior is any of your business."

"If my sister-in-law is playing the fool with a young man, it *is* my business. Then again, what should I expect from you, given the example set by Marianne?"

Margaret took a deep breath, willing herself to contain her emotion before it caused her to do something she would regret. "Think whatever you like, Fanny. Your opinion matters not at all to me." Her lightness was feigned, but it hit its target.

Fanny's face reddened. "You—"

"Good morning," said John, strolling into the room. Oblivious to the glares exchanged by his wife and his sister, he sat at the table and poured himself a cup of tea. "Today seems much more suitable for traveling than yesterday," he observed.

"Indeed," said Fanny.

Margaret made no answer, furiously stirring her tea, eyes cast downward.

"Good morning," said Mrs. Dashwood. "Margaret, have you prepared everything for our journey?"

"I have," Margaret replied.

Mrs. Dashwood made no comment about Margaret's terseness. "Good," was her only reply.

Not another word was spoken in the breakfast parlor until the sound of wheels clattering on the drive outside broke the silence. Margaret leapt from her chair and raced to the window. "The post-chaise has arrived!" she cried and rushed from the room.

"Margaret!" her mother called.

In the hallway Margaret stopped, knowing she was expected to say her goodbyes, and dutifully returned to the breakfast room. "Goodbye, John. Goodbye, Fanny," she said woodenly.

"Goodbye, Margaret," said John with something approaching real feeling.

"Goodbye." Fanny's voice held such a sharp chill that it made Margaret shiver.

"Thank you for your hospitality," said Mrs. Dashwood. Margaret marveled at her mother's civility.

"I shall see you into the carriage." John rose.

"Oh, that will not be necessary. But thank you, John. Margaret, shall we?"

Margaret smiled at the relief in her mother's voice. "Yes, Mama," she said.

Once settled in the carriage, Margaret turned to watch Norland retreat from her sight. She felt a pang of homesickness and dabbed at her eyes with her handkerchief.

"There, there, my dear," said Mrs. Dashwood, taking her hand. "Norland ceased to be our home when John inherited it. I, for one, would be happy never to see it again." She kissed Margaret gently. "Only think, my dear, of the much warmer reception awaiting us in London!"

"You are right, Mama," Margaret said. She tucked away her handkerchief. For the rest of the ride,

Margaret considered only the comforts awaiting her in London: a reunion with her beloved sisters, tea with Mrs. Bristlethwaite, and a chance to see Mr. Ellsworth.

The sun had barely begun its descent as the carriage carrying Margaret and Mrs. Dashwood arrived at the London townhouse of Marianne and Colonel Brandon. Margaret and her mother had just alighted when the animated voices of Elinor and Marianne met their ears. A moment later Margaret and Mrs. Dashwood were bound in tight embraces, the sisters and mother joyful at their reunion.

"Elinor!" cried Mrs. Dashwood. "We had no idea you would be here, too! Will we find dear Edward in London as well?"

"He will be here in a few weeks," Elinor replied. "But you must be exhausted from your travel." She looked from mother to sister, her concern for their well being clear.

"Yes, yes!" cried Marianne. "We must get you inside at once. Brandon will be delighted that you have arrived. He did not believe it possible before sunset, but you have proven him wrong. You rode in Phaeton's own carriage!"

With full hearts, Margaret and Mrs. Dashwood accompanied Marianne and Elinor into the house.

"Your trunks will be taken to your rooms, and I am sure you would like a moment's rest before joining us in the drawing room. Elinor and I will show you up." Marianne gestured for everyone to follow her.

As they climbed the stairs, Margaret listened with contentment to the happy chatter of mother and daughters, together after so many months apart. That her sisters thrived as wives and mothers was apparent to anyone who observed them.

"Here we are," Marianne said. "Margaret, this will be your room."

Margaret followed her into a large chamber filled with light from the enormous windows overlooking a park in the middle of the square. It seemed a peaceful spot, with benches placed around a central walkway. In the fading light Margaret could just see the outline of a little pond in the park's center.

"What a beautiful view," Margaret said.

Marianne placed a soft hand on Margaret's shoulder. "I knew you would appreciate it. We shall have tea in half an hour. Will that be enough time for you to refresh yourself?"

"More than enough!"

Marianne rewarded Margaret with a gentle kiss. "Come, Mama," she said.

Elinor lingered at the door. "It is wonderful to see you, Margaret."

"And you, Elinor "

Then Elinor followed Marianne and Mrs. Dashwood down the hall, leaving Margaret to examine her new quarters. The room was simply but beautifully decorated, with a wide hearth set for the evening fire. On the other side of the room stood a spacious bed, draped with soft blue curtains that matched the window hangings. Next to the window was a writing desk and chair. The floor was covered in a thick, blue carpet that softened every step. Marianne had spared nothing to assure her guests' comfort. Margaret was glad to be among family who loved her.

As she moved toward the basin to wash her face,

she noticed something on the desk. A closer examination revealed it to be a letter! She tore open the seal and began reading, elated:

My dear Miss Dashwood,

You can have no idea what joy your letter has given me! To hear from the daughter of Henry Dashwood has long been one of my dearest wishes. I shall make this short, as I anticipate seeing you very soon. Until such time, I await word of your safe arrival in London.

Your friend,

Mrs. Eugenia Bristlethwaite

"Wonderful!" Margaret sat down to write an immediate reply with the paper and pen she found generously supplied in the desk. With the letter sealed and addressed, she splashed a little water on her face and changed into a fresh gown. Then she hurried back downstairs to greet the rest of her family.

Everyone had gathered in the drawing room. Margaret took a seat next to her brother-in-law, Colonel Brandon.

"You look well, Margaret," Brandon said. "Did you enjoy your stay at Norland?"

Margaret gave an expressive sigh. Before she could answer, however, Marianne cut in.

"Tell me absolutely everything. Do not spare me a single detail!" Margaret almost laughed at the tragic mask Marianne's face had assumed. But remembering the pain *she* had felt upon first observing the new greenhouse, Margaret composed herself and reported all of Fanny's *improvements* to an increasingly agitated Marianne. When Margaret reached an account of the new greenhouse, Marianne gave a cry and suddenly ran from the room.

"Goodness!" Margaret said. "Is Marianne going to be all right?" She looked at her mother, who wore an odd expression for the circumstances: joy was painted in broad strokes across her face. "Mama?"

"My dear, I believe you are going to be an auntie again!" Mrs. Dashwood said.

"We can never hide anything from you for long," Elinor said, laughing.

"I do not understand!" Margaret glanced from her mother to her sister.

Mrs. Dashwood patted Margaret's hand. "I shall explain later. But you need not worry. Your sister is in perfect health."

Soon enough, Marianne rejoined the company and confirmed the joyous news. As talk turned to infants and their needs, Colonel Brandon, smiling broadly, hid behind a newspaper, and Margaret let her thoughts drift toward the two people she most wished to see now that she was in London.

Her musings were interrupted by her brother-in-law. "Margaret, a gentleman called on me yesterday. He said he had made your acquaintance at Norland and hoped that it would not be improper to visit you here."

"Did the gentleman leave a card?" Margaret asked, endeavoring and failing to keep from blushing.

Colonel Brandon handed her a card.

Mr. Weston Ellsworth it read in a lovely script.

"I told him that I saw no harm at all in allowing you to further your acquaintance, should your mother approve." Both he and Margaret looked at Mrs. Dashwood, each wearing a different expression.

"Of course!" Mrs. Dashwood said.

Margaret released her breath. "Oh, thank you, Mama! Brandon!"

"He seems a true gentleman. And he spoke quite highly of you."

That news made Margaret's blush deepen, but she did not care.

"I should hope so!" exclaimed Marianne. "We must invite him to pay us a call soon," she said to Colonel Brandon.

"I will write to him this evening," he promised.

The prospect of seeing Mr. Ellsworth again so soon nearly drove Margaret's desire to meet Mrs. Bristlethwaite from her mind. But then another letter from Mrs. Bristlethwaite arrived with the evening post, inviting her to tea the next day "if she felt up to it." Margaret's happiness was complete.

That night before she went to bed, Margaret consulted the atlas to plan her route from her brother-in-law's Berkeley Square townhouse to Mrs. Bristlethwaite's address in Mayfair. While searching the map of London for a safe place to appear, Margaret discovered the Corridor of Doors:

> *Devised in the seventeenth century, the Corridor of Doors provides a safe and secret conduit for sorcerers wishing to travel quickly across London without tiring themselves unnecessarily. (See page seventy-six for a detailed map of the Corridor's entrances located throughout the streets of London.) Travel is quite simple: enter from any of the marked locations and*

*walk through the Corridor until you find the door
that corresponds to your destination. A note of
caution: take care to enter and exit the doors without
being seen. Few non-magical people will notice, but
one can never exercise too much caution.*

Margaret searched the map for the nearest
entrance, which was located just a few yards from
Colonel Brandon's house. The door to Mayfair
appeared to open about a block from Mrs.
Bristlethwaite's house. "This should be easy enough,"
Margaret said, tracing the route with her finger.
Satisfied with her plan, she set the atlas aside and
blew out her candle. Feeling safe and warm, she
slipped into a peaceful sleep.

***

The following day Margaret managed to leave the
house without arousing any suspicions, claiming she
desired a walk around the square to admire the sights
that must already be so familiar to her sister. As
fortune would have it, no one wished to accompany
her, so with her atlas tucked in her pocket, Margaret
set out to visit Mrs. Bristlethwaite. She found the
hidden door to the Corridor with ease and passed
through it undetected. Once safely inside the
Corridor, Margaret gasped at what she saw. A stone
passage opened before her, its entire length lined with
wooden doors. She started down the passage, taking
note of the writing on the doors she passed, looking
for the one marked Bond Street. A shiver of awe ran
through Margaret as she realized that she walked in
the footsteps of hundreds, if not thousands, of

sorcerers and sorceresses. Having grown up largely without magical fellowship, Margaret found this notion comforting.

At last she reached the door she sought. She opened it carefully, peered out at the street, and then stole outside. A short walk took her to Mrs. Bristlethwaite's address, a handsome townhouse on a quiet street. A long-faced butler met Margaret at the door. She began to introduce herself, but he gestured for her to enter before she could speak. Wordlessly, he led her down a long hallway, its walls hung with portraits. Margaret only took in a few, the subjects of which had a jolly air about them, some plump with pink cheeks and wide smiles, others thinner but also wearing welcoming expressions. The hallway itself was wide and well lit, with polished wooden floors covered in exotically patterned rugs. Margaret longed to examine the portraits and furnishings closer, but the butler set a rapid pace.

At the door to the drawing room, the butler stopped. "I shall inform Mrs. Bristlethwaite of your arrival," he said in a dry voice. "Please wait in here."

"Thank you," Margaret said. The butler gave her a small bow and then left. Margaret, unsure of what was expected of her, remained standing and took in her surroundings. The same exotically patterned rugs covered the shining wood of the floors. Portraits and landscapes adorned the walls. The room itself was oval in shape with wide windows that looked out into a garden. Bright light streamed through them, making candles unnecessary. Plush-cushioned chairs stood around the room, accompanied by dainty-legged tables. An ornate mantelpiece hung over a wide hearth in which a fire burned merrily.

"Miss Dashwood!"

Margaret turned as a plump, handsome woman of middle age hurried toward her and pulled her into a close embrace. "How lovely to meet you!" Margaret was startled by Mrs. Bristlethwaite's display of affection. But the warmth of the older woman's arms soon comforted Margaret, and she began to feel at ease.

Mrs. Bristlethwaite released Margaret and held her at arms' length, studying her.

"You take after your dear father," she declared. "Come, sit," she added, leading Margaret toward the chairs by the fire. "I hardly know where to begin! I feel as though I have known you all your life. Your father wrote to me often about you, and now here you are!"

"It is a great pleasure to make your acquaintance, Mrs. Bristlethwaite," Margaret said. She looked at her hands, suddenly shy.

Mrs. Bristlethwaite cocked her head to one side. "I suppose dear Henry never got a chance to tell you about me, did he?"

"My father did not speak often about his past," Margaret rushed to explain. "He put his energy into my education. Then he grew ill and—"

"I understand, my dear. Of course." She was about to continue when a maid entered. Mrs. Bristlethwaite paused as the girl prepared their tea. "Thank you, Lucy."

Lucy bobbed a quick curtsey and then hurried off. Margaret and Mrs. Bristlethwaite sipped their tea in silence.

At length Mrs. Bristlethwaite set her cup in its saucer. "It was rude of me to bring up such a dreadful memory so soon after making your acquaintance, Miss Dashwood. I hope you will forgive me."

"Oh, of course, Mrs. Bristlethwaite," Margaret cried. "But what I meant to add was that after his death I learned about you in a letter from him that I found with some of his things at Norland Manor. I cannot tell you how much it means to me to meet a friend of my father and to—to make a friend of my own, I hope."

"I could never resist such a sentiment, especially coming from the daughter of Henry Dashwood," Mrs. Bristlethwaite replied.

The last traces of Margaret's shyness melted, and she felt she could say anything to Mrs. Bristlethwaite. "What was my father like as a young man?" she asked.

Mrs. Bristlethwaite's eyes sparkled. "Henry was a great sorcerer. He possessed one of the keenest intellects I have ever encountered. Even more important, however, was his curiosity. He was a visionary, Miss Dashwood. Far ahead of his time. His true talent was enchantment, but he was also an accomplished inventor of spells."

Margaret was conscious of the atlas stowed in her pocket. But she was not yet ready to reveal it to Mrs. Bristlethwaite. "How did you come to know my father?"

A look of nostalgia crossed Mrs. Bristlethwaite's face, softening its cheerful set. "We were members of the Mayfair Coven together," she began. "It was in the days when I was just Miss Richards, before I met my dear, now departed, Mr. Bristlethwaite. Henry and I were possessed of the same romantic nature." She chuckled, a low amusing sound that made Margaret want to join in, although she did not understand the source of Mrs. Bristlethwaite's mirth. "Ah, the zeal of youth. Nothing like it in the world." Mrs. Bristlethwaite's eyes glowed as she spoke. Then she shook her head. "We had no idea then of the lessons that awaited us." She gazed into the fireplace before turning back to Margaret. "Alas, I have become an old woman." She sighed. "Your father and I became close friends soon after joining the coven. The gossips who saw us together insisted that we were destined for marriage. The truth was far more mundane—your father was like a brother to me. I had lost my own brother a few years before, and Henry came to fill that place in my life. Then, of course, I met Mr. Bristlethwaite, and there was no one else in the world for me. You can imagine why," she said.

Margaret followed the direction of Mrs. Bristlethwaite's gaze to a portrait of a handsome man of about thirty years. He stood tall and straight with a mop of black curls framing a thin face of well-proportioned features. His blue eyes regarded Margaret with a friendly expression. Margaret could certainly understand Mrs. Bristlethwaite's regard for Mr. Bristlethwaite.

"He departed this world nearly ten years ago. I think you would have liked him, Miss Dashwood. My Mr. Bristlethwaite was a jolly man and so kind."

"Was he also a member of the Mayfair Coven?" Margaret asked.

"He was indeed. A magnificent sorcerer, my husband. There are times when I forget that he is gone and turn to ask him a question. But, of course, he does not answer. It is a pity he never had a chance to meet Henry Dashwood's daughter. But I have talked enough already. Tell me something about yourself, my dear."

"I do not think that there is much of interest to say, Mrs. Bristlethwaite," Margaret said. "I have lived a quiet life in Devonshire with my mother and my sisters until their marriages took them to their own homes. I enjoy my life, but—" She stopped herself, suddenly aware that she was speaking to a relative stranger.

"But what, Miss Dashwood? You need not be bashful with me."

"I should very much like to see more of the world. My little green corner of England is beautiful, but I can imagine what wonders await me in the wider world." Margaret stopped speaking and bit her lip. Should she share the atlas with Mrs. Bristlethwaite? Her father had encouraged her to make contact with his old friend. The time seemed as good as any. "My father knew my desire very well. That is why he made this for me," she said, pulling the atlas from her pocket and handing it to Mrs. Bristlethwaite.

The older woman took the book with an expression of reverence. She weighed it in her hands and caressed the cover before opening it. Margaret watched as Mrs. Bristlethwaite read the inscription, noting the tenderness of the older woman's expression. Then Mrs. Bristlethwaite began to look through the atlas, pausing to examine a map here, to take in the scent of a page there. At long last she looked up at Margaret.

"I had no idea the atlas would be so magnificent! The detail is astonishing, even with its much reduced size," Mrs. Bristlethwaite said. "Your father wrote to me about his project, but I could never have anticipated this masterpiece." Reluctantly, she returned the book to Margaret. "Miss Dashwood, you hold in your hands an object of immense power. I can see why it took such a toll on your father."

"What do you mean, Mrs. Bristlethwaite?" Margaret asked.

"Such a powerful object requires potent spells to sustain its magic. But only a few avenues for such a task exist. Blood magic provides that kind of power, but your father objected to that choice—with good reason. He chose instead to feed the atlas with his own magical energy. I do not know if even he understood what he was doing. I believe that in the making of the atlas, your father gave up too much of himself, leading him to succumb to his final illness."

Margaret looked at the atlas resting in her lap, tears pricking her eyes. "He told me in a letter that he had made it for me and that he was sorry that he would not be able to teach me to use it. He did warn me that it is a very powerful object and that it should be kept under close guard, but he made no mention of the atlas causing his death. I suppose he did not want me to regret its existence." The atlas took on a new weight with this knowledge, and Margaret could not help but feel deep sorrow that it represented all she had left of her father.

Mrs. Bristlethwaite handed Margaret a handkerchief. "I believe you are right, Miss Dashwood," she said kindly. "He made this book out of love for you. It is a gift."

Margaret dabbed at her eyes. "He also told me that you could help me learn to master it."

Mrs. Bristlethwaite beamed at her. "I should be honored to be of service to you, my dear. It will be lovely to see my old friend again." At the alarmed look on Margaret's face, Mrs. Bristlethwaite laughed. "All such objects contain a tiny bit of the sorcerer who enchanted them," she explained. "It is simply what happens when we put our energies toward enchantment. Some objects even take on the personalities of their makers, sometimes to rather amusing effect. At other times, however, it can be terrifying. I suspect we shall find more of the former than the latter."

Margaret's heart leapt at the possibility of encountering even the smallest echo of her father. "How soon may we begin?"

Mrs. Bristlethwaite fixed her with a searching gaze. "Why not right now?" she said.

"Now?" Margaret replied, all astonishment.

Mrs. Bristlethwaite nodded with such enthusiasm that Margaret found she could not resist.

"Where shall we go?" she said.

Mrs. Bristlethwaite took a sip of her tea. "Let us consult the atlas."

CHAPTER VI

Margaret glanced up from the atlas, awaiting Mrs. Bristlethwaite's response.

"Brilliant choice!" Mrs. Bristlethwaite cried. "I have not been to Wales in years. Read to me what the atlas says again."

Margaret, brimming with eagerness, complied:

Magic is woven into the very fabric of Wales. Wherever one travels within this mystical green country, one encounters sorcerers of the greatest skill. Much of the magic practiced in Wales concerns domestic life. But the purest Welsh magic resides in music. Bard Magic continues to thrive throughout the luscious hills. As the Welsh consider magic to be sacred, it is one of the few places in the world where its practice is not condemned. That is not to say, however, that a sorcerer or sorceress travelling to Wales should drop his or her guard. You must follow the course of action outlined in the introduction just as you would for a more dangerous part of the world.

Below you will find a complete history of Welsh sorcery as well as detailed drawings of the most enchanted locations in this beautiful country. I have also included a list of known sorcerers who welcome visits from foreign members of the magical community.

"Marvelous," Mrs. Bristlethwaite breathed. "Simply marvelous." She rose and extended her hand to Margaret. "Well, my dear Miss Dashwood, shall we?"

"We must choose a point of arrival before we leave," Margaret said.

"Of course! I will leave that to you." Mrs. Bristlethwaite waited while Margaret examined the map.

At length Margaret pointed to a spot. "Here." She held the map up for Mrs. Bristlethwaite to see.

Mrs. Bristlethwaite smiled. "An excellent choice. Well, then, would you care to do the honors, my dear?"

"Oh yes!" Margaret's voice quivered. She took Mrs. Bristlethwaite's hand, hardly believing that at long last she would be venturing away from England, even if only as far as Wales. She took a deep breath and closed her eyes. With a clear voice she said, "*Que Mayfair se replie sur le Chateau d'Aberystwyth!*"

As she finished the incantation, Margaret experienced the curious sensation of her body moving both very rapidly and not at all. When she opened her eyes, she gasped. She and Mrs. Bristlethwaite stood in the middle of a stony ruin. She could hear the sea lapping at the shore nearby. Gulls flew overhead, their forlorn cries carried on the wind. Dizziness overwhelmed Margaret, and she collapsed onto the ground.

"Oh dear," said Mrs. Bristlethwaite. "I forgot to warn you. The Folding Spell can be rather disorienting the first several times you do it. I find keeping my eyes open helps lessen the effects' severity. Never mind, my dear, you will be fine in just a moment, as soon as you get your bearings. Meanwhile, take nice deep breaths. There you are. Interesting choice, casting the spell in French. Fortunately for us you have a lovely and accurate accent!"

Margaret soon recovered and stood, casting her gaze about the quiet ruins. She and Mrs. Bristlethwaite had arrived in the center of a ring of small standing stones. A few yards away a small tower rose above the land, the remains of the castle wall. Other parts of the old castle still stood, but none of them appeared habitable. Margaret sighed. It was even more beautiful than the drawings in the atlas suggested.

Mrs. Bristlethwaite walked a few paces toward the ocean, visible from the ruins, and Margaret joined her. The two women gazed at the endless stretch of blue, the waves glinting in the reflected sunlight. "It is glorious," Margaret whispered. "Simply glorious."

"The world seems older here, does it not, Miss Dashwood? And the coast a little wilder."

Margaret nodded, her sensibilities nearly overcome with the pleasure of the wildness. The sea crashed into the retaining wall beneath them, sending up a misty spray.

From behind them someone called, a sudden sound causing the two women to whip around. A cold hand of fear clenched Margaret's stomach at the sight of a man trudging toward them. She reached out for Mrs. Bristlethwaite's hand, finding in its warmth a measure of comfort.

"Should we not hide?" Margaret said, controlling her panic. "I forgot to do the Many Tongues spell!"

Mrs. Bristlethwaite did not answer. She squinted at the stranger, but then her countenance shifted, brightening with a wide smile.

"Sir Berwin!" she cried.

The stranger answered her cry with a wave. As he drew closer Margaret could tell that the stranger was an older gentleman. Yet his back was strong and straight, his step, though aided by a staff, steady and sure. His white hair and beard were neat and well trimmed. When he arrived in front of them, the kindness in his blue eyes, adorned by deep wrinkles, set Margaret at ease.

"My dear Eugenia!" he said, grasping Mrs. Bristlethwaite by the hands. If she was bothered by his familiarity, she did not say.

"Sir Berwin! How splendid to see you again!" She turned to Margaret. "Miss Dashwood, this is Sir Berwin Llewellyn, a sorcerer and a bard."

Margaret curtsied. "I am pleased to meet you, Sir Berwin."

"And you, my dear," came his lilting reply. "What brings you to Wales?"

Margaret glanced at Mrs. Bristlethwaite who gave her an encouraging nod. "We wanted to see how this worked," she replied, offering the atlas to Sir Berwin. Margaret suffered a moment's doubt as she relinquished the atlas, remembering her father's exhortations to keep it safe. But she banished the worry; if Mrs. Bristlethwaite trusted Sir Berwin, Margaret decided she could as well.

The old gentleman studied the atlas. "Remarkable," he murmured. "How did you come to possess such an object?"

"My father left it to me," Margaret replied. "He made it." She could not keep the pride out of her voice.

"Henry Dashwood enchanted it," Mrs. Bristlethwaite added.

"Of course he did!" Sir Berwin exclaimed. "Who else would have done such magnificent work?" The last traces of Margaret's doubt evaporated. A light rain began falling. "Oh my, where are my manners? Please, come with me. We are not far from my house. Lady Jane will be thrilled to see you, Eugenia."

They followed Sir Berwin away from the castle. In front of them a manor house rose out of the soft green hills. As she breathed in the fresh, cool air, Margaret indulged in a romantic vision of settling in Wales, living her life in a small cottage tucked into the beautiful landscape. Another vision concerning a companion who would share her simple life in the Welsh countryside crossed her mind, and she blushed. Fortunately, Sir Berwin and Mrs. Bristlethwaite were engaged in conversation and did not notice.

"Welcome to Llewellyn Lodge," Sir Berwin declared as they approached the enormous manor house that Margaret had seen from the castle. It was an ancient dwelling of grey stone and dark timber.

"Oh my!" Margaret exclaimed at the sight of it.

"Yes, it is impressive, is it not?" Sir Berwin pushed

open the enormous wooden door and gestured them inside. The entrance was paneled in the same dark wood that Margaret had seen from the outside. But rather than shrouding them in gloom, it created a comfortable feeling, as though warm arms welcomed them inside. Portraits lined the walls in every direction.

"My ancestors," Sir Berwin explained. "Llewellyns, Davies, and Joneses—all solidly Welsh."

He led them into a comfortable parlor with a blazing fire and lamps lit against the day's growing darkness. A slim woman with white hair sat near the fire, a book open on her lap. At their entrance she looked up, and a smile creased her face.

"Eugenia!" Lady Jane moved with a speed Margaret never could have imagined in one so obviously beyond her prime years.

"Lady Jane," said Mrs. Bristlethwaite as the older woman pulled her into an embrace. "How wonderful to see you again!"

Lady Jane released Mrs. Bristlethwaite and held her at arms' length. "You look well, Eugenia," she declared. Then Lady Jane noticed Margaret. "And who is this charming young woman?"

"This is Miss Margaret Dashwood, my dear," replied Sir Berwin. "Henry's daughter."

"Oh my goodness!" cried Lady Jane. "Let me look at you, child." Margaret stepped forward and stood still while Lady Jane examined her. "I see Henry in your countenance, though you have much more delightfully arranged features." Before Margaret knew what was happening, Lady Jane had drawn her into the same tight embrace with which she had greeted Mrs. Bristlethwaite; the strength of it surprised

Margaret.

"Shall I call for tea, my dear?" said Sir Berwin.

"Yes, that would be lovely," said Lady Jane.

Sir Berwin rang the bell, and the ladies took seats near the fire.

"It is magnificent to see you again, Eugenia," said Lady Jane. "How long has it been?"

"Ten years?" said Mrs. Bristlethwaite.

"Goodness, that long? Alas, time passes so quickly now." Lady Jane sighed. "But never mind that. Tell me what brings you so suddenly to our little corner of Wales."

By the time Mrs. Bristlethwaite had finished her explanation and Margaret had shown Lady Jane the atlas, refreshments had arrived. Lady Jane perused the atlas as the maid laid the tea.

"Extraordinary!" she cried. "Have you seen this, my dear?"

"Only for a moment," Sir Berwin replied.

"You must examine it further." Lady Jane passed the atlas to her husband and then reached for her tea. "I assume by your presence in my drawing room that it works."

"We tried it for the first time today, and it works perfectly," Mrs. Bristlethwaite said. "I have never been particularly fond of the Folding Spell, but with the atlas there is almost no discomfort." She looked at Margaret. "I promise you will grow accustomed to the feeling of Folding, my dear. And what you experienced today does not compare to the spell's effects unaided by the atlas."

"Remarkable!" Sir Berwin said. "This will prove invaluable, I imagine. With all the places in the world you could have gone, what made you choose our sleepy little seaside?"

"Margaret chose the destination, and I agreed. It has been too long since my last visit." Mrs. Bristlethwaite sipped her tea. "What brought you to the castle, Sir Berwin?"

Sir Berwin gave her an arch look. "I wished to welcome you."

"Oh?" said Mrs. Bristlethwaite. "Have you perfected your Divination Spell at last, Sir Berwin?"

Sir Berwin merely smiled, but Lady Jane replied, "Heavens no! He saw you through the window."

Mrs. Bristlethwaite chuckled. "Naturally."

Margaret was not sure how to respond until Sir Berwin laughed along with Mrs. Bristlethwaite. She giggled.

"Divination Spells rarely work, Miss Dashwood," Sir Berwin explained. "But that minor inconvenience has not prevented my efforts to devise one." He turned to Mrs. Bristlethwaite, his face clouding. "But your arrival is a fortunate coincidence, Eugenia. I meant to write to you later today."

"Indeed?"

"There have been reports of disturbances at a few ancient magical locations in Wales. Someone tore apart a cairn thought to mark the place of a revered sorcerer's remains. If they took anything, we cannot yet tell—a complete inventory of the site has never been made as no one wished to disturb the sorcerer's rest."

"Of course," said Mrs. Bristlethwaite. "What other sites have been disturbed?"

"An old hill fort a few miles from the castle and a set of small standing stones near the southern coast," said Sir Berwin.

"But who would do such a thing?" Margaret cried.

Mrs. Bristlethwaite patted her hand. 'My dear, I understand your outrage. I am afraid the magical world has more darkness in it than one cares to admit."

"But to steal something from a *shrine*!"

"It is dreadful, Miss Dashwood, but it is the way of the world," said Lady Jane. "Not everyone you encounter possesses the honor of your father."

Margaret had never considered the possibility that darkness might grow in the hearts of sorcerers. She shivered, imagining what it would mean to meet with someone given over to such malevolence.

"Who else knows about the incidents?" Mrs. Bristlethwaite said.

"A small group of Welsh bards with whom I meet from time to time," said Sir Berwin. "We do not know much about the disturbances; I have set a few sorcerers to guard the more prominent locations. But I shall keep you abreast of the situation should it develop. There is always the chance that it is some poor man or woman who has no idea with what they toy."

"Though I doubt that to be the case," added Lady Jane.

"I shall send letters to Miss Cottlebury, Lady Isabelle, Mr. James, and Mr. Barrington. Perhaps we should reconvene?" said Mrs. Bristlethwaite.

"Thank you, my dear," said Sir Berwin. "I do not think we need to gather everyone together just yet. I shall keep you informed."

"I would like to help, too, Sir Berwin," Margaret said.

"Thank you, Miss Dashwood. I shall not hesitate

to call upon you."

Mrs. Bristlethwaite set her teacup down. "Miss Dashwood, perhaps we should return to London. I have letters to write, and no doubt your family will wonder where you have been if we stay away much longer."

Sir Berwin stood. "Allow me to accompany you as far as the ruins."

"Thank you, Sir Berwin. Lady Jane, thank you for the tea. It was splendid to see you again," said Mrs. Bristlethwaite.

"Of course, my dear. Let us not allow so much time to pass before meeting again. Miss Dashwood, I hope to see you again soon, too."

"Thank you, Lady Jane," Margaret replied.

They followed Sir Berwin back to the small standing stones where they had arrived.

"I shall write with whatever news we have, Eugenia. Stay safe," said Sir Berwin.

"And you, Sir Berwin," replied Mrs. Bristlethwaite. "Margaret?"

The two women joined hands. Margaret, eyes open, said, "*Que le Chateau d'Aberstywyth se replie sur le Mayfair!*" The physical sensations surprised her less this time, but Margaret was amazed to see Mrs. Bristlethwaite's drawing room appear before her. She turned her head quickly and saw the ocean disappearing behind her.

"How are you, Miss Dashwood?" Mrs. Bristlethwaite asked.

"I feel better this time. I left my eyes open."

"Good girl. And what did you think of our journey?"

"It was remarkable!" Margaret took Mrs.

Bristlethwaite's invitation to sit before continuing. "How happy a coincidence that Sir Berwin had thought to write you later today."

"Sometimes such coincidences befall those of us with magic. Have you never thought of someone only to see them or hear from them unexpectedly later in the day?"

Margaret considered Mrs. Bristlethwaite's question. "I suppose I have. Quite frequently in fact."

"Coincidence is another term for 'magical confluence of events,' my dear. What we experienced today fits squarely in that category." Mrs. Bristlethwaite paused, looking thoughtful. "I doubt that our choice of Wales was an accident."

"Indeed?" said Margaret. "But I simply happened upon that section of the atlas and the idea appealed to you."

"One can attempt to trace these confluences back from event to event and never arrive at their initiation. Perhaps you turned to the section about Wales because we were meant to travel there today. We could drive ourselves mad trying to trace causes and effects. No, we may as well simply accept that our journey to Wales today was necessary for reasons we cannot know yet."

Margaret nodded, though not quite understanding what Mrs. Bristlethwaite had told her. It seemed a great deal of information to absorb. Instead she turned to a question that had arisen during their visit with Sir Berwin and Lady Jane. "Who are those people you plan to write to today, Mrs. Bristlethwaite?"

"Ah, those are friends, former members of the Devonshire Coven."

Margaret could not believe what she had just heard. "The Devonshire Coven?" She could not keep the excitement from her voice.

"Yes, although it has been many years since we last met."

"But you are planning to meet again soon?" Margaret asked.

"It seems we may have to. I suppose it is past time for me to return to Devonshire."

Margaret wanted to ask if she could join the coven, but she did not know how to go about it without seeming too bold. She had longed for such a magical fellowship since her father's death, and perhaps now she had found one. She decided to speak. "Mrs. Bristlethwaite," Margaret began in a small voice. "Could—could I join the coven?"

"What a marvelous idea, my dear! I cannot imagine anyone would object to the daughter of Henry Dashwood as a potential member. Of course, the others will require you to undergo the usual steps, including the trial."

"Trial?" Margaret said through a suddenly constricted throat.

"Yes, a test of your magical abilities; it is required of all prospective members. From what you demonstrated today, I know you will fare well. Afterward, you will enter a year-long apprenticeship, honing your magical skills under our instruction."

"Oh," Margaret said. She opened her mouth to continue, but found she had not the words.

"What is it, Miss Dashwood?" Mrs. Bristlethwaite asked gently.

"Why does the trial come *before* the apprenticeship?"

"An excellent question! The work we do often demands magical expertise of the highest order. Therefore, we expect prospective members to demonstrate advanced abilities before we will consider taking them under our wings. The Devonshire Coven is one of the most highly regarded covens in all of England, largely because of these requirements." Margaret nodded to demonstrate her understanding. "But now, my dear," Mrs. Bristlethwaite continued, "you should be off home to your family. Shall we meet again? I am free early next week."

"I would like that very much!" Margaret replied.

"Excellent! I look forward to seeing you soon, my dear."

When Margaret returned to Berkeley Square, she found the house in an uproar. She hastened to the drawing room where the scene that met her stopped her in the doorway. Her mother and Marianne sat together on the sofa, weeping. Colonel Brandon knelt by his wife, trying to comfort her. Elinor paced restlessly in front of the fire.

"Goodness, what has happened?" Margaret cried.

Several heads turned toward her. There was a moment of silence then came the strangled voice of her mother.

"Margaret!"

"What is it, Mama?"

"You disappeared, and we had no idea where you were! You said you were going for a walk, but when you did not return, Colonel Brandon went to look for you. You were nowhere to be found!" Her voice rose as she spoke until it dissolved into a sob.

"Oh!" Margaret said, reaching for an explanation. "I—I am terribly sorry to have worried you, Mama! I must have lost track of time. I found a little park and sat reading until just a few minutes ago."

"Margaret, you must not wander off by yourself! London is not safe for young girls!" Colonel Brandon admonished.

"It is all right," Marianne said. "She is home. One cannot blame her for wishing to explore, can one?"

Margaret cast a thankful glance toward Marianne. "I do apologize, and I promise it will not happen again."

Her mother seemed satisfied with her explanation and made no more mention of the incident.

CHAPTER VII

*M*uch to Margaret's relief, by the following morning Mrs. Dashwood had made a complete recovery from the emotion of the day before. But at an announcement from Marianne, a more enjoyable agitation gripped the Dashwood ladies. As Margaret entered the breakfast parlor, Marianne greeted her with exuberance.

"Good morning, Margaret! I have some news for you."

"Indeed?" Margaret said as she took her place at the table. "And what is that news?"

"A certain Mr. Ellsworth will be dining with us this evening."

Margaret did not attempt to hide her elation. Her sisters exchanged an amused glance while her mother cried, "Wonderful news! Is it not wonderful news, Margaret?"

"It is, Mama."

"How nice it will be to see dear Mr. Ellsworth!" continued Mrs. Dashwood. Margaret could not look at her sisters, knowing they struggled to contain their laughter. Had she behaved so when Elinor and Marianne faced similar circumstances? Margaret did not believe she did, but she had been so young, perhaps she had not understood what was happening. She kept her eyes on her plate, but her smile betrayed her feelings.

"I am glad that the news pleases you, Margaret," Marianne said. "Edward arrives later this afternoon for a week's stay. We shall have such a happy family party!"

None of Margaret's usual occupations could hold her attention for long that day. After a morning of wandering absently from room to room, Margaret finally settled in the drawing room with her sisters and mother. She alternated reading her volume of Cowper with peeking out the window at the sound of every passing carriage. She knew that her mother and sisters observed her with some merriment, but she could not bring herself to be concerned by their reactions. The afternoon plodded along; every time Margaret checked the clock, she was disappointed to see that the hands had barely moved.

But time would not stand still, and just as Margaret could bear her anticipation no longer, Marianne spoke. "Margaret, my dear, it is time to dress for dinner."

"Oh, goodness! Thank you, Marianne," Margaret said before hurrying from the room. She ignored the laughter that followed her down the hall and onto the stairs.

Margaret took more care in dressing that evening than she ever had. By the time she arrived downstairs, everyone else in the family, including Edward, had already gathered, and their guest had long since arrived. As Margaret entered the drawing room, her eyes went directly to the tall figure of Mr. Ellsworth, who stood to greet her.

"My dear Miss Dashwood!" He strode toward her, his countenance even more handsome than Margaret had remembered.

"Mr. Ellsworth," Margaret said with only the slightest of trembles in her voice. She allowed him to take her hand and lead her to the fire.

"How thrilled I am to see you again! It seems an age since we last met. You—you look well." Mr. Ellsworth's eyes conveyed his meaning more fully than his words, and Margaret flushed with delight.

"As do you, Mr. Ellsworth," she said with feeling.

A moment's awkwardness descended between them as they realized they were the objects of close scrutiny. Margaret sensed her entire family's eyes locked on the two of them. She wanted to apologize for their attention, but knew not how. Mr. Ellsworth gave Margaret a shy smile into which she read a great deal of meaning. She returned a smile equally laden with significance.

"Shall we go in to dinner?" came Marianne's lovely voice, and the company rose as one.

Mr. Ellsworth extended his arm, and Margaret took it, feeling a rush of happiness. Unfortunately for the two, dinner afforded them little opportunity to speak. Instead, Margaret's family engaged Mr. Ellsworth in conversation.

"I understand you have changed your travel plans, Ellsworth, having meant to head west," said Colonel Brandon. "What brings you to London instead?"

"I found that my business could be conducted in London as easily as elsewhere," Mr. Ellsworth replied.

"And what is your business, Mr. Ellsworth?" Edward enquired.

"It is not so much a business as a passion. I am a collector."

"Oh?" said Elinor. "What do you collect?"

"Rare items. Artifacts, works of art, many objects from around the world."

"You do?" Margaret was intrigued.

Mr. Ellsworth nodded, obviously gratified by Margaret's interest. "Perhaps sometime I could show you my collection," he said with a hint of shyness.

"I should like that very much," Margaret replied.

"Mr. Ellsworth, I hear you are also an admirer of poetry," said Marianne.

"You have heard the truth," Mr. Ellsworth replied amiably.

"I hope that I can convince you to favor us with a reading after dinner," Marianne said.

"If you entreat, I cannot deny, although one whose reading far surpasses mine is among our company."

Marianne raised an eyebrow. "And who might that be?"

"Your sister, Mrs. Brandon. Miss Dashwood favored me with a reading of Cowper the likes of which I had never experienced."

"You have good taste, Mr. Ellsworth."

After dinner Mr. Ellsworth joined Margaret on the sofa near the fire. Again Margaret ignored the significant looks exchanged by her sisters and mother.

Marianne approached him with a book. "You promised," she said.

Mr. Ellsworth took the book, laughing. "Do you have a poem in mind, or am I at liberty to choose?"

"I bow to your choice." Marianne took her seat at her husband's side.

Mr. Ellsworth turned the pages in silence before settling on a poem. He looked at the company, his gaze lingering on Margaret before he began. His well-measured voice held them as if spellbound, and even Marianne approved of his reading.

"Excellently done, Mr. Ellsworth! You read with genuine feeling."

"Thank you, Mrs. Brandon."

When at last everyone had turned to other enterprises, Mr. Ellsworth addressed Margaret.

"I have been thinking about your desire to see the world, Miss Dashwood."

"Oh?"

"Yes. It seems a shame that a young man may go where he likes whereas a young woman must depend upon a chaperone—or someone else in a similar capacity—to take her."

"I have often considered the same inequality in the state of man and woman," Margaret replied. "I do not consider myself any gentler than most of the men of my acquaintance." Margaret could not believe her boldness, yet she continued speaking. "I have as hearty a constitution as my brothers."

"I am certain you do," Mr. Ellsworth agreed.

"As a child I often pretended to lead expeditions around the world." Margaret smiled at the memory. "My father used to say I had a restless heart."

Mr. Ellsworth fixed her with a gaze. "I wonder, Miss Dashwood. Do you still think it so?" His inflection hinted toward a deeper significance than his simple question conveyed. Margaret glanced around, but her sisters and their husbands were occupied at the card table while her mother watched them play and did her needlework. "I apologize, Miss Dashwood, if I have implied anything unfitting," Mr. Ellsworth added, appearing distressed.

"Oh, no, Mr. Ellsworth. You have said nothing that is not already well known about me. My father was right, of course." Margaret regarded Mr. Ellsworth, seeing the care in his blue eyes, so intent upon her, the solicitation of her good will. "When I was a child I could spend hours in his study, playing with an atlas that he had."

"Indeed? His atlas?" Mr. Ellsworth's eyes brightened. "What a curious plaything!"

"I enjoyed imagining what the different countries might be like. What sights or sounds or scents I might encounter." She paused, afraid she had revealed too much. "But that was so long ago."

"It is hard to let go of those things we cherished as children, is it not, Miss Dashwood?" Mr. Ellsworth's voice was gentle.

"Yes it is, Mr. Ellsworth."

"What became of your father's atlas?"

"I—I am not certain," Margaret replied. "It was such a long time ago." Margaret looked away, unable to meet Mr. Ellsworth's eyes.

"Your brother speaks highly of your father. I was most impressed by his library. I wish I had had a chance to know him."

"He was a wonderful man," Margaret said, her voice shaking.

"Oh, Miss Dashwood. Please forgive me! How heartlessly I brought up a subject that must cause you such pain!"

"Not at all, Mr. Ellsworth," Margaret said, grateful that he misunderstood the cause of her agitation. "I enjoy thinking about my father. I am always astonished, though, how much I still miss him."

"You have good cause."

Another companionable silence descended.

"Margaret," came Marianne's voice from across the room. "Would you favor us with something at the *pianoforte*?"

"Oh, yes, please, Miss Dashwood!" agreed Mr. Ellsworth with enthusiasm.

Margaret consented, allowing Mr. Ellsworth to the turn the pages of the music. They occupied themselves in this fashion until the hour grew quite late.

"Is that the time?" Mr. Ellsworth said. "How quickly the hours fly when one is surrounded by such company! I am afraid, however, that I must take my leave." He bowed to Marianne. "Mrs. Brandon, thank you for a most delicious dinner."

"You are most welcome, Mr. Ellsworth," said Marianne. "I look forward to hearing you read again."

Mr. Ellsworth turned to Margaret. "Miss Dashwood, I hope I shall see you again soon. I have business that takes me away from London for a day or two, but when I return I shall pay you a call."

"I would like that, Mr. Ellsworth," Margaret replied.

And with another bow, Mr. Ellsworth left the family to themselves. All eyes turned to Margaret, who braced herself for their gentle teasing.

"He seems a kind man, although I do not know how I could make a complete judgment of his character, having had so little opportunity to converse with him," said Elinor, eyes twinkling.

"As it should be!" cried Marianne.

Margaret slipped from the drawing room, accompanied by her family's laughter and made her way back to her room in near perfect felicity.

Margaret spent the next two days cheerfully ensconced in family life while in the evenings she read more of her father's notes and perused the atlas. As the week came to a close, she began to think about how she could slip away to Mrs. Bristlethwaite's house. But before she could form a plan, a note from Sir John Middleton arrived at the Brandon residence, driving all other considerations from her mind.

"Margaret," said Marianne. "Sir John and Lady Middleton have arrived in town and have sent an invitation to a ball for two nights from now."

"Splendid!" Margaret said, catching her sister's enthusiasm.

Marianne fixed her with a mischievous grin. "I have taken the liberty of informing Sir John of a certain new acquaintance of ours."

"Oh?" Margaret replied.

"Yes. And I believe an invitation has been sent to the gentleman."

Margaret's heart began to race. How marvelous it would be to dance with Mr. Ellsworth! Then a terrible thought struck her. "Will Mrs. Jennings be in attendance?"

Marianne laughed. "I am afraid so, my dear. You must brace yourself for some teasing. 'And whom do you favor, Miss Margaret Dashwood?'" said Marianne in a faultless imitation of Sir John's garrulous mother-in-law. "'I believe it is a Mr. E, is it not?'"

The entire family laughed, though Mrs. Dashwood looked a little abashed.

In a note later that morning, Mr. Ellsworth both confirmed his attendance at the ball and requested that Miss Dashwood save a dance for him. From that moment, time seemed to move with the speed of cold molasses. No matter her occupation, whenever Margaret looked at the hands of the clock they seemed not to have advanced at all. Finally she thought of the atlas hidden in her room, and making her excuses, headed upstairs.

Margaret spent an enjoyable afternoon engrossed in the atlas, reading about far-flung places such as Persia and India, only glancing up once or twice. She did not notice when someone arrived at her room.

"Is that Papa's old atlas?" Marianne cried upon entering Margaret's chamber. "It is!" Before Margaret could stop her, Marianne had begun leafing through the book. Margaret braced herself for Marianne's shock. "I remember this being so much bigger. I suppose it must have seemed so when we were small. How you loved this book, Margaret."

"I did indeed love it," said Margaret carefully.

Marianne read the inscription aloud. "How sweet," she whispered.

Margaret was beside herself with anticipation. At any moment Marianne was going to discover the book's magic. Yet her perusal of the atlas continued without any indication she knew what she studied. At last she set the book down and said, "Would you care to join us for tea?"

"I shall be down shortly," Margaret said in as

steady a voice as she could manage.

After Marianne left, Margaret flipped through the atlas, searching for some explanation. She found what she was looking for in an appendix titled "Additional Notes."

> *As an added precaution, I have included an enchantment that renders the magic of the atlas completely invisible to the non-magical. Nevertheless, I encourage you, whenever possible, to keep the atlas close to yourself.*

Her family would not be able to see the enchantment! Margaret was elated at the prospect of reading the atlas amongst them. Such was her anxiety over its discovery that she had not even attempted a cloaking glamour to hide it. But now she could keep the atlas with her at all times. Tucking the book into her pocket, she made her way down to tea.

CHAPTER VIII

No matter how slowly, time will pass, and at last the hour of the ball arrived. Margaret descended from Colonel Brandon's carriage and followed her family into Sir John Middleton's stately London residence. The sun had already set, and the townhouse glowed with torches. Guests filled the entrance, displaying with pride their finest attire. Margaret searched for a tall figure crowned with black curls. But through the crush of people she saw only Sir John, who stood talking to someone. When the person blocking her view shifted, Margaret recognized Sir John's companion as Mrs. Bristlethwaite. Excited, she hurried toward them.

"Miss Dashwood!" Sir John cried with delight. "How long it has been since last we met!" He turned to Mrs. Bristlethwaite. "Miss Margaret Dashwood is a charming neighbor of ours in Devonshire," he said. "And Mrs. Bristlethwaite is mistress of Barbary Hall."

"Miss Dashwood and I are old friends."

"Indeed? How fortunate for both of you!" He

leaned toward Margaret. "Mrs. Bristlethwaite has been away from Devonshire for far too long. Perhaps together we can convince her to return. What do you say, Miss Dashwood?"

"You speak nothing but the truth, Sir John. But I shall be opening Barbary Hall soon."

"Excellent news!" Sir John waved to someone nearby. A crowd of people parted to reveal Sir John's mother-in-law, Mrs. Jennings, bustling their way. Margaret saw no way to escape the jolly onslaught and so braced herself.

"Mrs. Bristlethwaite!" cried Mrs. Jennings. She turned toward Margaret. "And Miss Dashwood! Why are you standing here with the old people? The dancing has begun. Go on and find a partner!" She shooed Margaret toward the ballroom.

"Give the poor girl time to get her bearings, Mrs. Jennings," said Mrs. Bristlethwaite. "Her mother may not wish her to run off so quickly. Where is your mother, Miss Dashwood?" Mrs. Bristlethwaite winked at Margaret.

"I shall find her," said Margaret, relieved by this excuse to avoid Mrs. Jennings's inevitable teasing.

"Nonsense," countered Mrs. Jennings. "Miss Dashwood's mother would never come between a young lady and a dance! Come along, Mrs. Bristlethwaite, I shall introduce you, and you can judge for yourself. I just saw Mrs. Dashwood pass into the drawing room with your sisters, Miss Dashwood." Mrs. Jennings paused, her attention diverted. A familiar smile tugged at the older woman's lips, and Margaret felt a wave of dread. "I believe a gentleman approaches! I cannot imagine he aims to speak to us, Mrs. Bristlethwaite. Come with me." She herded Mrs. Bristlethwaite down the hall.

At the mention of the gentleman, Margaret's heartbeat quickened. Relieved that Mrs. Jennings had spared her the anticipated, though undesired, attention, Margaret turned to search for Mr. Ellsworth. Her efforts were immediately rewarded. The gentleman himself strode toward her.

"Miss Dashwood!" His greeting carried as much fervor as Margaret could desire. She held out her hand, upon which he laid a gentle kiss.

"Well, Miss Dashwood, it seems you are not lacking a dance partner after all," observed Sir John.

Mr. Ellsworth bowed to the older gentleman. "Weston Ellsworth," he said, extending his hand.

"Ah, the famous Mr. Ellsworth. I have heard a great deal about you," said Sir John, shaking the proffered hand. "Sir John Middleton. Welcome to my house. I suppose, however, that your interest lies in other company. Excellent choice. I shall leave you to it then." He bowed and then bustled off, chuckling merrily.

"Well," said Mr. Ellsworth. "Is he always so—"

"Yes, I am afraid he is," Margaret replied.

Mr. Ellsworth laughed. "Then I am glad to have rescued you, Miss Dashwood. Might I have this dance?"

"I would be honored, Mr. Ellsworth," said Margaret, taking his arm.

They entered the ballroom just as the next set was beginning and took their places among the company. The musicians struck the opening chords, and Margaret and Mr. Ellsworth were swept into the dance. For the first breathless moments they did little more than smile at one another.

"I was delighted to receive the invitation," Mr. Ellsworth said at length. "I believe your brother Colonel Brandon had something to do with securing it."

"He did," Margaret replied. "With my sister Marianne's help."

"They have risen even further in my estimation, then." They danced on in silence until Mr. Ellsworth spoke again. "Have you passed a pleasant week since we last met?"

"I have, though it was a quiet week."

"I am sorry to hear it, Miss Dashwood. You deserve adventure!" He paused, fixing her with his blue eyes. "Perhaps—no, that would be too forward of me."

"What were you going to say, Mr. Ellsworth?"

"I very much enjoy the theatre, Miss Dashwood, and I had hoped to take you to see a play. With your mother or another member of your family, of course."

"I would enjoy that very much," said Margaret. "And I am certain that we could persuade Mama or someone else to accompany us. Marianne is very fond of the theatre."

Mr. Ellsworth beamed at her response. Margaret's joy made her giddy. Already the evening promised to be better than she could have imagined.

When the dance ended, Mr. Ellsworth escorted Margaret to a table and promised to return with refreshments. Margaret took the opportunity to glance around the room. It was beautifully appointed, Lady Middleton's superior influence evident in the arrangement of furniture and the choice of wall hangings.

"There you are, Margaret!"

Margaret turned; her mother and Mrs. Bristlethwaite joined her. "I see Mrs. Jennings found you," Margaret said.

"She did," replied Mrs. Dashwood. "And she has introduced us. Did you know Mrs. Bristlethwaite is the mistress of Barbary Hall?"

"I did."

"I hope we shall see one another often once we have all returned to Devonshire," said Mrs. Dashwood.

"As do I, Mrs. Dashwood."

"Are you enjoying the ball, Mrs. Bristlethwaite?"

"I am, although I must say I am a touch too old for one," Mrs. Bristlethwaite replied. "I see you had a dance already."

"Did you?" said Mrs. Dashwood.

"Mr. Ellsworth has arrived, Mama."

"Splendid! Where is he?"

"He has gone for refreshments. He should return in a moment." And just as Margaret spoke, she saw him striding toward her, carrying two glasses.

"Mr. Ellsworth," said Mrs. Dashwood when he arrived at their table. "How good to see you again."

He bowed to the ladies. "Mrs. Dashwood. How lovely to see you!"

"This is Mrs. Bristlethwaite," said Margaret.

Mr. Ellsworth hesitated, as though suddenly shy. A hint of coldness passed over his face, but it was gone so quickly that Margaret was certain she had imagined it. He addressed the older woman amiably.

"Mrs. Bristlethwaite, I am delighted to make your acquaintance."

"As am I, Mr. Ellsworth," Mrs. Bristlethwaite

replied.

"Would you ladies care for some refreshment as well?"

"Oh no, Mr. Ellsworth. We have just been drinking tea in the drawing room," said Mrs. Dashwood.

"We have come to watch the young people dance," added Mrs. Bristlethwaite.

"I suppose we must not disappoint your mother and Mrs. Bristlethwaite," said Mr. Ellsworth.

"I suppose not," Margaret agreed, taking his arm.

"Is Mrs. Bristlethwaite a new acquaintance?" Mr. Ellsworth asked after they had started dancing.

"She is," said Margaret. "She, too, is a friend of Sir John's. She seems a jolly woman, does she not?"

"Jolly indeed!" said Mr. Ellsworth.

Toward the end of the dance, Margaret had the sensation of someone watching them. She searched the room but could not tell from what quarter the gaze originated.

"Are you looking for someone, Miss Dashwood?" said Mr. Ellsworth.

"Oh, no, not really." She sighed. "I suspect, Mr. Ellsworth, that we are being observed. By whom I am not entirely certain, but if I had to guess, I would say my entire family as well as Sir John and Mrs. Jennings." She blushed as she spoke.

Mr. Ellsworth laughed and said, "Perhaps I have strained the bounds of propriety by dancing with you twice in a row."

The music ended, and Mr. Ellsworth escorted Margaret to a small bench at the edge of the dance floor. "Oh, I doubt very much that anyone in my family worries terribly about the bounds of propriety," said Margaret as they crossed the room. "Except perhaps for Elinor."

Again Margaret was pleased by the amiable sound of Mr. Ellsworth's laugh.

"You have a charming smile, Miss Dashwood," Mr. Ellsworth said, suddenly growing serious. His blue eyes met hers, holding her in their gaze. She resisted the urge to look away.

"I have a confession to make, Miss Dashwood," he whispered, barely audible above the music. "I find myself quite enchanted by you."

Margaret's eyes widened. Had he discovered her secret?

"Have I said something wrong, Miss Dashwood?" said Mr. Ellsworth, an expression of concern on his face.

Margaret composed herself. "Not at all, Mr. Ellsworth."

"Good." He paused, weighing his words before continuing. "I do not know why, but I feel as if I have known you for years rather than weeks. How might such a thing be possible?" His eyes were soft.

"My sister Marianne is fond of saying that with some people that is the case—some people require little time to develop true intimacy, whereas others may know each other for a lifetime and remain mere acquaintances."

"I believe your sister to be a wise woman, Miss Dashwood. And you, do you share her beliefs?"

"I did not know before this moment, for I had no experience to rely upon. But now—yes, Mr. Ellsworth, I do think it possible." Margaret could not believe the daring with which she addressed this charming man. She was glad her mother was not near to hear their exchange.

"As do I, Miss Dashwood."

"Ah, Miss Dashwood!"

Margaret turned and saw Mrs. Bristlethwaite hurrying toward her, a look of worry creasing her normally cheerful features.

"What is it?"

"Your sister Marianne has taken ill. Your mother and Mrs. Ferrars have joined her in the carriage. I came to tell you; if you would like to remain here, I can easily convey you home. Otherwise, they await you."

Margaret turned to Mr. Ellsworth. "I—"

"Of course, Miss Dashwood; you must go with your family," said Mr. Ellsworth. "I shall call on you tomorrow."

"And I have invited you and your mother to tea, so we shall meet again soon, Miss Dashwood." Mrs. Bristlethwaite leveled a look at Margaret that she well understood.

"Thank you!" Margaret cried and raced out without making her apologies to Sir John.

She found Mrs. Dashwood and Elinor sitting with Marianne in the carriage.

"You need not have come, Margaret," said Marianne. "You were having such a fine time!"

"Nonsense!" Margaret took her place in the carriage. Marianne looked very pale, but remained upright, which Margaret hoped boded well.

The family together, they began their journey to Berkeley Square. As they travelled through the streets of London, Marianne grew fainter, made uncomfortable by the jostling of the carriage.

"Not much longer, dearest," said Elinor with a

worried glance to their mother.

Margaret searched her memory for a spell that might help, but she could think of nothing. She would consult her spell books for something that might ease Marianne's suffering as soon as she could. Meanwhile, Margaret watched her sister with growing concern. Marianne had always been more delicate than the other Dashwood girls.

Upon arriving in Berkeley Square, Colonel Brandon assisted Marianne to her room.

"Will you stay with her?" he implored Mrs. Dashwood.

"Of course, Colonel," Mrs. Dashwood reassured him.

"As will I," added Elinor.

"Thank you! Margaret, come with me."

Margaret followed Colonel Brandon downstairs where he instructed the footman to fetch the doctor. "As quickly as you can!" he insisted.

The footman bowed and raced away. Colonel Brandon turned to Margaret. "When the doctor arrives, will you bring him to Marianne's room? I wish to return to her immediately."

Margaret nodded and took his hand. "I am sure the doctor will help, Colonel," she said, hiding her worry as best as she could.

Brandon replied with a curt nod and then hurried back up the stairs.

Margaret paced the hallway, stopping frequently at the sound of carriages trundling by outside. At last the doctor arrived, bristling with competence. Margaret led him to the patient's room, and not wishing to be underfoot, remained outside. When it became apparent that no one would be leaving the room for some time, she abandoned her vigil.

Margaret returned to her chamber and poured through her magic books. After half an hour's fruitless search, she put aside her books and stared at the fire as her fatigue battled her worry. Her tangled thoughts suddenly gave way to clarity. How could she have forgotten Mrs. Bristlethwaite? She hastened to her desk and composed a short note, explaining the nature of Marianne's complaint as best she could. *I shall consult my spell books, but as my sister's condition is already delicate, I apply to you for guidance*, she wrote. She snuck downstairs to ensure that the letter would be sent with the morning post. Finally, she took herself to bed, hoping that she would wake to good news.

Margaret found her mother and eldest sister in the breakfast salon, looking much calmer, though quite tired.

"How is Marianne?"

"Marianne will be all right, my dear," Mrs. Dashwood assured her. "She tired herself and requires much rest. The doctor has ordered her to keep to her bed until her lying in."

"Will that not prove difficult for Marianne?" Margaret asked.

"I suppose it will, dearest," replied Elinor.

Her mother and sister's laughter convinced Margaret that Marianne was no longer in danger. Relief allowed her appetite to assert itself, and she ate a hearty breakfast.

After the morning meal, Elinor and Mrs. Dashwood retired to their rooms. Restless, Margaret paced in the drawing room as the rain prevented her from taking a walk in the square. But to her relief, a

letter from Mrs. Bristlethwaite soon set her mind at
ease.

My Dear Miss Dashwood,

*If I am not mistaken, you will find several spells,
charms, and potions commonly employed by
midwives in A Compendium of Magical Spells by
M. Langlois. While much of the Compendium is
given over to masculine matters, it is surprisingly rich
in sorcery concerning women's health. Marie
Langlois Girard, the author's sister, was a well-
known sorceress who specialized in a branch of
healing magic dedicated especially to childbirth, and
her influence can be clearly felt in her brother's book.*

*I shall send my carriage this afternoon to collect you
and your mother; if you have any need of assistance
with a spell, charm, or potion, we can find a way to
discuss it this afternoon.*

Fear not, my dear. All will be well.

Yours,

E. Bristlethwaite

Margaret hurried to her room and consulted
Langlois's *Compendium*. Mrs. Bristlethwaite's memory
had been correct. Margaret found an excellent charm
that would protect Marianne and the baby:

*Wrap a sprig of lavender, a dried lily, and a pinch
of myrrh in a cloth; tie with a ribbon, then utter the
words of the spell: "Bébé dort au chaud et en*

sécurité; maman repose apaisée." Translator's note: "Baby sleeps in warmth and security, mother rests secure." The English translation is just as effective, though perhaps less poetic.

"I prefer the French anyway," Margaret said. She copied the spell and tucked the paper into her pocket before dashing downstairs.

She found her mother in the drawing room. "How is Marianne?" Margaret asked.

"Resting, my dear."

"I am glad to hear it!" Margaret sat on the sofa with her mother. "Mrs. Bristlethwaite sent a note. The carriage will be here this afternoon."

"Oh, how lovely," said Mrs. Dashwood. "Alas, I believe I would not be good company, tired as I am after my long vigil last night. And I would like to stay close to Marianne. Will you make my excuses to Mrs. Bristlethwaite?"

"Would you rather I remained here, too, Mama?" Margaret asked, concern for her mother overcoming her desire to see Mrs. Bristlethwaite.

"You should go and enjoy yourself. I shall be fine," said Mrs. Dashwood. She tucked a curl behind Margaret's ear and then kissed her. "All will be well, my dear."

CHAPTER IX

*A*nother letter arrived for Margaret as she waited for Mrs. Bristlethwaite's carriage. Margaret recognized the handwriting and smiled. Mrs. Dashwood and Elinor glanced at each other, but remained silent. Margaret opened the letter.

Miss Dashwood,

You cannot know the pain I suffer in being the bearer of such news, but I am afraid I must break my promise to visit you today. I have been called away by some urgent business. I beg you to forgive me, Miss Dashwood; believe me when I say that if it were in my power, I would like nothing more than to stay in London for as long as you reside here.

I promise to call immediately upon my return, the time of which I cannot be certain. But you will be the first to know of my arrival.

Yours ever,

W. Ellsworth

As she read, Margaret's feelings swung from disappointment to elation. She would miss seeing Mr. Ellsworth, but she was thrilled by the loving tone of his note. She hated for him to feel pain, but took a small measure of joy that he shared her feelings. Her poor heart was strained, and though she felt nothing would remove her anguish, perhaps tea with Mrs. Bristlethwaite might assuage it somewhat.

The carriage's arrival distracted her, and Margaret bid her mother and sister farewell. She watched London pass as the carriage rolled through the streets. The ride was much shorter than she would have thought, given the distance they had to cross, and she wondered, as they stopped in front of Mrs. Bristlethwaite's house, if the coachman knew of a shorter route.

Mrs. Bristlethwaite was waiting in the drawing room, the tea already prepared. "Hello, Miss Dashwood," she said upon Margaret's entrance. "How is your sister?"

"She seems better today. She has been ordered to stay in bed, which I think she finds troubling. Marianne is a great lover of walking."

"Poor girl. But we shall do what we can to protect her."

Margaret smiled. "I found the perfect charm." She drew the paper from her pocket and handed it to Mrs. Bristlethwaite. The older woman perused it.

"Perfect. I have everything we need to make the charm after we have finished our tea. In the meanwhile, perhaps you could tell me about the gentleman with whom you danced. How did you come to be acquainted?"

Margaret could not hide her sigh. She tried not to notice Mrs. Bristlethwaite's amusement as she spoke. "Mr. Ellsworth is a friend of my brother John's. He came to dinner at Norland while my mother and I were visiting." Margaret was grateful to discover that speaking about Mr. Ellsworth relieved some of the heartbreak caused by his absence.

"If he is a friend of your brother then I doubt he is a sorcerer," Mrs. Bristlethwaite mused. "Your father told me that you were his only magical child and that John possessed very little in the way of imagination. He did not anticipate John crossing paths with any sorcerers."

"I do not believe Mr. Ellsworth to be a sorcerer." Margaret paused. "How does one generally know?"

"Sometimes you can tell by family name. Anyone who studies magical genealogy, for example, knows that Bristlethwaite is a prominent name among sorcerers. Hartbustle is another, though I think there is only one member of that family still alive. He has something to do with books.

"Secrecy is important as it is dangerous to reveal oneself to the nonmagical. On rare occasions you may meet someone whose magic cannot be hidden. But most of the time we guess. Then there are the Councils of Covens in which large groups of sorcerers come together. One often makes acquaintances in that manner."

"Have you been to a Council?" Margaret asked. There was so much her father had not taught her.

"Once or twice, although I prefer smaller groups,

especially as I grow older." Mrs. Bristlethwaite set her teacup on its saucer. "But we must get to work, Miss Dashwood. Come with me."

Margaret followed Mrs. Bristlethwaite down the hall and up a flight of stairs. They came to a door at the end of the corridor.

"Open," said Mrs. Bristlethwaite.

The lock tumbled and then the door swung open, revealing Mrs. Bristlethwaite's cozy study. Most of the walls were lined with shelves laden with books. A tall window opposite the door let in the afternoon sunlight. Much of the room was taken up by a large wooden worktable, which stood upon a thick rug woven in an arabesque pattern of deep red, blue, black and white. A small brass telescope sat at one end of the table, surrounded by what appeared to be maps of some kind. Margaret picked one up and examined it, but she could not read it.

"I have a number of charts of the heavens," Mrs. Bristlethwaite explained. "My late husband was fond of gazing at the stars."

"Oh yes, my father kept these, too, though he never showed me how they work."

"I do not believe your father put much store in reading the stars. To tell you the truth, neither do I. Although peering through the lens on a clear night can be an enjoyable way to spend an evening, I prefer more earthly pursuits." She indicated the mortar and pestle, set of scales, and small brass cauldron on the middle of the table. "I find charms and potions always work better when I prepare them myself."

"Can one buy them already made?"

"If you know which apothecary to visit, you can buy a variety of charms and potions. But one can never be certain of their potency. Have you never made a charm?"

Margaret shook her head. "I have read about them, but I have never had the chance to make one myself."

"Well then, we shall work together." Mrs. Bristlethwaite rolled up her sleeves and then gestured to the large cabinet set against the far wall. "You will find what we require in there. The jars are clearly labeled."

Margaret opened the cabinet. Several different scents rushed out to meet her. She gathered the jars marked lavender, myrrh, and lily and brought them to the table where Mrs. Bristlethwaite had laid the charm's instructions next to a piece of pink cloth and a pink ribbon.

"Everything is ready for you. It seems simple enough."

Margaret drew the ingredients out of the jars and placed them in the cloth, tying it with the ribbon. She held the small bundle in her hand and spoke the words of the charm, "*Bébé dort au chaud et en sécurité; maman repose apaisée.*" The charm grew heavier as if with the weight of magic. Pleased, Margaret turned to Mrs. Bristlethwaite.

"Interesting choice, Miss Dashwood. You spoke the Folding Spell in French, too. I have been meaning to ask you why you do not use English?"

Margaret colored under Mrs. Bristlethwaite's scrutiny, but she knew that Mrs. Bristlethwaite would expect an honest answer. "I prefer French because it is more poetic."

Mrs. Bristlethwaite raised an eyebrow. "What does poetry have to do with magic?" She spoke with curiosity rather than judgment.

Margaret could not believe Mrs. Bristlethwaite's question. "Is magic not the very essence of poetry? And is poetry not the very essence of magic? They are linked in beauty and power!"

Mrs. Bristlethwaite considered Margaret's impassioned speech. "I have never thought about it that way. I have always thought magic rather more practical than poetry. In my experience clarity offers the best results." She gave Margaret a kind look. "What did your father think?"

"He loved poetry, too. He encouraged me, I suppose."

Mrs. Bristlethwaite cocked her head to one side and observed Margaret carefully. "I suppose it will do no harm." Mrs. Bristlethwaite's countenance softened. "Your French is beautiful, Miss Dashwood, which explains your facility with spells cast in it. Be careful, though. Spells can easily go awry if you do something as simple as mispronounce one of the words."

"Oh, I can assure you that I am always very careful!"

"Then you should be fine. But perhaps, just as an experiment some time, you might try casting a spell or two in English to see what happens."

Torn between desire to please Mrs. Bristlethwaite and dedication to poetry, Margaret merely nodded. Mrs. Bristlethwaite, returning everything to its proper place, did not notice Margaret's reticence.

"Well, now, that was easy, was it not, Miss Dashwood?"

"Quite!" Margaret said, eager to agree with Mrs. Bristlethwaite.

"You should give that to your sister as soon as possible while the charm is at its strongest. Tell her that it will calm her mind and soothe her spirit. I imagine she will need that reassurance. It should provide sufficient protection as long as it remains in the room with her."

"Thank you, Mrs. Bristlethwaite."

"Of course, my dear."

With the charm in her pocket, Margaret followed Mrs. Bristlethwaite back to the vestibule. Outside, the carriage waited to take Margaret home.

"Good-bye, my dear," said Mrs. Bristlethwaite. "Do give my regards to your mother. When she feels well enough, we shall all have tea together."

"I will tell her. Good bye, Mrs. Bristlethwaite."

As soon as she returned to the house in Berkeley Square, Margaret went to Marianne's room. She found her sister propped in her bed with Elinor sitting in a chair next to her, reading.

"Margaret!" Marianne cried.

"Do not trouble yourself to get out of bed, Marianne," Margaret said, sitting next to her sister.

"I am sorry if I frightened you," Marianne said, taking her sister's hand.

"Do you feel better?"

"Worlds. But I do not know how I shall stand being kept in my bed for the next several months. I will go mad with wanting to go outside."

"I have brought you a little gift." Margaret handed Marianne the charm.

Marianne took in its scent. "I smell lavender. What else am I detecting?"

"A little lily and other dried flowers. I thought you might like a small bouquet to keep with you, since you cannot go outside. Dried flowers will not lose their scent so quickly."

"Thank you, Margaret!" Marianne set the charm next to her in the bed.

"Yes, dearest, it is a charming gift," Elinor said. "Very thoughtful."

Margaret stood to leave, but Marianne held firmly to her hand. "Oh, please stay. I have seen so little of you since you have been here."

"Of course," Margaret said. "I suppose I have been rather occupied."

Marianne gave her a coy smile. "I can certainly understand why! Mr. Ellsworth seems a lovely gentleman. He dances wonderfully."

"He does indeed," Margaret agreed.

A cloud passed over Marianne's countenance. "Do be careful, Margaret. Take care where you bestow your heart. Remember what happened to me—"

"Now, now, Marianne. Mr. Ellsworth is nothing like—" Elinor said.

"No, he is not. But I have learned that taking one's time can be the best strategy with love."

Margaret's eyebrows disappeared into her hair. "Have you indeed?"

The incredulity in her tone inspired her sisters to laughter. Soon the three of them were giggling much as they had when they were younger and lived together in their little cottage in Devonshire.

"Oh!" Marianne gasped.

"What is it?" Elinor and Margaret said together.

"Nothing, just a little pain in my side." She fixed them with a steady gaze. "I am fine. I think I just laughed a little too much. But it was marvelous—I felt like a girl again."

"You are hardly more than a girl now, though you

are married and have two children," said Elinor.

Marianne's eyes began to close. "I think I should rest."

"Would you like us to stay?" Elinor asked.

"Just until I fall asleep. Then would you send Brandon? I should like to wake up with him watching over me."

"Of course, my dear," said Elinor. She leaned over and kissed Marianne, much as she might have her own children. When they were certain that Marianne had fallen into a peaceful sleep, the two sisters slipped out of the room.

CHAPTER X

Margaret spent much of the following week engaged in quiet pursuits with her sisters and mother, always alert for Marianne's well being. She awaited each delivery of the post with eagerness, hopeful that Mr. Ellsworth would write again soon, but several days passed without a letter. She managed to hide her growing concern from her mother and Elinor. Marianne, however, had a far keener eye for the breaking of a heart. One morning as Margaret sat alone with Marianne, she caught her sister studying her. Margaret responded by bustling around the chamber in a show of good humor.

"What is troubling you, Margaret?" Marianne said.

"Oh, nothing at all," Margaret replied.

Marianne smiled. "Sit next to me." Margaret complied, and Marianne continued. "My dear, you need not keep your worries from me. I am not so delicate that I cannot help my sister to feel better."

Margaret struggled with her feelings, wishing to keep them a secret, but at length she confessed. "I have not heard from Mr. Ellsworth in more than a week." Rather than offering relief, admitting her distress brought tears to Margaret's eyes.

"My dearest!" said Marianne, patting Margaret's hand. "You must not fret. I am certain that he holds you in high regard. He is not like—well, he is an honorable gentleman, with a fortune all his own. You will hear from him soon."

"Oh, Marianne, I hope what you say is true! For I—I love him!" Margaret collapsed on the bed, sobbing.

"There, there, my dear. All will be well!" Marianne stroked Margaret's hair. "There is no shame in giving one's heart!"

Margaret nodded, her face still buried in the covers. Marianne waited for the storm to pass. When at last it did, Margaret sat up. "I never understood before—"

"No one can, my dear. Not until they have felt the pangs themselves. Perhaps you might take solace in your poetry?"

"I shall try." She dried her eyes. "Now you must rest," she added, seeing the strained look on Marianne's face. "I fear I have distressed you."

"Not at all, though I think a little rest would be a good idea. Would you come back this afternoon? And bring Cowper. I should like to hear you read."

Margaret kissed her gently. "I promise." She rose to leave. "Thank you, Marianne."

"Of course, my dear."

"How is Marianne?" Mrs. Dashwood enquired when Margaret joined her in the drawing room.

"Resting." Margaret took a seat near the fire and

stared at the flames. She knew Marianne meant well, yet Margaret continued to wonder why Mr. Ellsworth had not written. Perhaps she had been mistaken about his feelings. Or something horrible had befallen him! What if Mr. Ellsworth were ill or hurt? What if he needed her help?

"Margaret, a letter has come for you."

"What is that?" Margaret said, her fevered imaginings interrupted.

"A letter has come for you," Elinor repeated.

Margaret leapt up and took the letter. Relief coursed through her at the sight of the familiar handwriting, and she tore the letter open.

> *My dearest Miss Dashwood,*
>
> *I beg your forgiveness for my recent neglect and for the news that this letter bears. My business has called me unexpectedly to the Continent, where I am afraid I shall have to remain for some time. I wish I had been at leisure to bid you a proper farewell. Perhaps the promise of a visit in Devonshire will lighten the burden of this message. Sir John has invited me to stay with him and Lady Middleton at Barton Hall whenever I happen to find myself in his neighborhood. I shall do everything in my power to assure that occurs sooner rather than later.*
>
> *In the meanwhile, Miss Dashwood, would it be too forward of me to request a letter or two from you? You may direct any missives to my London address and they will be sure to reach me. I am certain correspondence with you will soften the pain of our separation.*

Until we meet again, I remain your most earnest admirer,

W. Ellsworth

Margaret read the letter again. She would miss Mr. Ellsworth's company terribly, but his assurances of regard filled her with joy.

A much more cheerful Margaret accompanied her mother to Mrs. Bristlethwaite's house for tea that afternoon. London glistened with new brilliance, every street offering an interesting view. Although he was far away, Mr. Ellsworth had written. All was right with the world.

"My word," said Mrs. Dashwood. "We have already arrived!"

Jenkins brought them down the long hallway past the family portraits into the drawing room.

"I am so glad you could join us," said Mrs. Bristlethwaite, rising to greet Mrs. Dashwood.

"As am I," Mrs. Dashwood replied. "Thank you for sending your carriage. I have never had such a quiet ride on cobbled streets!"

"My late husband designed the wheels to soften travel. One is always so exhausted after going any distance."

Margaret turned so that her mother would not see her merriment. She would ask Mrs. Bristlethwaite about the spell later.

"Perhaps you could share the design with Colonel Brandon? I know that his carriage causes him discomfort, though he never lets on."

"I shall do what I can," said Mrs. Bristlethwaite.

"Come sit by the fire. It is a blustery day!"

As usual Mrs. Bristlethwaite's kitchen had sent a superior tea. The maid finished serving and slipped out of the room, leaving the ladies to enjoy their refreshments and each other's company.

"How is Mrs. Brandon?" Mrs. Bristlethwaite said as she passed a plate of biscuits to Mrs. Dashwood.

"She improves, though the doctor has ordered her to remain in her bed for the duration. Marianne does not enjoy being confined."

"I imagine having her mother near offers some comfort," said Mrs. Bristlethwaite.

"I think so. Her elder sister Elinor is also a great help, but she has small children of her own and must return home soon. Marianne does not look forward to our departure with any enthusiasm."

"I wished to speak to you about just that subject. I shall be returning to Devonshire soon, and I would like to invite Miss Dashwood to join me, which I hope would allow you to remain with Mrs. Brandon." Mrs. Bristlethwaite looked at Margaret. "You may stay with me for as long as your mother is needed here."

Margaret's heart leapt at the idea of staying with Mrs. Bristlethwaite and finally seeing the inside of the mysterious Barbary Hall. She turned an eager face toward her mother, awaiting her reply.

"Oh, Mrs. Bristlethwaite, I could not put you to so much trouble!"

"Nonsense! It would be no trouble at all. I have grown very fond of your daughter, Mrs. Dashwood. She reminds me of my dear Anna."

Margaret heard the catch in Mrs. Bristlethwaite's voice. She had not known that Mrs. Bristlethwaite had any children.

Mrs. Dashwood favored Mrs. Bristlethwaite with a sympathetic look. "Your daughter?" she said softly.

"She would be Miss Dashwood's age, but she succumbed to consumption when she was only ten."

Mrs. Dashwood set down her tea and moved closer to Mrs. Bristlethwaite on the sofa. "I am so sorry, Mrs. Bristlethwaite. The loss of a child is such a dreadful thing."

"Thank you, my dear. She was a darling child. Spirited and bright, like Miss Dashwood."

"Margaret, would you like to return to Devonshire with Mrs. Bristlethwaite?"

"I would, Mama, as long as you can spare me."

"Of course, my dear. I shall rest easier knowing you are in Mrs. Bristlethwaite's care."

"Thank you, Mama!" Margaret turned to Mrs. Bristlethwaite, feeling a little shy. "Please call me Margaret, Mrs. Bristlethwaite."

"Of course, Miss—Margaret," said Mrs. Bristlethwaite. "I intend to leave in two days. Since I would like to depart early, I shall send the carriage for you at Colonel Brandon's house tomorrow evening. Will that give you enough time to pack your things?"

"Oh, yes!" cried Margaret. "I do not have much to pack."

The plans for Margaret's return to Devonshire settled, the conversation turned to mutual friends and shared tastes, although Margaret paid little attention, too excited by the prospect of visiting Barbary Hall and spending so much time with a magical companion. She could practice her magic in relative security, not worrying that anyone would interrupt. She could read her books in the drawing room without relying upon glamours to hide their true natures. When Mr. Ellsworth made his promised journey to Devonshire, she would be the most fortunate creature alive.

"My word," cried Mrs. Dashwood, suddenly.

"What is it, Mama?" Margaret said, having been pulled out of her daydreams.

"We have taken up far too much of Mrs. Bristlethwaite's time. Besides, Marianne will be wondering why we have not yet returned."

"My time has been most delightfully spent, but I understand your desire to return to your daughter." Mrs. Bristlethwaite rang for the butler. "Jenkins," she said when he slipped into the room, "please call the carriage for the Dashwoods."

Jenkins bowed and retreated.

"It will be but a moment." Mrs. Bristlethwaite rose to accompany Margaret and her mother.

"Thank you for a marvelous tea and for your kind offer," said Mrs. Dashwood.

"You are most welcome! And it will be lovely to have a young person in the house again." She turned to Margaret. "I shall send the carriage by six o'clock tomorrow, Margaret. I so look forward to our time together!"

"As do I, Mrs. Bristlethwaite," Margaret replied with sincerity. She sensed there was much more to learn about her father's old friend, and now she would have plenty of opportunities for discovery.

"What an admirable woman," proclaimed Mrs. Dashwood as the carriage glided away from Mayfair. "How lucky we are to have made her acquaintance! And how fortunate that she lives so close to Barton Cottage. Once Marianne has been safely delivered, I shall return home, and we can invite Mrs. Bristlethwaite to tea."

"I would like that," Margaret replied.

Mrs. Dashwood continued in her praise of Mrs. Bristlethwaite for the remainder of their journey to Berkeley Square, Margaret's enthusiastic nods punctuating her mother's effusions.

Upon arriving at the Colonel's house, Margaret returned to her room to reply to Mr. Ellsworth. She had no idea how to begin her letter and sat for some time with pen poised over the paper. She did not wish to seem too forward, but he *had* requested a correspondence. With that reassurance, she wrote:

Dear Mr. Ellsworth,

Let me remove your anxiety at once! Of course I forgive you, though to tell the truth, there was nothing to forgive. I confess that I was concerned about your safety, but the receipt of your letter removed my worry immediately.

May I also relieve you of the regret that you will miss me in London? For the day after tomorrow I, too, will no longer be here. I travel to Devonshire in the company of Mrs. Bristlethwaite to Barbary Hall where I will stay for the next several months.

In the meanwhile, I shall read our favorite poet every evening and think of you.

Your friend,

M. Dashwood

Margaret read over the letter, questioning whether it was a trifle too bold. In the end she let her heart convince her that it was not.

***

After a flurry of goodbyes and promises to write often, Margaret found herself seated in Mrs. Bristlethwaite's carriage en route to Devonshire. As soon as they had left London, she noticed that the landscape began to pass her window at a curiously rapid pace.

"How are we moving so quickly?"

"Magic, naturally," replied Mrs. Bristlethwaite. "My husband devised this spell; he called it the Winged Chariot Spell. It is the same reason that we do not feel the cobblestones and other irregularities in the road. The wheels merely give the impression of touching the ground. The horses pulling the carriage for long journeys such as ours are also magical, winged, though I have enchanted them to hide the wings from most people's sight."

"Does the coachman know?" Margaret was incredulous.

Mrs. Bristlethwaite shook her head, chuckling. "I suppose I am wicked to find his ignorance amusing, but he believes himself the finest driver in all of England. I simply do not have the heart to tell him otherwise."

"Do you not worry what he would do if he were to discover the truth?"

"I have found that most people will shape the truth to fit their own ends, Margaret. But I will confess to you that a few of my servants are aware of my magic. My butler, Jenkins and maid Lucy." Mrs. Bristlethwaite studied Margaret. "May I tell you a secret? Something you promise never to tell?"

"Of course!"

"As you know strict laws govern the practice of magic. I speak not of those decreed by the non-magical but of the laws set forth by the Sorcerer's Council, one of which forbids servants and others of the lower classes from practicing magic. There are very stiff penalties for anyone of the serving vocations found breaking that law."

Margaret nodded. Her father had told her about these rules.

"I think those laws are ludicrous," Mrs. Bristlethwaite proclaimed.

Margaret hid her astonishment as well as she could.

"Jenkins has served my family since I was a child, so I have always known about his magic. A few years ago I happened upon Lucy performing her daily tasks in the drawing room. She was alone and did not see me. It soon became clear that she was using a cleaning spell—quite an ingenious one at that! When I approached her, the poor girl was terrified. After I convinced her that she was in no danger from me, she admitted that her grandmother was an accomplished sorceress who specialized in domestic magicks. The spell I had seen Lucy performing was one of her grandmother's.

"I could not let such talent go to waste, so I took her under my wing and began training her. Not that she needed much help." Mrs. Bristlethwaite paused. "I hope I have not appalled you, Margaret."

"Not at all. I—I think you are terribly courageous

to do such a thing. And I promise never to speak of it to anyone else."

"Thank you, my dear. A few others do know, though one of them disapproves. We shall ignore him."

They rode on, enjoying one another's company. Much sooner than Margaret could have anticipated, the familiar landscape of Devonshire rolled past the windows of the carriage. She could not get enough of looking at the beloved sights. Next to her Mrs. Bristlethwaite sighed. "I had forgotten how beautiful it is here. I have been away far too long."

Barbary Hall soon loomed into view. From Margaret's position in the carriage, she could see only one wing of the house, but she could tell that it was a majestic structure—ancient and beautiful, made of grey stone polished by the years. The building's gabled roof and arched windows suggested that it had been built at least three centuries before, though Margaret suspected it was even older. A thrill passed through her. She had never been to such an ancient hall, and she longed to walk through it, running her fingers over the stone and feeling a connection to something older and bigger than she, a connection to history itself.

"How did Barbary Hall get its name?"

"Ah, that is an excellent question, Margaret. Mr. Bristlethwaite's great, great grandfather was something of an explorer. He spent a long time among the Berbers of North Africa, studying with their sorcerers. When he returned to England and settled in Devonshire, he wished to take a little piece of his adventure with him. He was a sentimental man, according to Bristlethwaite family history. My late husband shared that trait."

As the carriage drew closer to Mrs. Bristlethwaite's home, Margaret marveled at the expanse of Barbary Hall's park. Wide rolling lawns led up to the manor. In the distance stood a woodland that Margaret looked forward to exploring. The carriage crossed a stone bridge built over a wide river, and the whole of Barbary Hall towered into view. Margaret gasped. It was the most magnificent house she had ever seen.

"It is beautiful, is it not, Margaret?" said Mrs. Bristlethwaite.

"Sublime! I have never seen a more majestic building!" Margaret could not peel her eyes from the sight.

"I felt much the same way the first time Mr. Bristlethwaite brought me here. I could not believe that I was to be mistress of such a grand house."

The carriage swept up the long lane and arrived in the circular drive. A footman helped them down.

"Thank you, Carlson," Mrs. Bristlethwaite said. "Please see to our luggage. I believe the Westerly Room has been prepared for Miss Dashwood."

"Yes, Ma'am," Carlson replied and set about unpacking the carriage.

Jenkins stood next to the door. "Welcome home, Madame," he said with a bow. Turning to Margaret he inclined his head. "Miss Dashwood."

Margaret smiled nervously, not sure how to comport herself, knowing as she did now that he, too, was a sorcerer.

"And to you, Jenkins," Mrs. Bristlethwaite said. "What a long exile it has been!"

He nodded. "Shall I send Lucy to help the young

lady?"

"Thank you, Jenkins. And we shall take tea in the drawing room in half an hour."

"Very good," Jenkins replied.

Margaret followed Mrs. Bristlethwaite into the enormous hall. Sunlight poured through windows set high up in the walls, illuminating the stone floors. The walls were paneled in a dark wood that gleamed in the light.

"Watch your step, Miss Dashwood," said Jenkins. "The stones are a bit uneven in places."

"How old is this house?" Margaret asked, awestruck.

"The oldest parts, including this hall, were built in the thirteenth century, though the paneling was added recently. The turret has been standing since before the reign of Edward the Second," Mrs. Bristlethwaite replied proudly.

"Goodness!"

"Of course the Bristlethwaites have only been masters of the house for two hundred years. But after they acquired it, they made a number of additions. No doubt you will be able to discern the newer parts of the building. It has been cobbled together in some places—different architectural styles combining to make the marvelous mélange that is Barbary Hall."

They began climbing the wide stone staircase. Margaret was surprised that a house with so much stone could nevertheless feel so inviting until she noticed the portraits lining the walls. Generations of Bristlethwaites smiled down on her, as though welcoming her to their home. Mrs. Bristlethwaite stopped in front of a portrait of a thin man with wispy hair and blue eyes filled with a strange combination of mirth and sadness.

"This is William Bristlethwaite, Mr. Bristlethwaite's great, great grandfather, the first Bristlethwaite of Barbary Hall. I am especially fond of this portrait. The artist's rendition of his eyes is remarkable, is it not? They appear so alive. Mr. Bristlethwaite told me that in addition to being a great sorcerer, William was a gifted composer of sonnets."

Margaret lingered in front of the portrait, sad that she could not meet this man who had been dead for more than a century. Then she hurried to catch up with Mrs. Bristlethwaite and Jenkins.

At the top of the stairs, Mrs. Bristlethwaite turned to Margaret. "Jenkins will show you to your chamber, and Lucy will bring you to the drawing room for tea in half an hour, my dear," she said before bustling down the hall.

"Please follow me, Miss Dashwood," intoned Jenkins. He led her to an intricately carved wooden door set in an arched doorway. "The Westerly Room, Miss."

Margaret crossed to the tall French doors across from the doorway and stepped outside onto the stone balcony. She caught her breath at the sight that met her. The grounds of Barbary Hall spread out for miles in a magnificent view. She could see the woodland and the bridge over the river. The sunlight glinted off the water, making little jewels of light. She turned toward the road they had travelled and could just make out a horse and cart driving at a leisurely pace toward the little town nearby.

A cold breeze drove her back inside where the view from the south window drew her attention.

"Miss Dashwood?"

Margaret jumped.

"Oh, I am sorry if I frightened you. Jenkins sent me to help you with your things."

"Hello, Lucy," said Margaret.

The maid entered the room, followed by Carlson laden with Margaret's trunk. Perspiration dampened his brow, and Margaret experienced a pang of guilt, knowing the books inside her trunk made it so heavy. After he relieved himself of his burden, he bowed to Margaret, clearly glad to be rid of the trunk.

"Thank you, Carlson," Margaret said.

Carlson dashed away, leaving her alone with Lucy.

"Shall I begin unpacking for you, Miss Dashwood?"

"Please," Margaret replied. She felt rather shy around Lucy, never having known a servant who could do magic. Her father would have discouraged Norland's servants from using it if they had the ability. A giggle rose at the thought of one of the servants casting a spell on Fanny. If anyone might provoke the unlawful use of magic, it would be Fanny, a thought that led Margaret to conclude that none of Norland's servants were sorcerers.

"Where would you like me to put the books?" Lucy asked.

"Pardon me?" Margaret asked.

"The books in the compartments," Lucy said.

"You can see them?" Margaret was all astonishment.

Lucy smiled shyly. "I can. It is an old spell my grandmother taught me—to make sure that everything is clean."

Margaret returned Lucy's smile. "In that case, I suppose you could put them on the shelves."

"Mrs. Bristlethwaite will be expecting you in the drawing room," Lucy said after she finished putting all of Margaret's things into place. "I can bring you there. It takes a little time to learn your way around the Hall."

Lucy led Margaret downstairs and through a long hallway, making several turns before they arrived at the drawing room. Despite Lucy's reassurances, Margaret thought she would never learn her way around.

"Thank you, Lucy," said Margaret.

The maid curtsied and headed away to fetch the tea.

"Come in, Margaret," came the voice of Mrs. Bristlethwaite. "How do you find your chamber?"

"It is beautiful!" Margaret cried. "Thank you for putting me there. The view is astonishing!"

"It is one of the best rooms in the house. I always reserve it for my favorite guests."

Lucy returned with the tea. As Margaret waited for her refreshment, she examined the room. Her eyes were drawn immediately to the mantel over the fire where a transparent globe sat mounted on a filigreed copper base. Inside was a perfect miniature of Barbary Hall and the park surrounding it. Margaret moved closer to examine it. She could see that it matched the current state of the Hall perfectly.

"It was a gift," Mrs. Bristlethwaite explained, joining Margaret. "A potent protection charm from a French sorceress, Lady Isabelle de Fleur. She made one for each member of the coven. A rather ingenious charm, is it not? Not only does it envelop the manor in a magical barrier, but it also shows Barbary Hall at all seasons and in all conditions. See, it is raining inside the globe. I suppose you never noticed the one I keep in my London house. Pity— that one is quite as beautiful as this one."

"It is extraordinary," Margaret breathed. "So beautifully wrought."

"You will meet Lady Isabelle soon. I think you will like each other. She, too, is a lover of poetry."

"The tea is ready, Ma'am," said Lucy.

"Thank you, Lucy. Go and have a cup yourself. And one of cook's marvelous buns."

Lucy bobbed a small curtsy and returned to the kitchen.

Margaret took a sip of her tea and a bite of her bun. "Oh my!" she cried.

"What is it?" Mrs. Bristlethwaite said, alarmed.

"I believe this is the finest tea I have ever had," Margaret said.

Mrs. Bristlethwaite laughed. "Mrs. Crawford, Barbary Hall's cook, is something of a genius."

"Does she use magic, too?"

Mrs. Bristlethwaite shook her head. "No, she merely has a talent for making things delicious, which, I suppose is a sort of magic, is it not?"

Margaret nodded, her mouth too full to speak.

CHAPTER XI

*B*y the end of her first fortnight in Devonshire, Margaret had come to view Barbary Hall as another home. Mrs. Bristlethwaite proved such excellent company and the Hall so fascinating that she spared only a few moments every day to think about Mr. Ellsworth, who had expressed joy about their correspondence. She devoted much of her time to uncovering the Hall's many secrets. Lucy had hinted that somewhere in Margaret's chamber was a door that led to a secret passage, but even the True Vision Spell proved fruitless in helping her to find it. Then one afternoon during the third week of her visit, Margaret noticed something odd about her mirror. The sunlight streaming into the room had illuminated the frame, revealing an elaborate pattern of wooden swirls that formed a little handle! Delighted, Margaret pulled it open and stepped through.

The passageway was dark and musty. Margaret muttered "*Lumière,*" and a little light appeared in front of her. She followed the light as it led her around a bend and then downward until she came to another door. With a gentle push she opened it and stepped into the drawing room.

"Oh! Margaret!" cried Mrs. Bristlethwaite. "I had not expected you to find that passage so soon. Well done! You have arrived just in time for tea."

"Thank you," Margaret said. "Are there many such passages in the Hall?"

"I shall let you discover them for yourself."

While they were enjoying their tea, Jenkins arrived. "I beg your pardon, Madame, but this letter has just come for you. The man who delivered it insisted that you should read it at once."

"Thank you, Jenkins. Where is this man?"

"He is in the kitchen. Lucy has given him a cup of tea and a bun. He was rather travel-worn, having ridden for many hours. He looked as if he might collapse at any moment, so I have offered him my room in which to rest for the day."

"Very good of you Jenkins."

Jenkins bowed and left the room as Mrs. Bristlethwaite opened the letter.

As she read, a crease appeared between Mrs. Bristlethwaite's brows. When she finished, she handed the letter to Margaret.

Dearest Eugenia,

The situation about which we spoke in Wales has become rather urgent. I waited to write until I had more information, and now I am convinced that the thefts we discussed were not committed by an ordinary vandal or treasure seeker. It has become clear to me that a sorcerer is behind them, though what he stands to gain, I cannot be certain.

I wrote to a few of my overseas friends who guard artifacts of magical lore, informing them of what happened in Wales. I asked if they had experienced any suspicious activity in their area. Most of the replies indicated that nothing had occurred, but that they would inform me should they discover otherwise. A few, however, mentioned that there have been some thefts in their areas. Magical items have also gone missing from places, largely unguarded, in Ireland, Scotland, and France.

Then I received a letter from Mr. Sadik who guards the Staff of Adalet, which once belonged to a great Turkish sorceress. Mr. Sadik wrote of a battle he had with a sorcerer wearing a mask. Mr. Sadik escaped, though barely, and the Staff remains in his possession.

We cannot know where or when this masked sorcerer will strike again, but it has become clear that we must reconvene the coven, my dear. Lady Jayne and I offer our services, as always.

The man with whom I sent this letter will carry your reply to me as soon as he has rested.

We must act at once!

Yours in magical friendship,

Sir Berwin Llewellyn

Margaret finished the letter and looked aghast at Mrs. Bristlethwaite. The older woman wore a merry expression, which surprised Margaret given the seriousness of the matter. "You must understand that it has been so long since I have had a cause to enliven me. For much of my youth, I battled dangerous forces. I suppose I developed a taste for that sort of excitement. I have not felt so alive in years."

She retrieved a writing desk from a table in a corner. "I must reply to Sir Berwin at once. May I request your aid in writing to the other members of the coven? We should send those letters as soon as possible."

"Of course," Margaret replied, eager to be useful.

Mrs. Bristlethwaite rang for Lucy, who appeared mere moments later.

"Lucy, please bring another writing desk, some paper, ink, and a pen for Miss Dashwood."

"Of course, Madam."

The afternoon passed quickly, so engaged were they with their task. Once they finished writing the short notes informing the coven members that they were needed, Mrs. Bristlethwaite summoned Lucy to post them.

"There is nothing we can do now except wait for everyone to arrive."

"Why would someone wish to steal these artifacts?" Margaret asked, voicing the question that had been plaguing her all day.

"I imagine there are as many explanations as there are sorcerers. But if I had to guess, I would say for power, my dear. The items in question contain traces of their original owners' magic. Some of them also have a magic of their own, such as the Staff of Adalet, which was forged many centuries ago. The sorceress who made it, Dilan Adalet, carved it out of sacred juniper wood."

"What would a sorcerer do with so much power?"

Mrs. Bristlethwaite shook her head. "I forget how young and protected you have been. You believe in the goodness of everyone, do you not?"

Margaret nodded emphatically.

"It pains me that I must disabuse you of this notion. While most sorcerers do strive to better the condition of mankind, there are some who care solely about themselves. Power seduces. It drives some sorcerers to do unspeakable things."

Margaret shivered at the darkness in Mrs. Bristlethwaite's voice, the severity of her expression.

"Not everyone is as noble as your father."

The reference to her father pulled Margaret out of her shock. "I wonder," Margaret said, drawing the atlas out of her pocket. She turned to the index at the back of the book. "Yes!"

"What is it, Margaret?"

"The atlas contains information about the magical artifacts around the world." She skimmed a page in the section about France. "Here is one that remains unguarded. Some of them still have guardians, but others do not."

"Dear Henry! What a help he is even from beyond this world!"

Margaret felt a burst of pride in her father's work; he had given so much of his life to protecting the world. She turned to the beginning of the book.

"Shall we make a list?"

Mrs. Bristlethwaite pulled a sheet of paper out of

her writing desk and picked up her pen. "I am ready. Shall we begin with Britain?"

"I beg your pardon, Madam," said Jenkins. Both Mrs. Bristlethwaite and Margaret jumped.

"Jenkins!" exclaimed Mrs. Bristlethwaite, her hand clasped to her chest. "We must have been absorbed in our work. What is it?"

"I thought perhaps you and the young lady would like dinner brought in?"

"That would be perfect."

As the clock chimed six, Margaret glanced out the window. The sun had already set.

"We may as well continue until our meal arrives. Where were we?"

Margaret turned back to the atlas and read:

The Purple Stone of Dawlish, a particularly powerful and beautifully shaped amethyst, now resides in a remote location in Dartmoor (Consult the map below). Though the exact location is unknown, some say it rests in the belly of a stone giant. Legend suggests that the sorcerer charged with guarding the charm disappeared one night early in the seventeenth century, never to be found again. No replacement was ever secured. Nevertheless, all accounts suggest that the Stone remains undisturbed.

"And a location thought to be near the stone's hiding place is marked on the map," Margaret concluded, passing the atlas to Mrs. Bristlethwaite.

"Ingenious! When the coven convenes we shall act immediately to retrieve the Stone."

"What if," Margaret ventured.

"What is it?"

"Well, we have the atlas. Could we not retrieve the Stone ourselves? After dinner?"

Mrs. Bristlethwaite raised her eyebrows. "My word," she said. "You take after your father in so many ways, Margaret."

"What do you mean?"

"He would have offered the same suggestion, and he would have convinced me to go."

Margaret smiled, recognizing the invitation. "We know more or less where the Stone is. The bad weather should prevent anyone from stumbling upon us. As we are already so close to Dartmoor, we should suffer nothing from the exertion of the magic. And should we not prevent another object from falling into the hands of this mysterious sorcerer?"

Mrs. Bristlethwaite clapped. "A persuasive argument indeed!"

After dinner Margaret and Mrs. Bristlethwaite changed into warmer clothes. Margaret made sure the atlas was tucked safely in her pocket before she returned to the drawing room. Her heart pounded in anticipation of their adventure.

"Are you ready, Margaret?" asked Mrs. Bristlethwaite.

"I am!"

Mrs. Bristlethwaite took hold of Margaret's arm. "You shall have to work a little harder with the Folding Spell to get beyond Barbary Hall's protection charm, but as I am with you, it should part enough to let us through."

Margaret opened the atlas to the page of their destination, took a deep breath, and said, "*Que le*

Manoir de Barbarie se replie sur le Dartmoor!"

They met a moment of resistance before the cozy drawing room of Mrs. Bristlethwaite's house melted into the broad moorland. A strong wind chilled Margaret, who shivered from the effort of moving beyond the protection spell.

"Well done, Margaret! That was a remarkably smooth transition, especially considering the level of difficulty *and* your use of French for the incantation." Mrs. Bristlethwaite inhaled. "I do so love the moor, especially at night."

Margaret took in her surroundings: the dark shapes of hills rolling through the landscape, the moonlight touching everything with its silver glimmer, and the stars shining in the wide sky. The wildness of the moor welled up inside her, meeting her longing for poetry and beauty.

"So where is this stone giant?" Mrs. Bristlethwaite said.

Margaret consulted the atlas. "It seems to be a little north of here." She scanned the surrounding area, searching for something that met the description offered by the atlas. Nothing appeared.

"It must be somewhere nearby or your father would not have made this the arrival point. Shall we explore?"

Margaret gave a vigorous nod, the lingering effect of the Folding Spell giving way to enthusiasm.

They set off toward the north, moving carefully over the uneven, damp ground. A light mist had begun to form, gathering on Margaret's clothes like dew. She was exhilarated—searching for a magical treasure on the moonlit moor reminded her of something out of a sublime poem. With a pang, she wished she could tell Mr. Ellsworth about this adventure.

The two women walked for about a quarter of a mile before Margaret caught site of something promising.

"Mrs. Bristlethwaite, was there ever a castle on Dartmoor?"

"I do not believe so, my dear. Why do you ask?"

Margaret pointed to a pile of stones on a small hill, glimmering in the moonlight.

"Perhaps we have found our giant!" said Mrs. Bristlethwaite.

They hurried up the hill, Margaret's legs burning from the effort. As they neared the ruins, both Margaret and Mrs. Bristlethwaite stopped, amazed. The stones were far bigger than they appeared from a distance and stood balanced, one on top of another, making several small towers.

"Ancient magic," Mrs. Bristlethwaite said in a reverent voice.

Margaret approached one of the stones and looked up, craning her neck to see the top of it. In the shadow of the behemoth, Margaret felt tiny.

Mrs. Bristlethwaite walked around the circle, occasionally touching a stone.

"I can feel enormous power here. These must be the stone giants your father mentioned. But where is the amethyst?"

Margaret joined Mrs. Bristlethwaite in the search, running her fingers along the stones and feeling a hum of energy that tickled her. They searched for half an hour, but found nothing.

Margaret, growing ever more frustrated, suddenly remembered the True Vision Spell. "*Que le voile se retire; que la vérité soit révélée,*" she commanded.

Before Mrs. Bristlethwaite could comment, one of the biggest stones began glowing. Then a door appeared in its center, roughly carved into the stone. Margaret looked at Mrs. Bristlethwaite, elated.

"I suppose we have our answer," said Mrs. Bristlethwaite. "Shall we?"

Margaret opened the door. Together they passed into the stone. The sight that met them caused both Margaret and Mrs. Bristlethwaite to draw sharp breaths. They stood at the mouth of a long tunnel, lined with glowing stones that cast enough light for their safe passage. They started forward, their footsteps echoing around them. The path seemed to take them downward, and as they progressed, the air grew colder and heavier.

Their journey through the tunnel ended in an enormous chamber, filled with little pockets carved into the walls, each containing a candle that cast an eerie golden light around the stone, flickering in and out of shadow.

Margaret moved closer to study a candle. It had not melted, though the heat in the room suggested the candles had been lit for a long time. "How could they still be burning?"

"An eternal light spell, I should think," replied Mrs. Bristlethwaite, examining a candle across the chamber. "An inspired one at that."

They ceased their examination of the candles and turned instead to the center of the chamber where a crystal box stood upon a carved wooden pedestal. Inside the box glowed an amethyst of impressive size, a perfectly round sphere.

"The Purple Stone of Dawlish," Mrs.

Bristlethwaite breathed, inching closer to the pedestal.

"How do you suppose we get it?" Margaret asked.

"We try a few simple spells. We have to let it know that we mean only to protect it."

Margaret, confused, watched Mrs. Bristlethwaite approach the crystal box and lay her hand upon it, closing her eyes.

A moment later Margaret heard a click, and the lid of the box opened. Mrs. Bristlethwaite opened her eyes and lifted the amethyst from its home.

"You will be safe," she said gently as she dropped the stone into her pocket.

Margaret longed to ask a thousand questions, but before she could, they both heard an echoed footstep followed by something that sounded like a pebble being kicked. She and Mrs. Bristlethwaite looked at each other. Fear made Margaret's limbs numb.

"Quickly, my dear. The Folding Spell."

"But—"

"Yes, it will be difficult from here, but we shall do it together. Take my hand and use English."

Margaret obeyed.

"Fold Dartmoor into Barbary Hall!" they cried. Power surged through them, but the journey was far less smooth this time. Something tried to tear her from Mrs. Bristlethwaite's side. She clung to the older woman's hand and slowly felt the cold of the chamber receding. Just as the drawing room opened in front of her, an angry cry echoed from the chamber they had left. But when she turned to look, the chamber had disappeared. She and Mrs. Bristlethwaite had arrived at Barbary Hall.

"We retrieved the Stone just in time!" Margaret panted as she fell onto the thick carpet.

"That we did," Mrs. Bristlethwaite replied before collapsing into a chair.

Margaret struggled to her feet and made her way to Mrs. Bristlethwaite's side. She took her hand.

"Mrs. Bristlethwaite?" Margaret's voice sounded small. "Are you all right?"

Mrs. Bristlethwaite, her face pale and shiny, gave a small smile but did not open her eyes. "Send for Lucy, my dear." Her reply came in a faint whisper.

Fear banished Margaret's fatigue, and she pulled the cord to summon help. A few moments later, Lucy arrived. She gasped and rushed to Mrs. Bristlethwaite's side.

"Madam!" Lucy knelt in front of her mistress.

Mrs. Bristlethwaite struggled to open her eyes, which fixed in a hazy gaze on the maid. "The tonic, Lucy. Hurry."

Without a word Lucy raced from the room, leaving Margaret staring, wide-eyed, after her. Mrs. Bristlethwaite moaned. The sound brought Margaret back to herself. "Mrs. Bristlethwaite, the amethyst! Mrs. Bristlethwaite?" Margaret refrained from shaking the older woman. Instead, she reached into Mrs. Bristlethwaite's pocket and pulled out the amethyst. The stone felt warm and comforting. She opened Mrs. Bristlethwaite's hand, dropped the stone into it, and then closed the older woman's fingers around it.

"Please," Margaret whispered.

After a nearly interminable moment during which Margaret held her breath, Mrs. Bristlethwaite stirred. Her eyes fluttered open, and she took a deep breath.

"What happened?"

"I think the Folding Spell proved a little taxing," Margaret replied, relief coloring her voice.

Lucy came racing back, but stopped suddenly when she saw that Mrs. Bristlethwaite was conscious.

"Thank you, Lucy," said Mrs. Bristlethwaite. "Miss Dashwood's quick thinking restored me partially, but I do still require my tonic."

"Of course," replied Lucy. She brought a bottle and a glass to Mrs. Bristlethwaite, carefully measured out a dark liquid, and handed the glass to her mistress.

Mrs. Bristlethwaite sighed and then drank the liquid, making a face. "The tonic is restorative but its taste is hardly agreeable." She studied Margaret. "Actually, my dear, you look as though you could use a drop of it, too."

Margaret wished she could refuse, but she allowed Lucy to pour her some and drank it as quickly as she could. It burned a little going down, and she tried not to think about the taste, lest the tonic come right back up. But she had to admit that she felt better almost instantly.

"Excellent," said Mrs. Bristlethwaite. "Thank you, Lucy. You should take yourself to bed. Miss Dashwood and I have a little business to finish before we retire for the evening."

Lucy, looking relieved at her mistress's recovery, left them alone.

Mrs. Bristlethwaite opened her hand and stared at the amethyst. "What possessed you to put this in my hand?"

"I remembered the description of it in the atlas, and I know that amethysts have healing properties."

"That they do. It is a beautiful stone, is it not? Where should I keep it?"

"Some place very safe," Margaret replied. "Who do you suppose was coming toward us?"

"I imagine someone who was there for the same reason we were, although judging by the tenor of the cry we heard, perhaps not with the same benign intentions. We are lucky, Margaret. Had we lingered we might have faced real danger."

Margaret shivered.

"Goodness, my dear. You are exhausted! We shall speak more of this in the morning. Good night, Margaret."

"Good night, Mrs. Bristlethwaite."

Once she had returned to her comfortable chamber, Margaret sat staring out of her window toward the moor, despite her exhaustion. Somewhere out there was a very disappointed sorcerer.

CHAPTER XII

"Good morning, my dear," Mrs. Bristlethwaite said, looking up as Margaret entered the breakfast parlor. "I hope you are feeling better."

"I am. And you?"

"Absolutely, my dear! My tonic and a good night's rest set me to rights." She gestured to the pile of letters sitting next to her on the table. "It appears the members of the coven have all replied at once. I shall require your help with answering these letters and making the arrangements."

Margaret took her place at the table, and Lucy poured her a cup of tea. "But how did they manage to reply so quickly? Our letters could only have been sent with the evening post."

"You cannot imagine I relied on His Majesty's post, as marvelous as it is, for such urgent business?"

"Is there another way?"

"Of course. I had Jenkins deliver them." Mrs. Bristlethwaite turned to Lucy. "Lucy, the amethyst is safely stowed away?"

"It is, Madam."

Margaret was surprised that Mrs. Bristlethwaite had trusted Lucy with something so important. Then she chided herself for doubting Mrs. Bristlethwaite's judgment.

"Ah, wonderful!" Mrs. Bristlethwaite said, startling Margaret from her thoughts. Mrs. Bristlethwaite held up a light blue sheet of paper from which the scent of lilacs emanated. "Lady Isabelle has returned from the Continent. I am relieved; it is a bad time to cross the Channel. You will like her, Margaret. Lady Isabelle is from an old French family—the first sorceress they have seen in a very long time. I think we shall put her in the room next to yours." She gestured to the pen and paper next to Margaret's place.

Margaret made note of Lady Isabelle's room as Mrs. Bristlethwaite picked up the next letter. When she finished she chuckled and shook her head. "Miss Cottlebury, as full of vinegar as always. She will require a certain amount of privacy. It is the turret for her, then."

And so the morning continued—between sips of tea and bites of toast, Mrs. Bristlethwaite and Margaret made note of who would be coming and what rooms Lucy should prepare.

"Well, that is all of them. The entire coven has replied," Mrs. Bristlethwaite said. "That is the first time they have all responded with such alacrity," she added. "Lucy and the rest of the staff will have a busy few days. We shall stay out of their way and continue our work. Perhaps today we shall focus on the objects hidden around the Continent?"

Margaret took the atlas from her pocket.

"Curious," said Mrs. Bristlethwaite. "The entire

coven has been accounted for, so who sent this letter? Oh. It is for you, my dear."

At the sight of the handwriting, Margaret's heart leapt. Mrs. Bristlethwaite laughed as Margaret read.

Dear Miss Dashwood,

I hope my letter finds you well! Although I, too, have arrived in this fair county, I beg your forgiveness for my delay in writing to you—a slight fever has rendered me incapable of leaving my bed. But now I feel my health returning, and I long to pay a call on you. I understand from my generous, though gregarious, host Sir John that we are now neighbors! Nothing would soothe my soul more than the sight of you and perhaps the sound of your voice giving such life to our favorite poet's words.

With an anxious heart I await your response. Say the word, my dear Miss Dashwood, and I shall hurry to your side.

Yours ever in friendship and admiration,

W. Ellsworth

"Good news?" asked Mrs. Bristlethwaite.

Margaret looked up, her smile mirroring that of her hostess. "It is. Mr. Ellsworth is staying with Sir John and Lady Middleton at Barton Park."

"I did not realize that he and Sir John were friends. But then if they met at the ball, I can imagine Sir John insisting on hosting Mr. Ellsworth. At any rate, what made you beam so?"

"He would like to call on me," said Margaret,

glowing.

"We shall have him to tea this very afternoon!"

"Thank you!" Margaret cried.

"Of course, my dear. Any friend of yours will be a friend of mine."

Although Margaret found their work interesting, she did glance at the clock more often than she might have done on another morning. If Mrs. Bristlethwaite noticed Margaret's periodically wandering attention, she did not mention it, though Margaret caught the older woman smiling to herself from time to time. By the end of the morning their list of unguarded objects had grown considerably.

"It seems the coven faces an enormous task," said Mrs. Bristlethwaite, examining the list.

"I had no idea there were so many magical objects scattered around the world!"

"I confess that I would not have judged the number to be so large," said Mrs. Bristlethwaite. "And I am left to wonder again at your father's achievement."

Margaret perused the list of objects and could not help but imagine owning them. She could not quite suppress the thrill that ran through her at the idea of possessing so much power.

"Be careful what you wish for, Margaret. No one should have that much power. There must be balance, which is why most of these items remain scattered around the world rather than stowed in some place together."

"I—I," Margaret began, astonished that Mrs. Bristlethwaite had read her thoughts.

Mrs. Bristlethwaite took Margaret's hand. "Do not

feel so bad, child. We all face this desire. Who would not wish for more power? Especially in a world such as ours? But our choices matter, my dear. Do you understand?"

"I—I think so," said Margaret, though her head was spinning.

"We will speak more of this later. But for now I believe it is time for you to go make yourself even more beautiful. Your Mr. Ellsworth shall arrive soon."

As Margaret hurried to her chamber, she could hear Mrs. Bristlethwaite's laughter following her through the house.

When she returned to the drawing room, Margaret caught her breath at the sight of Mr. Ellsworth, who stood by the hearth and examined the globe containing the model of Barbary Hall.

"Mr. Ellsworth," Margaret said. He turned quickly, appearing agitated. "Oh, I am sorry I startled you!"

"Not at all, Miss Dashwood!" Mr. Ellsworth hurried over to take her hand. "You look well, Miss Dashwood! You have no idea how it pleases me to see you!"

Margaret blushed. "As much as it does me to see you," she replied.

"Ah, Mr. Ellsworth. How good that you could join us!" Mrs. Bristlethwaite said.

Mr. Ellsworth bowed and then took her hand. "It is wonderful to see you again, Mrs. Bristlethwaite. I am honored to be received at Barbary Hall. Sir John has spoken quite highly of it and of its mistress."

Margaret noticed with amusement the blush creeping up Mrs. Bristlethwaite's cheeks.

"Thank you, Mr. Ellsworth. You certainly know how to flatter a woman!" She took her seat and gestured for the others to join her.

"I mean no flattery, Mrs. Bristlethwaite. I have never seen a house as fine as yours. And with a little replica all of its own!" He indicated the globe on the mantel. "What a charming curiosity."

Margaret held her breath, hoping that he would not require more explanation.

"A dear friend had it made for me. It is a piece of art, indeed!" Mrs. Bristlethwaite betrayed no concern about Mr. Ellsworth's examination of the globe, so Margaret thought perhaps it worked like the atlas: only sorcerers and sorceresses could recognize its enchantment. When Mr. Ellsworth took his seat near her, Margaret let out her breath very quietly, relieved that he said nothing more about the globe.

Lucy entered with a tray and served their tea. For a moment the only sounds were the fire crackling in the fireplace and the clinking of spoons in cups.

"So, Mr. Ellsworth, what has brought you to Devonshire? This is hardly the time of year for holiday-making." Mrs. Bristlethwaite directed her gaze at Margaret.

Mr. Ellsworth, following Mrs. Bristlethwaite's eyes, smiled. "I must admit I do not usually travel here at this time of year, but I found compelling enough reason, in addition to a little business."

Margaret sipped her tea, conscious of their attention.

"Ah, yes, Margaret has told me you are a collector of beautiful items. How intriguing!"

"I suppose it is. Collecting suits my temperament," he replied. "I consider myself a connoisseur of beauty." He looked at Margaret.

"Miss Dashwood also informs me that you share

her love of poetry."

"Miss Dashwood speaks most truthfully," said Mr. Ellsworth with a tender glance at Margaret. "Though I bow to her considerably more sophisticated taste."

"I have not given much time to the study of poetry. Perhaps you both could convince me that I should."

"Miss Dashwood's abilities far surpass my own. I think we should entreat her to favor us with a reading."

"Oh yes, please do, Margaret!"

Mr. Ellsworth drew a small volume from his coat pocket. "I have just the poems," he said, handing her the collection.

"Have you any particular poem in mind?"

"Whatever you choose, Miss Dashwood, will suit."

Margaret took a sip of tea and then searched the book for the poem she wished to read. Settling on an old favorite, she cleared her throat and began, aware of Mr. Ellsworth's eyes fixed upon her.

When she finished, both Mr. Ellsworth and Mrs. Bristlethwaite clapped with enthusiasm.

"And now you, Mr. Ellsworth." Margaret handed him the book.

The afternoon progressed in this fashion until both Mr. Ellsworth and Margaret had grown nearly hoarse from reading. Mr. Ellsworth sighed and stood. "I wish I could stay longer, but Sir John has exhorted me to be home in time for dinner. He has another guest coming to whom he would like to introduce me—his brother-in-law Mr. Palmer. I cannot imagine that I shall enjoy his company more than that of my present companions, but as Sir John is my host, I must be gracious." He bowed to Mrs. Bristlethwaite who inclined her head. Then he turned to Margaret. "I hope to see you again soon, Miss Dashwood."

"As do I, Mr. Ellsworth."

He bowed over her hand, bestowing the gentlest of kisses upon it. Then he took his leave.

"I do not know when I have spent such an enjoyable afternoon," said Mrs. Bristlethwaite, breaking the silence that had lingered in the wake of Mr. Ellsworth's exit. "Mr. Ellsworth and you both read so beautifully. I am almost brought round to your way of thinking about spells, Margaret. Certainly such beautiful language carries a power of its own."

"I am glad you think so, Mrs. Bristlethwaite." Margaret could still feel the light touch of Mr. Ellsworth's lips on her hand.

"Mr. Ellsworth seems a charming man." Mrs. Bristlethwaite fixed Margaret with a significant look. "And quite taken with you."

Margaret could do nothing but smile and blush.

"We shall be sure to invite him to see us again soon. In the meanwhile, we have business to discuss." That statement commanded Margaret's full attention. "I plan to nominate you for an apprenticeship during our next meeting, Margaret."

"Oh?" Margaret experienced a curious mix of elation and terror at the notion.

"Under ordinary circumstances," Mrs. Bristlethwaite continued, "we ask prospective apprentices to attend meetings for several months before setting a trial. But as these are not ordinary circumstances and you are no ordinary sorceress, I am certain that the coven will agree to overlook that detail."

"I cannot begin to thank you, Mrs. Bristlethwaite."

Margaret's voice caught on the lump in her throat.

"Nonsense, my dear. For Henry Dashwood's daughter we would make allowances anyway, but you have proven yourself to me already. I wish that would satisfy the coven. But I know that a few members will not be convinced by my word alone. So you will be given a task to demonstrate your fitness for apprenticeship."

Margaret's mouth grew dry and her hands damp. "What sort of task?" she asked in a small voice.

"That will be determined by the coven." Mrs. Bristlethwaite took Margaret's hand, her expression growing serious. "I will not lie to you, my dear. The task will be difficult. But I believe you are more than a match for whatever trial you will face."

Margaret took small comfort in this reassurance. She remembered the exhaustion and sickness she had experienced when they returned from the stone giant of Dartmoor and the pallor of Mrs. Bristlethwaite's face as Margaret waited to see if the stone would revive her. But Margaret put on a brave face and nodded.

"In my day we did not have trials, of course," said Mrs. Bristlethwaite.

"Why was that?"

"We were at war."

"With France?" Margaret asked.

"No, no. Well, yes, England seems always to be at war with France. But English sorcerers faced a different threat. Your father played a key part in fighting a coven from the Continent engaged in some fiercely dark magic."

The references to battle in Mr. Dashwood's diaries made sense at last. "Is that how you lost Mr.

Bristlethwaite?"

"Alas, my dear. It was. He fought nobly, though, and managed to take the opposing coven's leader with him." She spoke the last with pride.

Margaret longed to ask a thousand questions, but hesitant to cause Mrs. Bristlethwaite additional grief, kept her silence.

"Some day, my dear, I shall tell you about it. But now we have a pressing matter of our own to sort out."

Not for the first time, Margaret was startled by her hostess's ability to discern her thoughts.

"The members of the coven should be here in time for dinner tomorrow, after which we will have our first meeting. I have a task in mind for you, though I am not at liberty to divulge it to you until the coven has agreed. Let us just say that if you spent the next day or so reading your atlas it would not be time misspent."

CHAPTER XIII

"*M*argaret, my dear," said Mrs. Bristlethwaite, looking up from her book. "Perhaps you should take a turn around the park." She glanced out the window. "I think the rain will hold off for a while yet. You could do with some fresh air."

Margaret stopped pacing in front of the fire. "I am sorry, Mrs. Bristlethwaite. I suppose I am more anxious about the coven's arrival than I thought."

"No need for nerves, my dear. Go on—before the clouds open and drench you." Margaret laughed as Mrs. Bristlethwaite shooed her away.

After retrieving her pelisse, Margaret set off through the garden, which was still wet from the night's rain. Clouds glowered overhead, but Margaret did not mind. The fresh air and new sights provided her with necessary distraction. She had just started on the path toward the woodland when she spied a familiar shape.

"Mr. Ellsworth?" she called.

The figure turned. "Oh! Miss Dashwood," said Mr.

Ellsworth. He glanced around but did not approach her.

Margaret ventured a little closer. "I did not expect to see you today, but this is a lovely surprise."

"Yes, indeed. Lovely." Mr. Ellsworth's expression surprised Margaret; ordinarily his face lit up when he saw her. But today he appeared distant.

"I hope I have not interrupted you."

"Of course not, Miss Dashwood!" Mr. Ellsworth hurried forward. "I must apologize. When you called to me I was deep in thought. I hope I did not offend you in any way." He offered her his arm.

"Oh, no!" Margaret took his arm. "I—I merely worried that you were not well."

"On the contrary. Now I could feel no better! Shall we?"

They walked in silence, Margaret's worries about the coven forgotten.

"The walk from Barton Park to Barbary Hall is beautiful," Mr. Ellsworth said at length. "And once I was nearby I could not resist wandering the grounds. I saw so little of them yesterday."

"The weather has been dreadful, has it not?" said Margaret. "I have not had much opportunity to explore the grounds until today."

"Is that so? Then I am glad that I am here to share your adventure."

They strolled on, coming to the top of a hill that afforded them a splendid view of the Hall. A carriage arrived in the circular drive. Margaret turned toward the road where two more carriages approached.

"It seems that Mrs. Bristlethwaite has more visitors," observed Mr. Ellsworth.

Although Margaret longed to tell Mr. Ellsworth

the truth, she said only, "I believe a few dear friends are arriving. It should be a lively visit!"

"If they are anything like Mrs. Bristlethwaite, I must say you are correct."

Their perambulation of the grounds continued for another half an hour before Mr. Ellsworth turned to Margaret. "I am afraid, Miss Dashwood, that I should be getting back. I hope I shall see you again soon."

"As do I, Mr. Ellsworth."

Mr. Ellsworth replied with a gentle kiss to Margaret's hand and bowed before taking his leave. Margaret followed his progress, admiring the strength of his stride and the straightness of his back. When she could no longer see Mr. Ellsworth, Margaret returned to Barbary Hall. Before she reached the house, the clouds burst and drenched her in the downpour.

After changing out of her wet clothes, Margaret went in search of Mrs. Bristlethwaite and her guests. When she arrived at the drawing room, she found a young man of about nine and twenty staring out the mullioned windows. He was of medium height with brown hair and ordinary features. The young man turned and met Margaret's gaze with sad eyes of deep brown. When he smiled, however, all traces of sadness disappeared, and Margaret wondered how she could have found him plain.

"You must be Miss Dashwood." He had a low, rich voice. "Edward Barrington," he said, with a slight bow.

"It is nice to meet you, Mr. Barrington," said Margaret.

"Shall we take advantage of being the first to

arrive?" He gestured toward the two chairs nearest the fire. "Are you enjoying your stay at Barbary Hall?" Mr. Barrington asked when they were seated.

"Very much! Have you visited the Hall often?"

"I have, though some time has passed since the coven last met here." He glanced around the room. "I have always loved this room. It is so cozy and inviting." He turned his attention back to Margaret. "I hear you are to be made an apprentice to the coven."

"I hope so!" Margaret worried that her response had been a bit too enthusiastic.

"According to Mrs. Bristlethwaite you have already proven yourself, so I cannot imagine your trial will be too difficult."

"Perhaps you and Mrs. Bristlethwaite flatter me," said Margaret.

"And you are perhaps too modest," he replied. "Young ladies often pretend to be less than they are, afraid of what society might say should they embrace their talents."

Stung by his statement, Margaret looked away.

"Oh, Miss Dashwood, I did not mean that as a reprimand," he said quickly. "I meant what I said in earnest. I can see no reason why young ladies cannot be proud of their accomplishments. You see—"

Whatever he had to say would have to wait, however, as Mrs. Bristlethwaite, Sir Berwin, and Lady Jane arrived. Mr. Barrington rose.

"Edward," said Mrs. Bristlethwaite, moving toward him. With a wide smile, Mr. Barrington bowed to Mrs. Bristlethwaite. "Let me look at you, my boy." He stood patiently as Mrs. Bristlethwaite examined him. "You grow ever more like your father, but you still have your mother's eyes. Octavia was a dear woman. I was sorry to hear of her death."

"Thank you," said Mr. Barrington.

"A new apprentice? And one so *young*? Do you really think that is wise, Mrs. Bristlethwaite?" Margaret searched for the speaker and found her standing in the doorway. She was a small, terribly thin woman with greying hair pulled away from her pinched face. Her clothes hung about her, draping more like a sack than a dress. But Margaret could see that despite the woman's seeming frailty, she possessed great vigor.

"Miss Cottlebury, meet Miss Margaret Dashwood," said Mrs. Bristlethwaite.

Miss Cottlebury waved away Mrs. Bristlethwaite's civility. "You have not answered me, Mrs. Bristlethwaite. Do you think it wise at such a time as this to invite another person—a relative stranger—into the coven? And so soon after making her acquaintance!"

Sir Berwin tutted, and Lady Jane shook her head.

"We shall discuss this after dinner, Miss Cottlebury. But, yes, given the sorceress in question, I think it *very* wise." Mrs. Bristlethwaite held up her hand. "I will not hear another word about this matter, Miss Cottlebury."

Miss Cottlebury sniffed and stalked over to the window as the remaining members of the coven arrived.

"Lady Isabelle, Mr. James! Now we are complete." Mrs. Bristlethwaite motioned for Margaret to join her. "Miss Dashwood, come and meet Lady Isabelle de Fleur and Mr. Adolphus James."

Margaret hastened to Mrs. Bristlethwaite's side and curtsied to the new arrivals.

"*Enchantée*, Mademoiselle Dashwood," said Lady Isabelle. She held out a soft, white hand. Margaret had never seen such a beautiful woman. Lady Isabelle was dressed most fashionably in a blue gown that perfectly complimented her deep blue eyes. Her dark hair tumbled in curls about her beautiful face. Her welcoming smile immediately set Margaret at ease.

"So good to meet you, Miss Dashwood," chirped the birdlike man at Lady Isabelle's side. "I was quite fond of your father," he added. "Such a dreadful loss!" He looked as if he might weep.

Margaret gave him a sympathetic smile. "Thank you," she said.

"Jenkins informs me that dinner awaits," announced Mrs. Bristlethwaite.

Margaret found herself next to Mr. Barrington, who proffered his arm. "May I accompany you to dinner, Miss Dashwood?"

"Thank you, Mr. Barrington."

Mr. Barrington led her down the hall to the grand dining room. Margaret had not yet taken a meal there, as she and Mrs. Bristlethwaite preferred the more intimate arrangement of the breakfast parlor or drawing room. She gasped at the sight of the beautifully appointed room. A large mahogany table set for eight, though it could have accommodated at least twice that number, stood in the center. Crystal goblets gleamed in the dancing light of the candles, which illuminated the room from a chandelier hanging above the table.

Mr. Barrington helped Margaret to her seat before taking his place across from her. On her right sat Lady Isabelle, on her left Mr. James. When the servants brought the first course, Mr. James's eyes widened. "Oh my! What bounty," he said.

Lady Isabelle laughed. "Though you would never know to look at him, our Monsieur James has a prodigious appetite," she whispered. Mr. James gave no indication that he heard. "I, too, was quite fond of your father, Mademoiselle Dashwood," Lady Isabelle continued. "I can see the resemblance in you." Her soft voice filled with kindness. "Madame Bristlethwaite tells me you share his talent."

"I hope Mrs. Bristlethwaite does not embellish the truth," Margaret said. She bit her lip, wishing she had not spoken so, for Mr. Barrington had glanced at her.

"Madame Bristlethwaite never does, *ma chère*," said Lady Isabelle. "She also told me that you prefer to use French for casting your spells. I believe we shall grow to be close friends." Lady Isabelle's laugh reminded Margaret of gentle bells.

"I should like that," Margaret replied with feeling.

With each course, Mr. James grew more and more delighted. "Have you ever seen such wonders?" he asked Margaret when the fish course was laid upon his plate.

From across the table, Mr. Barrington said, "It is quite a feast, Mr. James. Do you not agree, Miss Dashwood?"

"Indeed, I do. And I imagine more delicacies await us. I have grown rather fond of Mrs. Crawford." Both Mr. Barrington and Lady Isabelle laughed.

"With good reason, Miss Dashwood!" said Mr. Barrington.

As dinner progressed Margaret grew aware of Mr. Barrington's gaze. Each time she felt his eyes upon her, she glanced at him, but rather than looking away, he smiled. Despite her better judgment, Margaret found his attention agreeable, which caused her some consternation. After all, she had already given her heart to Mr. Ellsworth. She managed to convince herself that he was merely being polite and that, although he had lovely eyes, he lacked Mr. Ellsworth's grace and charm.

"Are you well, Miss Dashwood?" Mr. Barrington said, startling Margaret out of her thoughts.

"Oh, yes, I—I was just—"

"I understand," he said gently. "I, too, was nervous before my first meeting with the coven. But rest assured, we are all on your side." He glanced down the table at Miss Cottlebury. "Even if we do not all *seem* to be."

Margaret said nothing to correct his misinterpretation of her agitation.

After dinner the company retired to the drawing room for their meeting. A table had been moved to the center of the room, and Mrs. Bristlethwaite took her place at the head of it. The others joined her. Margaret remained standing, uncertain how to proceed.

"Margaret," said Mrs. Bristlethwaite. "You may take the seat nearest me."

After Margaret had settled herself, Mrs. Bristlethwaite rapped on the table with a small mallet. "I call this meeting of the Devonshire Coven to order. Miss Cottlebury, I assume there are no minutes to read, the last meeting having been so long ago?"

"No, there are not," said Miss Cottlebury, laying a piece of paper and a pen on the table.

"Are you prepared to take notes?"

"I am," replied Miss Cottlebury. "Mr. James, I

would appreciate it if you could refrain from unnecessary interruptions."

Mr. James said nothing, but slumped in his seat, clearly hurt. Next to him Lady Isabelle patted his arm. "Really, Mademoiselle Cottlebury," she said.

Miss Cottlebury replied with a glare.

Mrs. Bristlethwaite cleared her throat dramatically, and all eyes turned toward her. "As you know we have gathered because magical objects have begun to disappear from their hiding places, and we must put a stop to it. Sir Berwin and Lady Jane have already done some work in this direction. Miss Dashwood and I have also made a number of pertinent discoveries. Margaret, would you show the coven the atlas?"

Margaret, surprised by being called upon in her first meeting, drew the atlas from her pocket and passed it to Mrs. Bristlethwaite.

"Henry Dashwood made this extraordinary piece of enchantment," Mrs. Bristlethwaite explained, handing the book to Mr. Barrington. He examined it with reverence.

"It is so small!" he said. "I thought atlases were generally much larger books."

"That is part of the enchantment," Margaret explained. "So I can keep it with me while I use it."

"Of course. Ingenious!"

Mrs. Bristlethwaite resumed her explanation as the atlas continued around the table. "As you will see, the atlas contains a large amount of important information, including the location and status of a number of magical objects. Margaret and I have spent the past few days cataloging that information. I propose that our first order of business, after seeing to Miss Dashwood's trial, will be to locate the unguarded objects and either bring them here for safe-keeping or find appropriate guardians for them."

Silence met Mrs. Bristlethwaite's proclamation. Then Miss Cottlebury dropped her pen and crossed her arms.

"Mrs. Bristlethwaite, you know how I feel about allowing strangers to attempt their trials."

"We all know how you feel, Miss Cottlebury," said Mrs. Bristlethwaite, her patience wearing thin. "So you need not speak again on this matter." She ignored Miss Cottlebury's agitated muttering and turned to Mr. Barrington.

"I see no reason that Miss Dashwood should not be allowed to perform her trial," he said.

"Nor do I," agreed Sir Berwin.

"I suppose it would be all right," said Lady Jane, examining Margaret. "But she is so young!"

"My dear, you were only nineteen when you passed your trial," said Sir Berwin.

"I remember, but we seemed so much older in those days, did we not?"

"Every generation feels so about themselves. I remember Sir Herbert's reaction to my joining the coven," said Mrs. Bristlethwaite. "He thought that I was far too young at one and twenty. It is the way of the world. But I assure you, Lady Jane, Margaret is up to the task."

"Then I have no objections," Lady Jane said.

"Mr. James?" asked Mrs. Bristlethwaite after a short silence.

"What are we discussing?" said Mr. James, looking up from the atlas.

Mrs. Bristlethwaite sighed. "Whether or not to let Miss Dashwood attempt her trial after only one meeting, Mr. James."

"Why not? She seems a perfectly capable young lady. And we all knew her dear father." His voice cracked, and a sob escaped him. "Thank you," he said when Lady Isabelle handed him a beautifully wrought handkerchief.

"Yes, well," said Mrs. Bristlethwaite. "And what do you say, Lady Isabelle?"

"If you believe her capable, Madame Bristlethwaite, then I have no objections."

"There we have it. Miss Dashwood, I must ask that you leave so we may decide the form your trial will take. Do not wander too far; we will call you back shortly."

Margaret, not knowing where else to go, meandered down the hall into the library. Mrs. Bristlethwaite had an impressive collection of magical texts, so Margaret chose one from the shelves and perused it as she waited. She was reading about love potions when Mr. Barrington appeared in the doorway.

"Miss Dashwood?"

Startled, she slammed her book shut. "Oh, Mr. Barrington! Are you ready for me?"

"We are." Mr. Barrington offered his arm.

The smiles of everyone but Miss Cottlebury greeted Margaret when she returned on the arm of Mr. Barrington.

"Miss Dashwood," said Mrs. Bristlethwaite, her voice taking on a formal tone. "We have set a task for you. Are you ready to hear it?"

"Yes," replied Margaret, her voice shaking only a little.

"You are to retrieve the Jaguar Mask from the

savage jungles of the New World and return it to the coven for safekeeping. Will you accept this charge?"

"I will!" Margaret was happy that her voice remained steady. She could barely contain her elation; she would be going to the New World!

"Excellent!" Mrs. Bristlethwaite cried. "As we do not have the luxury of time, we shall expect you to embark on this task tomorrow. To that end, I suggest that you retire to your room at once and begin your preparations." She handed Margaret the atlas.

Margaret nodded and turned to leave.

"Good fortune, Miss Dashwood!" came a chorus of voices.

She looked over her shoulder. "Thank you," she said before hurrying to her room to prepare.

CHAPTER XIV

A merry fire awaited Margaret in her chamber; a pot of tea and a plate of cakes sat on the table next to the hearth. She sank into the comfortable chair, grateful for the obvious care afforded her. She poured a cup of tea and sampled one of the cakes. Then she consulted the atlas about the Jaguar Mask:

> *The jungles of the Americas hide many secrets. One such secret can be found on a peninsula laden with magic and mystery. Many years ago powerful mages lived there. Only ruins now remain, rising majestically out of the surrounding wilderness. Few people outside the peninsula know of its existence, but those few feel the pull of the place's power. Although the area boasts some remaining population, neither the extent of the inhabitants' magic nor their friendliness to foreign sorcerers has been demonstrated. One is urged to exercise caution.*

Rumors suggest the Jaguar Mask resides in the ruin, hidden within an ancient temple. Its guardian disappeared many years ago, though there have been reports of a formidable beast defending the mask's hiding place. Some suggest that the beast is the spirit of the former guardian mage, Mr. Balam Paal, haunting the area for eternity after his brutal murder. I have found no evidence to support this gruesome claim. Fearsome beasts, however, have been known to wander this area.

Next to this description was a drawing of the mask, rendered in such detail that on her first glimpse of it, Margaret brought her hand to her chest in shock. Carved from a dark, almost black, wood, the head of some large cat sneered up at Margaret, its mouth open wide to reveal fierce teeth. Giant eyes pierced Margaret from the page.

"Goodness! It appears to be alive!" Margaret looked up from the book and shivered. "I have never seen anything like it!" But as she was to retrieve it, she swallowed her trepidation and resumed her work. On the following page she found the instructions for arrival.

As the weather differs significantly from our climate, the sorcerer travelling to this part of the world should don lighter clothes. But as bloodthirsty insects abound, keeping the skin covered is advised. Rest assured, these insects have no magical properties and so may be easily crushed to avoid further discomfort.

In fact the jungle teems with a wide variety of fauna, including enormous snakes and ferocious felines, which may see you as prey. Take care to avoid them. The jungle's dense foliage creates something of a difficulty as well. The wide canopy often obscures the sky, which can disorient the traveller.

"Oh my!" Margaret whispered to herself, staring at the words in horror. What sort of place had such dangers? How would she ever succeed in her trial? With growing apprehension, she continued reading.

Several locations are marked on the map as secure arrival and departure points. No matter which you choose, you face a trek of a short distance. It is never advisable to Fold directly into a place of significant power, as one never knows what one will face, and as far as anyone can determine, the Temple of the Jaguar was once the site of prodigious magical workings. Much of that power may linger, so I urge caution. A slight tingling sensation throughout your body will alert you to the presence of such magic.

No matter which arrival location you choose, you may employ the "Show Me" spell to guide you to your destination. The incantation is simple: "Show me." For more accuracy, simply be specific about what it is you wish to be shown.

Before you embark on your trek to the Temple, be sure to speak the Many Tongues spell, though the wise sorceress will avoid any company.

Despite the fire's cheerful warmth, Margaret grew terribly cold. She pulled a shawl tightly around her shoulders and sat steadying her breath. When she had composed herself, she examined the map and found a safe arrival location marked near a drawing of a pyramid. "Perhaps that is the temple that I seek. I may as well choose this place to arrive."

She braved the atlas again, growing more agitated with each page. Finally she set the atlas down and attempted to still her heart's wild beating. When she could not, she rose and began pacing her chamber, trying to reassure herself. "For goodness' sake," she said. "I am not a new born babe, completely helpless in the world." She felt steadier. "If all else fails, I can always cloak myself in darkness." Margaret paused. "On the other hand, a little extra preparation could not hurt." She collected Langlois's *Compendium* from her desk and returned to her place by the fire. After she freshened her tea, she consulted the table of contents. "Excellent," she said and turned to the section marked "Protecting Oneself."

Margaret awoke with a start at dawn. She could not remember climbing into her bed the night before, but she must have, for here she lay, though still dressed. She left her bed and looked in her wardrobe for something suitable for her day's work. She found an old muslin dress and a small jacket. Reluctant to disturb Lucy, she put another log on the fire and poked the still smoldering coals. Soon the log caught, and Margaret sat reviewing the spells she had learned the night before. By the time Lucy arrived with a tray of breakfast, Margaret felt confident that she could perform each of them.

"Good morning, Miss Dashwood," said Lucy as she set Margaret's breakfast on the table near the hearth. "Did you sleep well?"

"I suppose I did. I must have exhausted myself

preparing for today."

Lucy gave Margaret a shy smile. "I am sure you will do very well."

"Thank you, Lucy. I hope so."

"Mrs. Bristlethwaite would like to see you in the drawing room at half past eleven," Lucy said before curtsying and hurrying away.

"Margaret! How are you feeling?" said Mrs. Bristlethwaite when Margaret arrived in the drawing room.

"I must admit I am a little apprehensive," Margaret replied.

"I should think so. I would be more worried if you felt perfectly fine." Mrs. Bristlethwaite inspected Margaret in silence and then took her hands. "Are you ready, my dear?" Mrs. Bristlethwaite's tense voice betrayed her anxiety.

Margaret's limbs went cold, and her throat contracted. Nevertheless, she nodded.

"Well, then," said Mrs. Bristlethwaite. "It is time for you to depart." She pulled Margaret into an embrace. "We shall look for you to return this afternoon with the Jaguar Mask. I wish you good fortune, my dear."

Margaret considered asking what would happen if she did not return, but decided against it; she did not wish to add to Mrs. Bristlethwaite's worry. "Thank you," she said, steadying her voice as best she could. Then, with a deep breath, she opened the atlas and said, "*Que le Manoir de Barbarie se replie sur la Jungle du Jaguar!*"

The tasteful furnishings of Mrs. Bristlethwaite's drawing room disappeared, replaced by strange trees and wild plants. Only a little early morning sunlight streamed through the densely packed leaves. The hot, misty air oppressed Margaret, and she struggled to catch her breath. She gazed at her surroundings, searching unsuccessfully for anything familiar. Strange sounds issued from all around her: chittering, screeching, and buzzing. Margaret imagined that hundreds of animals waited in the impenetrable forest to pounce on her. Her fear, heightened by the disorienting effects of the Folding Spell, nearly sent her right back to Devonshire. But she took a steadying breath and muttered, "*Que les Bras de Protection m'entourent.*" Inside the sphere of the Protective Arms spell, Margaret calmed and remembered to speak the Many Tongues spell, "*Que les sons deviennent mots, que les mots deviennent sons.*"

Satisfied that she had prepared herself against whatever dangers she might encounter, Margaret, hands shaking, set about determining a path. The jungle seemed to extend in every direction. She turned round a few times but could not decide which way to go. So she consulted the atlas and whispered, "*Montrez-moi le chemin de la pyramide.*" A small glowing mark appeared on the map. When the mark began to move, Margaret started in the direction it indicated.

Margaret made slow progress through the jungle, stopping often to struggle with the vegetation that had overgrown what slowly revealed itself to be an ancient road. Perspiration dampened Margaret's brow, and she wished to remove her jacket. But at the sight of several enormous insects, she resisted. "Blood-thirsty?" she whimpered. Several times Margaret had the sensation of someone—or something—watching her. She stopped and glanced around, her heart pounding in agitation, but saw nothing, and so continued her laborious journey. Slowly the vegetation grew less and less dense until Margaret's path cleared.

"Oh!" Margaret cried suddenly. A tingling sensation had begun in her fingers and toes and slowly spread throughout her body. "I suppose I must be nearing the Temple." A moment later Margaret stopped in her tracks and stared at the sight that met her.

In front of her loomed a giant stone pyramid, rising out of the jungle floor. A grand stairway led to the flat top, which was crowned with a square edifice. Margaret stood, awestruck by the silent ruin, aware of the power emanating from it. "This must be where the Jaguar Mask is hidden," she whispered.

The climb proved difficult, as the stone had broken away in several places. Margaret had to choose her footing carefully. Once she almost fell, and after catching herself, sat panting before resuming her climb. At last she reached the top of the pyramid. She sat at the edge of the stairway and caught her breath, gazing at the vista that spread beneath her. Her heart swelled with the savage beauty of the jungle, lit by a strong sun in a deep blue sky lightened by a few wispy clouds. To the east she caught a little glimmer of light. She brought her hand to her eyes, shielding them from the sun. It took her a moment to realize that she gazed upon a vast body of water, the waves reflecting the light.

"I shall never forget this sight," she vowed.

After composing herself, Margaret turned her attention to the stone structure atop the pyramid. The building appeared intact. Margaret approached and noticed etchings on the walls. Amazed, she ran her hands over the stone, power humming under her fingertips. At the entrance she found a carving that took her breath away: a man with the head of large cat sat on a throne, surrounded by supplicants. "This must be the Jaguar Temple!" Margaret cried. Excited, she peered inside. Darkness met her, and Margaret hesitated, afraid of what she might find. Then she steeled herself and commanded, "*Éclairez le chemin.*" A faint glow preceded her into the temple.

A profound silence encircled Margaret as soon as she entered. Centuries of dust muffled her cautious footsteps. She glanced at the atlas and then up. The corridor led to a raised dais at the back of the temple, on which stood a small golden casket. Margaret walked down the long aisle lined with pillars stretching from floor to ceiling. She had almost reached the dais when a large black shape leapt into her path. Margaret screamed and backed away; the creature followed her. Despite her alarm, Margaret remembered another of the spells she had learned the night before. "*Bouclier!*" she cried, lifting her hands in a smooth gesture.

The beast hurtled toward her as she spoke, but then flew backward in mid-air, tumbling head over heels and smashing against a pillar. It lay there, dazed, but glaring at her. Margaret took in its sleek, midnight black coat, glowing golden eyes, and razor sharp claws. Perhaps this was the beast rumored to guard the mask?

The jaguar stood and shook itself and then began pacing in front of her barrier, growling. Frustrated, Margaret looked toward the mask. Even if she could get to it, the jaguar could easily prevent her from leaving. She did not think she could Fold her way out of the temple, either. Too much power protected it.

The jaguar's growls grew louder with its every step. Was it her imagination or did the growls have some sort of form to them? Margaret listened carefully. The great cat fixed his eyes upon her. She had not imagined anything.

"Who arrre you?"

Margaret, speechless, continued to stare.

"I shall rrrepeat myself just this once; who arrre you?"

Somehow Margaret found her voice. "M—Margaret Dashwood," she replied, surprised by the sounds issuing from her mouth. She spoke no language she had ever heard.

The jaguar cocked its head. "I do not know you. How arrre you keeping me from you?"

"A barrier spell," she replied, still too nonplussed to do anything but answer the questions.

"You arrre a mage?" The jaguar's tone of disbelief angered Margaret.

"A sorceress!" Margaret drew herself up to her full height, her indignation pushing aside her fear.

"And is yourrrs a darrrk or a light mageek?"

"Light!" Margaret cried. "Of course!"

The jaguar bared its teeth, and Margaret inched backwards.

"Then what business do you have in the Temple of the Jaguarrr? In *my* temple?"

"You are the mask's guardian? So the stories are true?"

The jaguar closed its mouth and regarded her. "You have hearrrd of me?" He sounded gratified.

"Well, I have read that there were rumors of a

beast guarding the mask after the mage disappeared."

"Ah. But you still have not answered my question. What arrre you doing in my temple?" His eyes had narrowed, and Margaret suffered a moment of dread.

"I came to—to get the mask." The jaguar growled, and Margaret rushed to continue. "Not to steal it! To protect it. You see, there is a sorcerer—at least we think he is a sorcerer—who is taking magical items that have been left unguarded. We do not know why he is doing it, but we have decided to put a stop to it."

"Who has made this decision?"

"The coven—the Devonshire Coven."

"And you arrre parrrt of this coven?"

"Well, not yet. This is my trial. I was to come here, retrieve the mask, and bring it back to Devonshire for safe-keeping."

"Where is this place—this Dev-on-sheerrr?"

"It is in England."

"I have neverrr hearrrd of such a place."

"Here—I have a map." Margaret opened the atlas to a map of the world. She held it up to the barrier. "Here is where we are, and here is England."

The jaguar's eyes grew wide. "This is powerrrful magic," it growled.

"The atlas is enchanted; it made the journey much easier," Margaret said, at a loss for any other explanation. "I mean you and your temple no harm. I just want to help."

The jaguar studied Margaret for a long moment. Then he swept into a bow, surprising Margaret even further. She regained her senses, however, and curtsied.

"I apologize forrr frightening you, Sorrrceress," said the jaguar. "I am honorrred to welcome you. My name is Balam Paal, Mage of the Jaguarrr Temple."

"So it is true! You did not disappear after all!"

Mr. Paal shook his sleek black head.

"Where are my manners? I am honored to make your acquaintance, Mr. Paal." And as a further courtesy, Margaret removed the barrier spell. "Mr. Paal, how did you come to be in this form?"

"I was currrsed during a battle with anotherrr mage who had come to steal the mask. As I cast the spell that vanquished him, he hit me with the transformation spell that left me in this form. I have yet to find a way back to my human body."

Margaret grew thoughtful. "Mr. Paal, perhaps I could help."

"Do you know anything about transformation spells?"

"Not really. But I am a quick study, and if you tell me what to do, I can do it," she said with more confidence than she really felt.

"Though I have grown fond of this body's strength, I can better guarrrd the mask in my own form." He looked at Margaret. "We shall try, Sorrrceress. First you need to take that cup from the altarrr and fill it with rain water."

"But the sky is clear!"

"Ah, Sorrrceress, you do not understand this land. It rains every day. Listen."

Margaret cocked her head. She heard the faint patter of raindrops splashing on stone. "Oh." She retrieved the simple wooden cup from the altar and took it outside. The rain poured from the sky. Drenched, Margaret returned inside with a full cup.

"I have it," she said, wiping water from her eyes with her free hand.

"Good. Come up here and pourrr a circle around me, chanting 'Water from the heavens purifies all that lies within the circle.'"

Margaret nodded to show she understood. "Then what?"

"After you have marrrked out the sacred circle with the water, you will lift the enchantment. First stand directly in front of me, and then place your arrrms at your sides, palms facing up. You will see the edges of the circle glowing around me if you have laid it correctly. Slowly raise your arrrms, imagining that you also lift a circle of light to surround me. Bring your arrrms all the way above your head, hands together. The light should envelop me completely. Then swing your arrrms back down as quickly as you can and cry, 'Release!' If you concentrate all yourrr effort on the circle of light and on the intention of restoring me to my former forrrm, the disenchantment should work. Do you understand what you must do?"

"I do."

"Rrrepeat back to me everything that I have said."

Margaret repeated his directions three times before Mr. Paal was satisfied that she understood them.

"All right, Sorrrceress. Shall we begin?" Mr. Paal took a place in the center of the Temple, sitting perfectly still.

Margaret walked in a slow circle around him, chanting Mr. Paal's incantation. Although she understood the sounds she made, she knew that they were foreign to her English tongue. Gently she drew her attention back to her task. Having completed the circle, Margaret stood in front of Mr. Paal. She looked at the ground around him and was thrilled to see a faint glowing. She took a breath and then slowly lifted her arms, willing the light that surrounded the jaguar to move up and around him. By the time her hands were clasped above her head, the jaguar had completely disappeared beneath a tent of bright, pure light. Rapidly she pulled her hands down and cried, "Release!" A rush of sound accompanied the light, which flew down and away. When Margaret's vision cleared, she saw a man sprawled in front of her. She experienced a painful moment, certain that she had killed him. Then he sat up, and Margaret blushed furiously.

Mr. Paal looked at Margaret, perplexed. Then he caught sight of his transformed body. "Ah, yes. I have returned to my own form without my clothing." He strode toward the back of the temple. When he reappeared he wore splendid robes fashioned from a material Margaret did not recognize.

"Sorceress, how may I thank you?" he asked.

"Could you come back to England with me—just to prove that I accomplished my task? We could bring the mask to show the coven that it is safe, and then I could return you to your temple."

Mr. Paal considered her request, a grave expression on his face. But then he retrieved the mask from its gold casket. "If that is how you wish me to repay my debt, then I will accompany you." His face darkened. "But how will we get there?"

"We shall use the Folding Spell—it allows sorcerers to travel huge distances quickly. I think we shall have to go outside. The temple's magic might interfere with our efforts."

"After you, Sorceress," Mr. Paal replied.

Margaret led Mr. Paal into the pouring rain. Then

she held out her hand, which Mr. Paal took, and said, "*Que la Jungle du Jaguar se replie sur le Manoir de Barbarie.*"

A moment later she and Mr. Paal stood dripping in the well-appointed drawing room of Barbary Hall. The coven surrounded them.

Miss Cottlebury screamed.

CHAPTER XV

"Oh for Heaven's sake, Miss Cottlebury," said Mrs. Bristlethwaite. She hurried forward, relief etched on her countenance. Both Margaret and Mr. Paal swayed, dizzy after the journey from the Jaguar Temple.

"But she has brought back a savage!" protested Miss Cottlebury, pointing.

"Miss Cottlebury," Margaret said, steadying herself on the back of a chair. "This is Mr. Balam Paal, the guardian of the Jaguar Mask and mage of the Jaguar Temple."

A nervous murmur ran through the coven.

"What did she say?" asked Mr. James.

"I said," Margaret began, raising her voice.

"Margaret," said Mrs. Bristlethwaite. "You are under the Many Tongues Spell, my dear. Perhaps you could cast it on the rest of us so that we can understand, too?"

"Oh!" Margaret cried, "Of course!" She focused her attention on the group, willing them understand. "Sounds become words and words become sounds," she said in the strange tongue of Mr. Paal. "Do you understand me?"

"Much better," said Mrs. Bristlethwaite. Then she turned to Mr. Paal. "Welcome to my home, Mage," she said.

Mr. Paal bowed. "Thank you, Madam Sorceress. It is a beautiful home." He took in the room, his eyes wide with wonder. "I apologize for appearing without a gift."

Mrs. Bristlethwaite dismissed his concern with a wave of her hand. "But you have brought a gift. You have seen Miss Dashwood safely home." She turned to Margaret. "Go change into something dry, Margaret. I shall attend to Mr. Paal. Come directly back here, and we shall hear your tale."

"I will return soon, Mr. Paal," Margaret said. "You are safe with Mrs. Bristlethwaite and the rest of the coven."

"Thank you, Sorceress."

By the time Margaret returned, Mr. Paal was seated near the fire, wrapped in a blanket. Most of the coven gathered around him. Even Miss Cottlebury, who kept her distance, listened with interest. Lady Jane examined the Jaguar Mask, wearing an expression of awe. When Mr. Paal noticed Margaret, he stopped speaking and stood.

"Ah, Margaret, very good," said Mrs. Bristlethwaite. "Mr. Paal has just told us that you transformed him back to his human form."

"Very impressive, Miss Dashwood," said Sir Berwin. "Some outstanding magic, that."

"Oh yes," agreed Mr. James with an enthusiastic nod of his little head. "Quite astonishing."

Margaret looked down and smiled, moved by their praise. She felt someone's gaze and looked up, catching Mr. Barrington's eyes. "You demonstrated great bravery, Miss Dashwood. I am not certain I would have faired so well."

"Of course you would have, Barrington," scolded Miss Cottlebury. "But I must say, Miss Dashwood, I am impressed. I did not think you had the mettle; you have proven me wrong."

Margaret raised her eyebrows.

"Goodness, Mademoiselle Cottlebury, that is high praise indeed! Actually, Mademoiselle Dashwood, from Mademoiselle Cottlebury that *is* the highest praise that you are likely to receive."

"Your father would be very proud, Margaret," said Mrs. Bristlethwaite.

Margaret thought she might burst with happiness.

"Sorceress Dashwood," Mr. Paal said. "It is time for me to return the mask to the Temple. There is much work for me to do."

"Of course!" Margaret replied.

Lady Jane handed the mask back to Mr. Paal, who replied with a bow.

"I shall return shortly," Margaret promised. "Shall we, Mr. Paal?"

He took her proffered hand. "Good bye and thank you for your kind reception," he said to the coven.

Margaret spoke the words of the Folding Spell, and Barbary Hall melted away. Much to Margaret's surprise, they arrived just outside the Temple. The sun shone, all traces of rain gone but for the steam in the air. Margaret swayed a little but remained on her feet. Mr. Paal appeared queasy but otherwise unperturbed by the journey.

"I cannot thank you enough, Sorceress," he said.

"It was an honor, Mr. Paal."

"I owe you a debt for your generous aid. Without you, I probably would have remained in my jaguar form for the rest of my days." A hint of wistfulness appeared in his eyes. "That form had some benefits, of course, but I could not perform my duties as Mage of the Jaguar Temple." He bowed to Margaret. "Know that you will always be welcomed here, Sorceress."

"Thank you, Mr. Paal." Margaret stopped speaking as tears welled in her eyes and a lump formed in her throat.

Mr. Paal cocked his head, a curious expression on his face. "We shall meet again, Sorceress Dashwood." He bowed to her and then stepped into the Temple.

Margaret dried her eyes, lifted the Many Tongues Spell from herself, and returned to England.

"Congratulations, Margaret!" cried Mrs. Bristlethwaite.

Margaret wobbled and then toppled over, exhausted from performing so much magic in one day.

"Miss Dashwood!" Mr. Barrington raced to Margaret's side, helped her to her feet, and led her gently to a chair near the fire.

"Bring her something to eat," suggested Mr. James.

"Margaret, can you tolerate tea?" Lady Jane asked.

"I should like a cup of tea and a biscuit better than anything," Margaret replied.

"Here you are, my dear. This will revive you."

Margaret sipped her tea, conscious of everyone's eyes upon her. She smiled over the teacup. "I shall be fine."

"Of course. We should give the poor girl some air," said Mrs. Bristlethwaite. The coven stepped back, all but Mr. Barrington, who remained at her side. Margaret could not decide if she was pleased or worried by his proximity.

"Margaret," said Mrs. Bristlethwaite after Margaret had taken a bite of her biscuit. "We have a little business to finish." She gestured for Margaret to join her in front of the coven. With shaking legs, Margaret complied, still clutching her biscuit. "Miss Dashwood, having passed your trial, you begin the next stage in your journey toward membership in the Devonshire Coven. But I must warn you: an apprenticeship with us must not be undertaken lightly. Are you prepared to face the rigors such an enterprise entails?"

"I am," Margaret replied. Though she trembled with elation, she adopted Mrs. Bristlethwaite's solemn tone.

"Then on behalf of the coven, I name you apprentice!"

"Welcome!" cried Lady Jane and Sir Berwin in unison.

"*Oui, bienvenue,*" said Lady Isabelle while Mr. James nodded his head vigorously.

Even Miss Cottlebury gave a little cheer, which drew broad smiles from the others.

Mrs. Bristlethwaite kissed Margaret on her brow. "You may begin tomorrow, my dear. This evening, we celebrate your accomplishment! Mrs. Crawford has prepared a feast in your honor."

"But how did she know I would succeed?" Margaret asked.

"She did not. But I felt certain you would. And if

you had not, well, I suppose a fine meal would have provided some consolation."

Margaret smiled at the twinkle in Mrs. Bristlethwaite's eyes, although she could not bear to think about how little consolation she would have taken in food had she failed her trial. A wave of exhaustion passed suddenly over Margaret, and she yawned.

"My dear, you must go up to your room and rest. I shall send Lucy with a little tonic for you as well." Mrs. Bristlethwaite examined her. "Yes, that will be just the thing."

Dinner that evening was an enjoyable affair. Margaret, who had recovered nicely through a combination of nap and tonic, felt like Mr. James—astonished by the many courses laid out one after another and enchanted by the fine wine from Mrs. Bristlethwaite's cellar. The conversation turned largely around Margaret's trial, although Mr. James interrupted from time to time to exclaim about a dish that he sampled.

"Were you not terrified when the jaguar leapt at you, Miss Dashwood?" asked Mr. Barrington midway through the meal, admiration dancing in his eyes.

"To be honest, Mr. Barrington, I was completely terrified," Margaret admitted with a hiccough.

"And yet you demonstrated such presence of mind," said Lady Jane. "According to Mr. Paal—a charming man, really, despite the *disadvantages* of his savage existence—you acquitted yourself admirably. He said you cast some sort of protection spell that formed a barrier around you. What inspired your choice?"

"Langlois's *Compendium*," Margaret replied. "I consulted it the night before my trial."

"Ah, Brava, Mademoiselle Dashwood," said Lady Isabelle. "*C'est un livre magnifique*! Perfect for nearly every magical occasion, *n'est-ce pas?*"

"Yes, well, I *suppose*," said Miss Cottlebury. "If one likes *foreign* things."

"Miss Cottlebury," admonished Mrs. Bristlethwaite. "Must you always be so rude? Margaret has just passed her trial; you could make a show of *fellowship* from time to time."

Miss Cottlebury blushed but said nothing. Margaret, shocked by Mrs. Bristlethwaite's tone, felt a sudden burst of compassion for Miss Cottlebury and patted her hand gently. Miss Cottlebury looked at Margaret with surprise, but then her expression shifted.

"I thought your father a wonderful man," she said quietly.

"Thank you, Miss Cottlebury," Margaret replied, touched by Miss Cottlebury's softened manner.

Miss Cottlebury took a sip of wine. Margaret glanced at Mrs. Bristlethwaite, who then patted Miss Cottlebury on her other hand. "There, there, my dear. I am sorry for my outburst. You know we all adore you, do you not?" Mrs. Bristlethwaite said.

Miss Cottlebury nodded, dabbing at her eyes with a handkerchief.

"Oh, look at that cake!" exclaimed Mr. James, dispelling the uneasiness created by Mrs. Bristlethwaite's scolding.

Over cake and Constantia wine, conversation turned to speculations about the thief of magical items.

"Mrs. Bristlethwaite said he nearly caught up to you in Dartmoor," said Mr. Barrington.

"I think so. At least *someone* arrived at the chamber while we were there. I thought it best not to remain in case we faced any danger."

"Quite sensible of you, Miss Dashwood," approved Mr. Barrington.

"It is a pity that neither of you saw the person you heard," said Sir Berwin. "That might have given us a better sense of whom we face."

"It seems rather apparent that a fairly accomplished sorcerer is responsible for the thefts," Mr. Barrington said.

"Or sorceress," countered Lady Jane.

"True. Although did we not hear from Monsieur Sadik that the thief is a sorcerer?" Lady Isabelle offered.

"A clever sorceress could easily disguise herself as a man. In fact, this sorcerer probably does disguise himself or herself. He—or she—could even be among us," said Sir Berwin, his tone ominous.

Mrs. Bristlethwaite chuckled. "Surely you do not believe that one of us is robbing magical sites around the world, Sir Berwin? I think it possible that you have had a little too much wine."

"Here, here," said Mr. Barrington, raising his glass, to general laughter.

After dinner everyone retired to the drawing room, where card tables had been set out. Margaret was amazed to see members of the Devonshire Coven gathered around the tables prepared to do something as ordinary as play whist.

Mrs. Bristlethwaite interrupted her thoughts. "Margaret, would you care to entertain us with something on the *pianoforte*?"

"I would be happy to!"

Margaret sat at the instrument and after a short pause to consider what piece to play first, brought her fingers to the keys. She lost herself in the music, content to play for her own amusement. When she finished, she found a rapt audience staring at her.

"Lovely!" exclaimed Lady Jane.

"Indeed," agreed Sir Berwin.

A small sob escaped from Mr. James. Even Miss Cottlebury voiced her approval. "Well done, Miss Dashwood!"

"Music has a magic all its own," said Mr. Barrington softly from behind Margaret. "Would you mind if I sat with you while you played? I find no entertainment in cards."

"I would not mind at all, Mr. Barrington," Margaret said with real feeling. Then she bit her lip. What would Mr. Ellsworth think?

"Are you well, Miss Dashwood?" asked Mr. Barrington.

"Yes, I am fine," said Margaret, endeavoring to dismiss her concerns. Surely allowing Mr. Barrington to sit with her as she played the *pianoforte* was hardly a betrayal of Mr. Ellsworth.

"Are you certain?"

"Yes, of course. But I thank you for your concern." She chose a piece that Mr. Ellsworth had enjoyed, reminding herself of *his* regard for her and of *her* great affection for *him*. Soon enough, her worry melted away.

"Enchanting, Miss Dashwood," said Mr. Barrington when she finished. "You play with such passion and sensibility."

"Thank you, Mr. Barrington. Music is very dear to me. Music and poetry both. Do you have a favorite poet, Mr. Barrington?"

"I must confess to an embarrassing ignorance of poetry. And my appreciation of music goes no deeper than understanding that certain sounds appeal to me and certain others do not. I have not your knowledge of these things of beauty."

"But it is not difficult to learn," said Margaret.

"Is it not?"

"No! One must only pay attention to how words affect one's feelings. I shall show you." She collected her book of Cowper's poems from a nearby table. "Here." She handed Mr. Barrington the book.

"What am I to do with this?"

"Read the lines. Aloud is best, of course, but if you are shy, you may read them silently."

Mr. Barrington took the book and then glanced at Margaret before turning to the page. He read silently and then looked dutifully back at her. "It seems lovely. But it has no effect on me."

"You cannot be serious, Mr. Barrington," said Margaret, nonplussed. "Poetry affects everyone. You simply do not know how to feel it."

"Is Margaret attempting to turn you into a poet, Mr. Barrington?" said Mrs. Bristlethwaite. "Margaret, my dear, Mr. Barrington is many things, but a poet is not one. You would be better discussing magical battle strategy with him."

Mr. Barrington laughed, but it was a kind laugh, not at all at Margaret's expense, so she could not help but feel cheered. "I am not completely convinced that I cannot convert him," Margaret declared. Then she brought her hands to her mouth. She had possibly drunk a little too much wine.

"I might just believe you could, Miss Dashwood," said Mr. Barrington. "Only time will tell."

CHAPTER XVI

At half past ten the following morning, Mrs. Bristlethwaite called the meeting of the Devonshire Coven to order, adding, "I hope everyone has recovered from last night's festivities."

Margaret surveyed the coven. Everyone looked pale. She had awoken feeling rather dreadful, but after a cup of tea and a bun, her condition had improved significantly.

"Only a little worse for wear," said Sir Berwin.

"I suppose so," said Mrs. Bristlethwaite. "We may as well get right to the business of this meeting." She placed her hand on a stack of papers on the table. "When we returned to Devonshire, Margaret and I occupied ourselves with compiling a list of magical items that lacked guardians. We discovered a great many. I suggest that we collect as many as possible for safekeeping until we can be certain that they are no longer in any danger of being stolen." She looked around the table. "The topic is now open for discussion."

"It seems a reasonable idea," began Sir Berwin. "With the aid of the atlas, we can work quickly." Lady Isabelle and Mr. James indicated their approbation. Margaret, who also agreed with Sir Berwin, felt it best that she remain a quiet observer as the conversation unfolded.

"I have one reservation," said Mr. Barrington. "Should we gather all those objects of power into one place? We do not know what they do or how they might react to one another."

"I agree with Mr. Barrington," Lady Jane said, ignoring the look from her husband. "We also do not know how their absence will affect the places from which we take them."

"We can solve the first problem by storing them in various locations. Each of us could take one or two into our homes," Sir Berwin suggested.

"But does that not just make them more difficult to guard?" Mr. Barrington replied.

"Mr. Barrington and Lady Jane make very good points," said Mrs. Bristlethwaite. "I agree with you, Mr. Barrington, both about the danger of gathering them together and about the difficulty of guarding them if we then separate them again. As for Lady Jane's concern, ours is a temporary solution. We shall return the objects to their rightful places as soon as possible. I think any effects on the land would take longer to appear."

Nods and muttered agreement met Mrs. Bristlethwaite's declaration.

"I hope that you are correct, Mrs. Bristlethwaite. But I do suppose that in the end keeping the objects away from this sorcerer must outweigh any other concerns," said Lady Jane.

"Do you not worry about temptation, Mrs. Bristlethwaite?" Miss Cottlebury's voice was quiet but crisp.

"My dear, I forgot. Of course, we must all take precautions against temptations." She gave Miss Cottlebury a searching glance. "We would all understand if you would like to find another way to aid the coven."

Margaret looked from Mrs. Bristlethwaite to Miss Cottlebury and then around the table. The other members of the coven fixed their eyes downward, except for Lady Isabelle who gazed at Miss Cottlebury with sympathy. Miss Cottlebury cleared her throat. "We should explain to Miss Dashwood."

Mrs. Bristlethwaite's eyebrows rose. "Are you certain?"

Miss Cottlebury turned to Margaret, placing a gnarled hand over Margaret's smooth one. "Miss Dashwood, it is no secret among the coven members that I nearly succumbed to a terrible temptation." She drew a breath and met Margaret's eyes. "Many years ago, when I was a much younger and even more foolish woman, I strayed from the coven, not satisfied with the power I found among them. I had stumbled upon an amulet that once belonged to a powerful Scottish sorcerer. Some say he could charm a Selkie away from her skin. I cannot say if that rumor is true. I do know that he fashioned an amulet that granted the bearer incredible power. I found that amulet and kept it for myself." She shivered at the memory, the hand resting on Margaret's growing cold. "Imagine doing magic without suffering any fatigue or illness. But the amulet began to leak away my human warmth. It turned me to stone inside. I cared little for anyone or anything but the power.

"I was nearly lost, and then Mrs. Bristlethwaite saved me. She cast the amulet into the sea." Miss Cottlebury's face paled. "My recovery took years; some might argue it continues still." Tears stood in Miss Cottlebury's eyes, and Margaret wrapped an arm around the older woman. Miss Cottlebury faced Margaret with a sad smile. "You have been far kinder to me, than I deserve, Miss Dashwood."

"Margaret has her father's gift, Agnes, and she sees your heart. It is a good heart, my dear." Mrs. Bristlethwaite's voice contained a gentleness that Margaret had never heard.

Miss Cottlebury sniffled, and Margaret drew out her handkerchief, handing it to Miss Cottlebury without a word. A sob erupted from the other end of the table. Margaret turned as Mr. James laid his head down, shoulders shaking. Lady Isabelle patted Mr. James on the back.

"There, there, Monsieur James. All will be well," she murmured.

Miss Cottlebury dried her eyes and took a deep breath. "I would like to help. Where shall I go?"

Around the table, faces brightened.

"Here, here," cried Sir Berwin.

"But Mr. Barrington's point has not been addressed. We must keep the objects separate," Lady Jane protested.

"Mrs. Bristlethwaite, what about the passages in Barbary Hall?" Mr. Barrington asked.

"What about them?" Mrs. Bristlethwaite countered.

"They could serve as hiding places. They are secret even from each other. Perhaps that secrecy will prevent any magical complications."

"Brilliant idea, Monsieur Barrington!" said Lady Isabelle. "I think that might work."

The others agreed.

"All that remains is to decide who will recover which objects," Mrs. Bristlethwaite declared.

"I propose working in teams of two," said Miss Cottlebury.

"I agree," said Mrs. Bristlethwaite. "Any objections?"

No one spoke. "All right. I shall work with you, Agnes, if that is acceptable."

"Yes, it is," Miss Cottlebury replied.

"Lady Jane and I shall work together," said Sir Berwin.

"Lady Isabelle, would you accompany Mr. James?" said Mrs. Bristlethwaite.

"Of course!" Lady Isabelle gazed fondly at Mr. James.

"That leaves Mr. Barrington to accompany Margaret," said Mrs. Bristlethwaite.

"I shall be going, too?" Margaret said.

"Of course, my dear! Unless you would rather not?"

"Oh, no! I want to help! I just thought—"

"In ordinary circumstances we would ease you into your apprenticeship, but we do not have that luxury now. We require all the power we can muster. Do you feel yourself fit for this challenge?"

Margaret nodded vigorously. "I do."

"Good. No one will provide better protection for you than Mr. Barrington, Margaret, and I am certain that he will appreciate your skill in this task."

"I look forward to the adventure, Miss

Dashwood," said Mr. Barrington.

Mrs. Bristlethwaite continued, "As for your assignments." She consulted her list. "We may as well begin at the beginning. Agnes, you and I can take my carriage to Wales to recover the Bard's Amulet. According to Margaret's atlas, it is hidden in a cave in southern Wales."

Miss Cottlebury took the paper from Mrs. Bristlethwaite.

"Sir Berwin and Lady Jane, I shall send you to Cornwall for the Pixie Runes."

"My dear, how do you prefer to travel?" Sir Berwin asked.

"We shall fly, I think, as it is a short distance," Lady Jane replied.

"Very good. I never was particularly adept at Folding."

"Lady Isabelle and Mr. James, the Orb of Loch Leven awaits you."

Mr. James let out a delighted cry. "I do so adore Scotland at this time of year." He stood and took a few steps toward the door.

"Mr. James, not yet," said Lady Isabelle. "We should make a plan first."

Mr. James's face fell. "I suppose so," he said.

"Margaret, I shall have you and Mr. Barrington take advantage of your atlas and begin retrieving the items located farther away." She consulted the list. "Ah, yes, this should do. The Urn of Osiris, housed in the Egyptian desert."

Margaret blanched at Mrs. Bristlethwaite's statement. So much time alone with Mr. Barrington! What might Mr. Ellsworth think if he knew?

"Indeed?" Mr. Barrington breathed.

"Not to worry, Mr. Barrington. Margaret has grown quite adept at magical travel."

"I trust that she has. But I thought the Urn of Osiris was a legend."

"No, Mr. Barrington, according to the atlas it is very much a real item. It passed out of magical use several centuries ago; its last guardian disappeared." Mrs. Bristlethwaite turned back to the coven. "Are there any questions?" When no one spoke, she continued, "Excellent. You know your tasks. Margaret and I copied down all the details you will require; you will find them on the sheets of paper I handed to you. I suggest all partners take some time to discuss their approaches, but leave as soon as possible. I propose meeting again in two days—that should allow everyone ample time for recovery. If anyone is missing, we shall form search parties."

Margaret's stomach fell at this statement, her worries about Mr. Ellsworth driven from her mind.

"Good luck, everyone," said Mrs. Bristlethwaite. "Take care of each other."

The coven rose from the table and made their way out of the drawing room. Mr. Barrington waited for Margaret by the door.

"I thought we could work in the garden," said Mr. Barrington.

"That sounds like a lovely idea, Mr. Barrington."

The day was bright and warm for the season. At first they walked in silence, each lost in thought. At length, however, Mr. Barrington spoke.

"We have quite a task to accomplish, would you not say, Miss Dashwood?"

"Indeed! I must confess a slight trepidation about it," Margaret replied.

"I understand your feelings, and to be perfectly honest, I share them. But I comfort myself by remembering that I have a strong and talented ally in this enterprise. And we have that ingenious atlas to aid us."

"That we do." Margaret spied a bench lit with sunshine. "Shall we sit and consult the atlas?"

"Absolutely. No time to dawdle even on such a fine day."

They settled themselves upon the bench, and Margaret turned to the section about Egypt. A warm blast of faintly musty air greeted them as they bent, heads together, over the page describing the Urn of Osiris.

A very powerful vessel, the Urn of Osiris was constructed from clay taken from the banks of the Nile. The sorcerers and sorceresses who served in the Temple of Osiris included their own blood in the mixture, sealing the Urn's power and connecting it to the bloodlines of the Egyptian gods. The Urn of Osiris has several uses, none of which is particularly savory. Suffice it to say that anywhere you see the Urn of Osiris, you can expect dark magic nearby.

"Oh!" cried Margaret. "I did not realize it was such a dangerous item."

"Did you not read about it when you and Mrs. Bristlethwaite compiled the list?"

"No. We put our attention on practical matters: determining arrival points, hiding places, and the like."

"Where is the Urn kept?"

"It is in a tomb beneath a pyramid." Margaret

turned to the map on the page facing the picture of the Urn. "Here it is."

"Miss Dashwood?" A shadow fell across the map.

Margaret and Mr. Barrington looked up. With a gasp, Margaret sprang to her feet, dropping the atlas.

"Mr. Ellsworth! I had not expected to see you today," she said. "What a splendid surprise!" she hastened to add.

Mr. Barrington stood and bowed. "Allow me to introduce myself." He held out his hand. "Edward Barrington. I am an old friend of Mrs. Bristlethwaite's." Margaret was amazed at the smoothness of Mr. Barrington's voice. He did not seem at all unnerved by Mr. Ellsworth's sudden appearance.

"Splendid to meet you, Mr. Barrington. I am Weston Ellsworth."

The gentlemen dropped hands and a short silence ensued. Mr. Ellsworth glanced at the ground.

"Miss Dashwood, you have dropped your book." Mr. Ellsworth bent forward, securing the atlas before Margaret realized what he was doing.

"Thank you, Mr. Ellsworth," Margaret said in a rush, reaching for the book.

But Mr. Ellsworth had already turned it over after glancing at the cover. "Is this your father's atlas? How curious! I always thought they were rather unwieldy books." He turned a few pages, examining them carefully. "To what use would one put so small a map?"

Margaret gave a nervous laugh. "It fits easily in one's pocket."

"I suppose it does." Mr. Ellsworth turned another page, and his eyes widened.

Margaret held her breath, wondering if he had seen the enchantment. But Mr. Ellsworth's expression softened. "I am amazed at the craftsmanship; though the maps are rather small, the lines are so fine and the detail of rivers and mountains impressive." Margaret exhaled, certain that he had not detected the atlas's magic. Mr. Ellsworth returned the book to her. "I apologize for my interruption; I will leave you to your reading."

"Oh, no, that is not necessary, Mr. Ellsworth!" Margaret looked at Mr. Barrington, appeal in her eyes. "Mr. Barrington, would it be terribly rude of me to excuse myself for just a little while?"

Mr. Barrington looked from Margaret to Mr. Ellsworth. "No, Miss Dashwood. I have business inside. We can continue our discussion of cartography later." He smiled. "I am something of an amateur cartographer," he explained to Mr. Ellsworth. "And Miss Dashwood wanted to show me her father's atlas, did you not?" He fixed her with a significant look.

"Pardon me? Oh, yes, yes I did. Mr. Barrington has been so helpful!" Margaret felt a little twinge of guilt for being untruthful, but reassured herself that it was for the best. There were some truths she was not yet ready to share.

"How gallant of you, Mr. Barrington," said Mr. Ellsworth. "Miss Dashwood, will you join me in a turn around the garden? It seems ages since I saw you last."

"Yes, I would like that."

"A pleasure meeting you, Barrington," said Mr. Ellsworth.

"And you, Mr. Ellsworth." Mr. Barrington bowed to Margaret. "Miss Dashwood, I look forward to continuing our conversation." Then he strode toward the house.

Margaret and Mr. Ellsworth set off around the garden. Margaret had no idea how to explain what she was doing with Mr. Barrington, so she was relieved when Mr. Ellsworth changed the subject entirely.

"I have been remiss in my visits to you, Miss Dashwood! I must apologize."

"I understand, Mr. Ellsworth! Your collection is so important. Have you made any progress in acquiring that—what was it you were trying to acquire?"

"A trifle, Miss Dashwood. Certainly not something you need concern yourself with." He stopped in the middle of the path and brought her hand to his lips. "I would rather hear about how you have been faring with Mrs. Bristlethwaite and her guests."

"Oh," Margaret said, searching for an answer that would betray nothing. "We have had a splendid time—dinners and conversation. Nothing out of the ordinary, of course."

"I am glad that you have been enjoying yourself. How long will the guests be staying?"

"I am not certain. At least a few more days." They rounded a bend in the path and suddenly were in full view of the entrance to the Hall.

"Curious," said Mr. Ellsworth. Margaret followed the direction of his gaze. Mrs. Bristlethwaite's horses and carriage stood in the drive. She cast an uneasy glance at Mr. Ellsworth. "Is one of the guests leaving?" Mr. Ellsworth asked.

"I suppose it is possible." Margaret heard someone approach.

"Mr. Ellsworth! How lovely to see you again."

Mr. Ellsworth bowed. "Always a delight, Mrs.

Bristlethwaite."

"I wish I could invite you in to tea, but I am afraid that I must be off. I have promised Miss Cottlebury a turn in the country." Miss Cottlebury stuck her head out of the window and narrowed her eyes at Mr. Ellsworth. "She has not been well, I am afraid. I hope that the drive will do her some good," Mrs. Bristlethwaite said quietly.

Margaret remained silent, amazed at Mrs. Bristlethwaite's ability to cover the truth so smoothly.

"I wish you an agreeable afternoon and your friend a complete recovery."

"Thank you, Mr. Ellsworth." Mrs. Bristlethwaite turned to Margaret. "Perhaps we could invite Mr. Ellsworth to tea another day?" She gave Margaret a significant look, more, Margaret thought, for Mr. Ellsworth's benefit than for her own. Once again Margaret admired Mrs. Bristlethwaite's resourcefulness.

"Of course," Margaret said.

"I should like nothing better." Mr. Ellsworth took Margaret's hand and planted a light kiss on it. "I await another meeting with bated breath."

Margaret and Mrs. Bristlethwaite watched him walk down the drive and disappear onto the road to Barton Hall. "My word. That was a precarious situation, was it not, Margaret?"

"Mrs. Bristlethwaite, we must hurry!" Miss Cottlebury called from the carriage.

Mrs. Bristlethwaite responded with a wave. "Margaret, I wish you good fortune in your travels."

"And I, you, Mrs. Bristlethwaite," Margaret said. After a warm embrace, Mrs. Bristlethwaite joined Miss Cottlebury. Margaret waved as the carriage carried Mrs. Bristlethwaite and Miss Cottlebury off to Wales.

"Shall we resume our preparations?" came a voice from behind Margaret. "Pardon me, Miss Dashwood, I did not mean to startle you."

"That is quite all right, Mr. Barrington." Margaret, recovered from Mr. Barrington's sudden reappearance, allowed him to lead her back to the garden bench.

"Have you and Mr. Ellsworth long been acquainted?" Mr. Barrington said, breaking the awkward silence that had fallen between them.

Margaret shook her head. "Not terribly long."

"He seems an affable gentleman."

"He is," Margaret replied, blushing.

Mr. Barrington looked away. "Perhaps we should return to our work."

"Yes, good idea. Where were we?"

"We had just read a description of the Urn, I believe."

"Of course." Margaret opened the atlas. "There are several points of arrival. I suggest this one." Margaret indicated a spot on the map. "I imagine the closer we arrive to the Urn's hiding place, the more difficult it might prove to Fold, but the more quickly we can accomplish our task."

"I am certain that with our combined strength we can manage the difficulty." Mr. Barrington smiled at her. "I hope we encounter no danger, but we should both be prepared to defend each other if necessary."

Margaret's stomach grew icy, but she nodded.

"Not to worry, Miss Dashwood. I shall do my best to see that you return safely." His brown eyes were so kind.

"And I shall do my best to ensure your safe return, Mr. Barrington."

"Excellent!" He stood and held out his hand. "Shall we, Miss Dashwood?"

Margaret took his hand and stood. "We shall."

"Would you care to do the honors?"

Margaret opened the atlas to the correct page and said, "Hold on tightly, Mr. Barrington." He squeezed her hand as she said, "*Que le Manoir de Barbarie se replie sur la Pyramide d'Osiris*!

The cool air of Devonshire gave way to the dry heat of the desert.

CHAPTER XVII

*M*r. Barrington swayed and then fell, pulling Margaret down into the hot sand. They lay next to each other, dazed, until Mr. Barrington turned to Margaret, anxiety creasing his brow.

"Are you hurt, Miss Dashwood?"

Margaret sat. "I do not believe so, Mr. Barrington."

Mr. Barrington placed a strong hand on her shoulder and leaned toward her. "Are you certain?" His voice was soft, and his eyes were gentle. Margaret forgot where she was.

But then the sand shifted beneath her, and she scrambled to stand, mortified by their compromising proximity.

"I am quite well, Mr. Barrington." Eager to change the subject, Margaret glanced upward at the structure towering over them. "Another pyramid."

"What is that?" Mr. Barrington asked.

"I have encountered more than the usual number of pyramids this week. At least we do not have to climb this one."

"How do you suppose we get inside?"

Margaret examined the pyramid. "Perhaps there is a door on the side?"

Mr. Barrington took a step, but Margaret stopped him. "First I must cast the Many Tongues spell." To his puzzled look she replied, "In case we encounter anyone."

"Of course!" said Mr. Barrington. "By all means—"

"*Que les sons deviennent mots; que les mots deviennent sons,*" Margaret said.

"You have the most impressive French, Miss Dashwood. I am afraid I do not share your fluency. How would you translate that spell to English?"

"Thank you, Mr. Barrington. It means 'sounds become words and words become sounds.'"

"A clever spell indeed! I cannot imagine casting spells in any language but English. But you manage so well. What made you choose French?"

Margaret blushed. "It is a beautiful language, and I want my magic to be beautiful."

Mr. Barrington cocked his head and studied her. "Yours is a romantic soul, Miss Dashwood," he said quietly. Margaret thought she detected a note of sadness in his voice. But before she could question him, Mr. Barrington continued, "Shall we?"

"Yes!" Margaret's reply was enthusiastic. They began their search for an entrance, keeping a slow pace and remaining alert for anything unusual. The wind whipped sand around them, stinging their faces.

They had not made much progress when Margaret stopped. "Mr. Barrington."

"What is it?" Mr. Barrington turned.

Margaret pointed at the sand. "Footprints." She met Mr. Barrington's eyes, unsettled by her discovery.

Mr. Barrington knelt to examine the prints. "I imagine they are recent."

"What makes you think so?" Margaret said.

"The wind would have erased them otherwise."

"What should we do?"

"Continue our search, but be wary. We may well encounter someone who shares our purpose, though not our intent." Mr. Barrington started walking, motioning for Margaret to follow. Trembling, Margaret stayed right behind him.

They met no one as they crept onward, and on the other side of the pyramid they found an entrance. Several steps led downward into the structure's stone foundation where an immense bronze door stood slightly ajar. Cool, musty air met them as they approached it. Margaret's heart leapt—whether from fear or exhilaration, she could not tell.

"We must proceed carefully, Miss Dashwood," Mr. Barrington whispered.

"Of course," Margaret replied. "Wait," she added, taking Mr. Barrington's hand. When he started to speak, she shook her head and held her finger to her lips. "*Que les Bras de Protection nous entourent!*"

Mr. Barrington raised an eyebrow. "What was—?"

"It is the protection spell that saw me safely through the jungle during my trial."

"Well done, Miss Dashwood!" His praise was earnest, and again Margaret's cheeks pinked. But a pang of guilt soon replaced the pleasure Margaret took in Mr. Barrington's praise.

"We should continue, Mr. Barrington," Margaret said.

"Yes. Of course." Mr. Barrington stepped into the pyramid's darkness. "Light," he murmured. A small glow illuminated the entrance, revealing more footprints in the dust covering the floor.

Margaret grasped Mr. Barrington's arm. With wide eyes she indicated the footprints. He held his finger to his lips.

"But will the light not reveal us?"

"Only we can see it. It is an ingenious spell. I shall teach it to you after we have returned." His voice was barely audible.

"Thank you, Mr. Barrington," Margaret breathed.

As they started down the low tunnel under the pyramid, Margaret noticed strange carvings decorating the walls. The cool darkness must have preserved them for centuries. She recognized many of the shapes but could make no sense of their arrangement, astonished by their intricate detail.

Again Margaret reached for Mr. Barrington's arm. "What do you suppose these signify?"

He stepped up to the wall. "I have no idea," he admitted at length. "Perhaps they tell the story of the pyramid? They are rather curious, are they not?" The hissing of his whisper echoed off the walls, and they stared at each other, standing still and waiting to be discovered. When no one came, Margaret exhaled.

They continued down the passage, stopping occasionally to examine the walls. As they approached the center of the pyramid, Margaret sensed the weight of the stones pressing downward. Afflicted by horrible thoughts about the stones collapsing and crushing Mr. Barrington and herself beyond recognition, she shuddered.

At length they came to another door that led into a

wide chamber filled with furniture, boxes of treasure, and what Margaret could only guess were bodies wrapped in ancient cloth. She shivered, though the air no longer held a chill, and glanced at the floor. Someone else had already passed this way. Mr. Barrington caught her eye and gestured to the arch at the end of the chamber. An urn was carved into the center of the arch. Her trepidation warring with excitement, Margaret followed Mr. Barrington into the next chamber, both of them alert for signs of another's presence.

"I think we are alone, Mr. Barrington," said Margaret, surprised by the strength of her relief. She glanced around the chamber, peering into the darkness at the back. "Oh no," she said.

"What is it, Miss Dashwood?"

Margaret pointed to the floor. Footprints led to a large table against the wall. She dashed over and scanned the table. A ring where something round once stood was clearly visible on its surface.

"I think the urn has already been stolen."

"We must have just missed the culprit." Mr. Barrington took Margaret's hand. "We were probably better off not encountering the sorcerer searching for the urn."

"But now we shall have to disappoint the coven," Margaret said, her voice trembling with barely controlled emotion.

"My dear Miss Dashwood, you need not worry about that." Mr. Barrington's voice was kind. "We could not predict that the urn would be missing." He stopped speaking and looked thoughtful. "I wonder, though—" He examined the table. "There would be fresh dust here, would there not, had it disappeared longer ago. It does seem a strange coincidence that it vanished so recently."

Margaret watched him, her eyes widening. "You cannot think that someone in the coven—"

"Of course not. I do not know what has happened except that we were not in time to protect the urn. I think we better return to Barbary Hall and await the others; this incident must be reported at once."

They sped through the corridor and emerged into the strong sunlight.

"Will you do the honors again, Miss Dashwood?" Mr. Barrington said.

Margaret opened the atlas, took Mr. Barrington's hand, and said, "*Que la Pyramide d'Osiris se replie sur le Manoir de Barbarie.*"

The desert disappeared, replaced by Mrs. Bristlethwaite's comfortable drawing room.

"Miss Dashwood? Mr. Barrington?" Lucy said. "Yours was a quick journey—none of the others have returned."

"Unfortunately, Lucy, Miss Dashwood and I met with no success." He glanced at Margaret. "Perhaps you could bring us some tea?"

"Of course, sir," Lucy replied.

Margaret remained in the drawing room with Mr. Barrington for the rest of the afternoon, her anxiety over their failure to retrieve the urn driving her to seek company. As Mr. Barrington read, Margaret stared out the window brooding over the day's events. Had she not desired to speak to Mr. Ellsworth, they would have arrived at the pyramid sooner, and perhaps they would have succeeded in their task. She gasped. What if her choice led the coven to dismiss her?

"Do you feel well, Miss Dashwood?" Mr. Barrington asked.

"I—yes, Mr. Barrington," she lied.

"Something troubles you." Mr. Barrington closed his book and set it on the table next to him.

Margaret kept her back to Mr. Barrington, unable to meet his gaze. "I fear that the coven will withdraw my apprenticeship." She paused, miserable. "I am to blame. Had I not delayed us in order to speak to—"

Mr. Barrington hastened to her side. "That is not true, Miss Dashwood! We had no way of knowing what we would find. I think you handled yourself admirably."

Margaret looked at him.

Mr. Barrington smiled. "Do you think the coven so harsh in their judgment that they would expel a promising sorceress for such a simple thing?"

Margaret relaxed, her worry almost disappearing. "I am being a bit silly, am I not?"

"No, Miss Dashwood," Mr. Barrington said kindly. "Not silly at all."

"Margaret! Mr. Barrington!" Mrs. Bristlethwaite bustled into the drawing room. "You have returned safely."

"We have, Mrs. Bristlethwaite," said Mr. Barrington. "Unfortunately, we returned empty-handed. Someone had already gotten to the urn."

Mrs. Bristlethwaite's eyes widened. "But how?"

"We have no idea."

"Where is Miss Cottlebury?" asked Margaret.

"She is in her room being tended by Lucy. She took rather a hard knock to her head."

Margaret started toward the door, but Mrs.

Bristlethwaite caught her arm. "Miss Cottlebury will be fine, my dear. Lucy has administered the tonic, and now Miss Cottlebury must rest, though I am certain she will appreciate your concern. Now, both of you sit down, and tell me exactly what happened."

By the following day the rest of the coven had returned—all with more success to report than Margaret and Mr. Barrington. Mrs. Bristlethwaite, to soften Margaret's disappointment, invited Mr. Ellsworth to tea that afternoon. While awaiting his arrival, Margaret studied the atlas, searching for some clue that would help to solve the mystery of the urn's absence.

"Miss Dashwood?" Mr. Ellsworth said, startling Margaret, who had been too absorbed by her reading to realize he had arrived.

"Mr. Ellsworth!" Margaret's delight radiated from her. With little thought, she set the atlas on the table next to her and stood.

Mr. Ellsworth took her hand in greeting, the joy of his countenance matching that of hers.

"So wonderful to see you again, Mr. Ellsworth," said Mrs. Bristlethwaite. "Forgive me for not inviting you to join us sooner. I must also apologize that a few of my guests are indisposed."

"There is no need for an apology, Mrs. Bristlethwaite," said Mr. Ellsworth with a friendly bow. "I understand completely."

"And who is this gallant young man, Mademoiselle Dashwood?" enquired Lady Isabelle.

"Mr. Ellsworth, may I present Lady Isabelle de Fleur and Miss Cottlebury?" Margaret said.

"*Enchanté*," Mr. Ellsworth said to the ladies,

earning the approbation of everyone but Miss Cottlebury, who sniffed and returned to her seat.

Mr. Ellsworth raised his eyebrows at Margaret, but said nothing. Margaret gave him a small smile and shook her head. After all the ladies had resumed their seats, Mr. Ellsworth sat next to Margaret.

"Please forgive my lateness. I was seeing to Mr. James," said Mr. Barrington.

"And how is Monsieur James?" asked Lady Isabelle, rising from her chair as if to dash away.

"He is fine, Lady Isabelle," said Mr. Barrington. "A little hungry, but otherwise fine."

Satisfied, Lady Isabelle returned to her chair. Margaret noticed that Miss Cottlebury regarded Mr. Ellsworth through narrowed eyes, just as she had done from the carriage. If Mr. Ellsworth felt Miss Cottlebury's glare, he gave no indication.

Mr. Barrington approached Mr. Ellsworth. "A pleasure to see you again," he said, his voice formal.

"And you," said Mr. Ellsworth.

Margaret looked from gentleman to gentleman; although they both wore neutral faces, she felt something stir beneath their interaction. Each had an expression in his eyes that she could not entirely comprehend.

Lucy entered with the tea tray and all attention turned toward the refreshments, dispelling any lingering unpleasantness.

"Mademoiselle Dashwood says you are something of a collector, Monsieur Ellsworth," said Lady Isabelle.

Mr. Ellsworth set his teacup on the table between himself and Margaret. "I am, though my collection hardly impresses anyone but me."

"Nonsense, Mr. Ellsworth," said Mrs. Bristlethwaite. "I imagine, Lady Isabelle, he puts on a show of modesty but really means nothing by it."

"I do admit to a certain pride in my collection, though I doubt that anyone else would understand it."

"And why is that?" demanded Miss Cottlebury. Margaret winced at the coldness in her voice.

"It is largely composed of trinkets that have value only to me."

"I see," snapped Miss Cottlebury.

"How is everyone at Barton Park?" Margaret asked.

Mr. Ellsworth turned a twinkling eye to Margaret. "As loquacious as usual."

Margaret laughed.

"Will you be staying much longer in Devonshire?" asked Mrs. Bristlethwaite.

Mr. Ellsworth again looked at Margaret. "I should hope so. I find Devonshire to be filled with charm and enchantment."

Margaret noticed a dark glance exchanged between Miss Cottlebury and Mr. Barrington; she wished she could reprimand them for their rudeness, but instead she turned her attention to Mr. Ellsworth.

"We are glad to hear it," said Mrs. Bristlethwaite.

A crash from across the room drew everyone's attention. Lady Isabelle's teacup had fallen and lay in pieces on the floor. "*Mon Dieu*!" she cried. "How did that happen?"

"Never mind, dear," said Mrs. Bristlethwaite. She rang for Lucy who, with a quick look at Mr. Ellsworth, bent and began cleaning up the pieces. Margaret wondered how long it had been since Lucy had last cleaned without using magic. Next to her Mr.

Ellsworth reached for his teacup.

"Oh!" said Margaret, pressing her hand to her forehead.

"Are you ill Miss Dashwood?" Mr. Ellsworth knelt in front of Margaret, concern in his eyes.

"I—I just felt very dizzy for a moment, but I feel better now."

"I hope you do not have a chill coming on," said Mr. Ellsworth.

"No, not at all." Margaret regarded the other members of the coven. "I assure you. It was a momentary dizziness, nothing more." She was touched by their obvious care.

Mr. Ellsworth gave her a searching look before returning to his seat.

The mess cleaned and the drama of Margaret's dizziness over, conversation resumed. "Lady Isabelle," Mr. Ellsworth said. "From which part of France do you hail?"

"My family lives near Rouen. We have an ancient *chateau* in the country."

Margaret listened to their conversation with contentment, Mr. Ellsworth's observations about Nature's sublime beauty once more charming her. She hardly noticed the time passing.

At length, however, the afternoon came to an end. Mr. Ellsworth rose with the others.

"Thank you for a delicious tea," he said to Mrs. Bristlethwaite. He cast his glance around the rest of the company. "I enjoyed meeting you all."

"As did we, I am sure," said Lady Isabelle. Margaret was surprised to see Miss Cottlebury nodding along. Mr. Barrington observed the entire company with a look of confusion.

"I shall walk you out, Mr. Ellsworth," said Margaret.

Mr. Ellsworth smiled and offered his arm. "Thank you, Miss Dashwood."

Once in the hallway Mr. Ellsworth said, "I thought at first that some of Mrs. Bristlethwaite's friends did not care for me. But in the end most of them seemed amiable enough."

"Miss Cottlebury takes her time to warm to people. In fact, she came around to you much quicker than she did to me. As for Mr. Barrington, he has some important business on his mind, and perhaps that is what you noticed?" Margaret did not understand Mr. Barrington's coolness, but she wished to assuage Mr. Ellsworth's fears.

"I hope that you are correct, Miss Dashwood. I should be upset if anyone dear to you did not care for me. It is so important that your loved ones approve of me." He turned a passionate face to Margaret. "You cannot know how important, my dearest, dearest, Miss Dashwood."

Margaret held his gaze, overwhelmed by the feelings flooding through her. "I think I do understand, Mr. Ellsworth. And you must know that I share your feelings."

Mr. Ellsworth clasped Margaret's hand and kissed it more tenderly than he ever had before. "Miss Dashwood," he said, his voice quavering with emotion. "You do me a great honor." He kissed her hand again. "I shall call on you tomorrow morning." And then he was gone.

Margaret floated back to the drawing room where she interrupted a lively discussion.

"Mademoiselle Dashwood," said Lady Isabelle.

"What a charming man!"

"Indeed," said Miss Cottlebury. "At first I cared nothing for him. He struck me as rather—" Her voice faded. "Well, I cannot remember what it was." She touched her bandaged head gingerly. "That wound must have confounded my mind." She gave Margaret one of her rare smiles. "He really is enchanting."

Mr. Barrington coughed.

"What was that, Mr. Barrington?" Mrs. Bristlethwaite's expression was arch.

"I said nothing." Mr. Barrington reddened.

"But you do not approve," said Lady Isabelle.

"I think it is too soon to judge."

"We all know why you feel that way." Mrs. Bristlethwaite lifted an eyebrow at Mr. Barrington but said no more. Mr. Barrington looked away.

Margaret glanced from one to the other. "Why?" she said.

"Never mind, my dear," replied Mrs. Bristlethwaite. "It does not signify."

Margaret returned to her chair, suddenly struck by a need to retrieve something, but she could not remember what it was. She looked around hoping to gain inspiration. What had she been doing before Mr. Ellsworth arrived? Reading, but what? She searched her mind, attempting to dispel her confusion. Of course, the atlas! She remembered reading it, but what had she done with it when Mr. Ellsworth arrived? Ah, yes, she had set it down on the table. She went to retrieve it, but it was not there. She began searching frantically.

"What is it, my dear?" Mrs. Bristlethwaite's voice held concern.

"I cannot find my atlas." Margaret struggled to

control the emotion in her voice.

"Are you certain that you left it there? Perhaps it is in your room?"

"I was reading it here this afternoon before tea. At least I thought I was." Confusion clouded her mind. "Perhaps I misremembered?" She hurried from the drawing room, Mrs. Bristlethwaite and Mr. Barrington behind her. They arrived in her chamber just after she did.

Margaret searched her room, pulling out drawers and rifling through the wardrobe, but the atlas was not to be found. She took a steadying breath and closed her eyes. "*Que le voile se retire; que la vérité soit révélée*," she said. When she opened her eyes, she looked around the room, but discovered no sign of the atlas.

She turned to Mrs. Bristlethwaite, tears pricking the corners of her eyes. "It is not here!"

Mrs. Bristlethwaite embraced her. "Not to worry, my dear. We shall find it."

Margaret's confusion mounted. "Maybe I left it in Egypt?" she said, no longer certain she could trust her thoughts. Every time they turned toward her activities before Mr. Ellsworth's arrival, a cloud formed in her mind.

"I doubt that, Miss Dashwood. Our return journey would have been very difficult had you done that."

"But why can I not remember?" Margaret's distress sharpened.

"Hush, my dear. It will be all right. You have the coven to help you. Take a little time to rest and compose yourself. We shall discuss this problem at our meeting in the morning. Have a nap and then come down to dinner. You will feel better after some sleep and some food."

Margaret nodded through her tears, although she was not sure that Mrs. Bristlethwaite was correct in this instance. How could she feel better knowing that she had misplaced her father's atlas? The gift he had given his life to make for her? As soon as she was alone, Margaret threw herself onto her bed and sobbed.

CHAPTER XVIII

*T*he first rays of sunlight woke Margaret. Her early morning peace was fleeting, replaced immediately by her memory of the previous day's events. She had lost the atlas. She lay still, tears collecting on the pillow. Only the prospect of Mr. Ellsworth's promised visit encouraged Margaret to rise and perform her morning ablutions. She dreaded facing the coven and lingered over her preparations until she could avoid going downstairs no longer.

Lady Isabelle's lovely countenance met Margaret in the breakfast parlor. "*Bonjour, ma chère amie,*" she said. "Come, sit with me. We shall break our fasts together."

Margaret, a little less wretched, joined Lady Isabelle. "Where are the others?"

"Most of the coven have already eaten. I thought you might like some company."

"Thank you," Margaret said, relieved by the reprieve from the coven's attention.

"You need not worry, Mademoiselle Dashwood.

No one faults you for the loss of the atlas. We all understand its significance to you."

Tears trailed down Margaret's cheeks. "My father gave his life for it. I must find it."

Lady Isabelle took Margaret's hand. "We will find it, *ma chèrie*. All will be well. Now you must dry your eyes. Your Monsieur Ellsworth will pay a visit this morning, *n'est-ce pas?*"

Margaret could not help but smile. "*Oui*," she replied.

After breakfast, a more cheerful Margaret awaited Mr. Ellsworth's arrival in the drawing room. Mrs. Bristlethwaite and Miss Cottlebury sat nearby in quiet conversation. Margaret endeavored to read Cowper's poems, but paused frequently to glance at the mantel clock. As the morning slipped away and Mr. Ellsworth did not appear, Margaret grew concerned. She set aside her book and strode to the window, watching the lane for approaching visitors.

"He must have been detained, Margaret," said Mrs. Bristlethwaite.

"But he would have sent a note," Margaret replied, her voice wavering.

"Perhaps some business prevented his writing. You need not worry, my dear. Mr. Ellsworth has made his feelings about you quite clear."

Margaret nodded, though she took little comfort in Mrs. Bristlethwaite's reassurance. She resumed her vigil at the window, glad that neither Mrs. Bristlethwaite nor Miss Cottlebury commented further.

The clock's chimes announced the hour of the coven's meeting, startling Margaret out of her vigil. "It is time, Margaret," Mrs. Bristlethwaite said. Margaret turned reluctantly from the window, still hoping to hear Mr. Ellsworth's approach.

Mr. Barrington arrived, followed soon after by Mr. James and Lady Isabelle.

"Sir Berwin and Lady Jane will be here shortly," announced Lady Isabelle, with a glance at the clock. "No more than a quarter of an hour." She studied the mantel and then gasped. "Oh!"

"What is it, Lady Isabelle?" Mrs. Bristlethwaite rushed to her side.

"The protection orb I made for you! There is a crack!"

Mrs. Bristlethwaite peered at the crystal. "How could that have happened?"

Margaret, her worries about Mr. Ellsworth momentarily forgotten, joined the two ladies. The crack ran the length of the charm. The space within the orb had gone smoky and dark. "What does this signify?" asked Margaret, alarmed.

"Someone has removed our protection from harmful spells," replied Mrs. Bristlethwaite.

"Only a powerful sorcerer could have done this," Lady Isabelle added.

"But who—" Margaret began.

"One of the servants." Sir Berwin stood in the doorway. "I would wager a great deal on that guess."

Mrs. Bristlethwaite glared at him. "How can you say such a thing?"

"I have told you again and again, Eugenia. You are too lenient with your servants. They should not be allowed to perform magic. The Sorcerer's Council has forbidden it, with good reason!"

"I will not believe that either Lucy or Jenkins

would do this." Mrs. Bristlethwaite gestured toward the broken orb.

Lady Jane took Sir Berwin by the arm. "For goodness sake, Berwin, you have known Jenkins and Lucy for years. They are completely loyal to Eugenia," she scolded. Sir Berwin grumbled but said nothing more. "Do you agree with me, my dear?" Lady Jane's eyes glinted, and her tone brooked no argument.

Sir Berwin sighed. "As I always do, my dear." He approached Mrs. Bristlethwaite. "Eugenia, I apologize. I should not have leapt to such a conclusion." He held out his hand, which Mrs. Bristlethwaite shook. "The question still remains, however: who *did* destroy the protection charm?"

The coven took their seats. Lady Isabelle cradled the broken charm in her hands. "Could it have been an accident?" asked Margaret. "Perhaps someone knocked it from the mantel, and it cracked on the hearth."

"*Non, chère amie*; my charms are much more durable than that."

"Lady Isabelle, how quickly can you repair it?" asked Mrs. Bristlethwaite.

Lady Isabelle examined the crack again. "I shall need an afternoon at least. I will begin directly after our meeting."

"In the meanwhile, we shall add solving the mystery of the cracked charm to our growing list of tasks," said Mrs. Bristlethwaite. "But first, I am thankful to see everyone returned, mostly unscathed, from your adventures and that you managed to obtain most of the objects."

"Is it true, Eugenia, that the atlas has gone missing?" asked an incredulous Sir Berwin.

"I am afraid it is, Sir Berwin," replied Mrs. Bristlethwaite with a sympathetic glance at Margaret. "We shall come to that."

Margaret lowered her eyes, ashamed.

"Miss Dashwood, I have something that will make you feel better." Mr. James, one arm in a sling and a bandage across his cheek, placed a brilliant red sphere in front of himself. "It is wondrous, is it not, Miss Dashwood?" he whispered, gazing at the Orb of Loch Leven. Margaret nodded, unable and unwilling to look away from the garnet crystal. A desire to touch it overwhelmed her. As Margaret reached out, Mrs. Bristlethwaite took her hand and returned it to her side. Lady Isabelle laid a handkerchief over the orb, and Margaret blinked, confused.

"You must not stare at the Orb of Loch Leven, Margaret," Mrs. Bristlethwaite explained. "What were you thinking, Mr. James?"

"I wished to cheer Miss Dashwood."

Lady Isabelle patted his arm. "A noble sentiment, Monsieur James."

"Indeed," said Mrs. Bristlethwaite. She rapped on the table. "Shall we begin?"

A chorus of voices replied in the affirmative. Margaret glanced at her fellow sorcerers, wincing at the bruises and bandages, but proud of their courage and tenacity. Several had sustained injuries, and yet they returned successful in their quests. Lady Jane arranged a small pile of luminous, blue stones in front of her. Strange, crooked figures adorned each of them. Mrs. Bristlethwaite held a large silver charm, depicting a hand grasping a harp. Miss Cottlebury averted her eyes from the objects on the table, studying the ceiling's fresco instead.

"There is no need for us to recount our journeys," said Mrs. Bristlethwaite. "After the meeting we shall hide the objects in Barbary Hall's secret passages." Muttered agreement met her statements. "Barrington, could you tell the others what happened at the Temple of Osiris."

Mr. Barrington complied, and the coven listened to his story in rapt silence.

"But you never saw the person who left the footprints?" asked Sir Berwin when Mr. Barrington's tale was finished.

"No, but I believe that we just missed whoever took the urn."

"It is rather a curious coincidence that the urn and the atlas went missing in such rapid succession," Miss Cottlebury asserted.

"Do you think so, Agnes?" asked Mrs. Bristlethwaite.

"Yes, I do. It seems too much a coincidence, in fact, to be one."

"What is your point, Agnes?" Mrs. Bristlethwaite's patience was wearing thin. Margaret, however, had a dreadful sense that she understood Miss Cottlebury perfectly well.

"Is no one going to address the obvious candidate for the thief?" Miss Cottlebury demanded.

"I am sure we do not know what you mean, Miss Cottlebury," returned Mrs. Bristlethwaite.

"Oh for goodness' sake. The only stranger present when the atlas went missing was Mr. Ellsworth."

Margaret's stomach clenched. "But he is not a sorcerer!"

"Do you know that for a fact?" Miss Cottlebury asked.

Margaret blinked. "He saw the atlas, and—and he said nothing about the enchantments. Only those with magic can see the enchantments." As Margaret spoke, she realized how silly she sounded.

"And you believe what you saw? Heavens, girl! The man is charm itself. What page did he see?" Miss Cottlebury leaned toward Margaret.

"I—I cannot be certain."

Mr. Barrington cleared his throat. "We were examining the notes about the Urn of Osiris before Mr. Ellsworth approached."

"Aha!" Miss Cottlebury raised a triumphant finger.

"Mademoiselle Cottlebury, please," admonished Lady Isabelle.

Margaret's eyes filled with tears. Had she been foolish to believe Mr. Ellsworth's protestations of love? Had she learned nothing from Marianne's experience with Mr. Willoughby?

Miss Cottlebury began a retort, but Mr. Barrington interrupted her. "We will know nothing until we recover the atlas. Do you not consider that undertaking more important than speculation about the thief?"

Margaret looked at Mr. Barrington with gratitude.

"Precisely," agreed Sir Berwin. "But how do you propose we find the atlas, Barrington?"

"My father's diaries!" Margaret exclaimed. "They contain extensive notes about the atlas. Perhaps he left some hint that will help us recover it."

"Excellent, Margaret!" said Mrs. Bristlethwaite. "I shall send Lucy and Jenkins to help you collect them. While Lady Isabelle repairs the protection charm, the rest of us will search for any clues left by Henry."

The afternoon advanced rapidly as the coven poured over the diaries.

"I wish I could find a clear order to Dashwood's notes," said Miss Cottlebury, closing one volume with a sigh and pulling another closer to her. "I suppose with a task so daunting as creating the atlas, however, order goes out the window."

"Ah!" cried Sir Berwin. "I think I have found something!" He read silently for a moment. "Alas, he merely elaborates on the charm for shrinking the atlas."

Margaret's hope, which had been inspired by Sir Berwin's outcry, sank. The atlas had been gone for more than a day and still the coven had found nothing. She rubbed her eyes and resumed work. A couple of pages later, she gasped.

"What is it Margaret?" asked Mrs. Bristlethwaite.

Margaret looked up, hope revived. "A map," she said, turning the book so the others could see. "And a spell for locating the atlas." No one made a sound while she read her father's notes:

> *My work is nearly complete. I have only precautions left to finish. My strength diminishes, but I shall soldier onward. Yesterday I devised a charm for locating the atlas should it be lost. My poorly sketched map on the preceding page shall suffice for experiments. Though the spell is complex, the incantation is simple: "Atlas, please show me where you are." When I tried it this morning, a small spot appeared on the map, hovering over Norland. I can only hope that it proves as effective across greater distances.*

"Genius!" breathed Miss Cottlebury.

"What are we waiting for?" said Mrs. Bristlethwaite. "Margaret?"

Margaret drew a breath. There was no time to translate to French. She spoke the incantation and then held her breath as a small but bright circle of light immediately appeared on the map. "The Hebrides," Margaret cried, pointing.

"Well, shall we?" said Sir Berwin, rising.

"Wait a moment, dear." Lady Jane took his arm; Sir Berwin sat. "Do you think it wise simply to rush toward the atlas? Some of us are injured, and we have no idea what awaits us."

"I agree. We must consider the best approach," said Mrs. Bristlethwaite.

Margaret clenched her hands under the table, certain she would go mad if she had to wait any longer to confirm the coven's suspicions about Mr. Ellsworth.

"Mrs. Bristlethwaite," said Mr. Barrington. "I think we should act sooner rather than later. Why not send those of us who are well? If our speculation is correct, then we know there is only one person whom we chase. Surely four or five of us should be enough to recover the atlas."

Margaret agreed, eager to put an end to her uncertainty.

"I do not think you should be roving around the globe without at least having your tea!" exclaimed Lady Jane, horrified at the notion. Mr. James nodded vigorously, shock rendering him speechless.

"I believe such tasks are better undertaken in the morning," said Mrs. Bristlethwaite. She held up her hand to stop the protests from Mr. Barrington and

Lady Isabelle. "I will not put a single member of this coven at risk by dashing off without considering your welfare. We shall go tomorrow morning. In the meanwhile, tea will be served shortly."

During tea Margaret again consulted her father's coarse map. The atlas was now in Yorkshire. Her heart sank; Mr. Ellsworth's manor was also in Yorkshire. She had nurtured a hope of some day becoming its mistress.

"What is it, Margaret?" inquired Mrs. Bristlethwaite.

"The atlas—it is now in Yorkshire."

"Is that significant?" Miss Cottlebury said.

"Mr. Ellsworth resides in Yorkshire, does he not, Margaret?" Mrs. Bristlethwaite's tone was gentle.

Through her tears, Margaret nodded.

Lady Isabelle, who had returned with the repaired protection charm, patted Margaret's arm. "There, there, *ma chèrie*! I am certain many sorcerers also call Yorkshire home. We must not make assumptions."

Margaret gave Lady Isabelle a watery smile.

"You must eat something, Margaret," admonished Mrs. Bristlethwaite. "I will not allow you to face whatever dangers await if you have not taken enough sustenance."

Margaret longed to cry, *And what good is sustenance for my body when my heart is breaking? What good is my life without love?* But she held her tongue and stopped her tears with great effort. Instead she sipped some of her tea and took a tiny bite of a scone, forcing it through the lump in her throat.

"Shall we make a battle plan?" suggested Mr. Barrington into the silence.

"Whatever we do should be quick," offered Sir Berwin. "We must assume we face grave danger."

"I agree," said Lady Isabelle. "Mademoiselle Dashwood, have you any knowledge of battle spells?"

"I learned one or two for my trial," Margaret replied. Appetite lost, she set down her scone.

"Excellent!" Sir Berwin's enthusiasm was unnerving. "After dinner you may demonstrate."

"My dear, do not frighten the poor girl!" said Lady Jane. She turned to Margaret. "Never mind him, Miss Dashwood. I have no doubt that you are prepared—especially after you handled your trial with such grace and courage."

"Indeed!" added Mr. Barrington, favoring Margaret with a wide smile.

Margaret's smile was much less generous. The others believed her far more prepared for battle than she felt, especially if she had to face Mr. Ellsworth. Could she cause him harm?

"I think that is enough talk about the morning's tasks for now," said Mrs. Bristlethwaite. "Margaret, would you play something for us on the *pianoforte*?"

Margaret longed to refuse and run back to her room. Instead, she stood and crossed to the instrument. Mr. Barrington pulled over a stool and sat with her. As Margaret played, gratitude to Mrs. Bristlethwaite replaced her disquiet; the music proved a welcome balm to her troubled spirit.

Margaret slept not a wink that night. Her mind would not cease turning around the question of Mr. Ellsworth's guilt or innocence. As the sun's first light crept into her chamber, Margaret, unable to bear the uncertainty, rose, dressed, and consulted the map.

The atlas was in northern France. With care, she tore the map from the diary and tucked it into her pocket. Then she snuck down to the garden. Before she could change her mind, Margaret took a deep breath, turned her thoughts to the French countryside, and said, "*Que le Manoir de Barbarie se replie sur Rouen.*"

Margaret gasped at the effort required to Fold without the atlas's aid. When she finally arrived in the cool grey morning light of northern France, she collapsed on the dewy grass, panting. As her breath settled, Margaret took in her surroundings. She hated to think about her reason for visiting this seemingly tranquil place. A vine-covered stone cottage stood at the edge of the field. It appeared long abandoned, yet a thin curl of smoke unfurled from the chimney. Margaret knew she would find the atlas inside.

CHAPTER XIX

*T*he cottage door stood ajar. Holding her breath, Margaret crept toward it. Footsteps sounded from inside. A heavy object clattered to the floor, followed by a frustrated exhalation. "Where is it?" a man hissed. Next came the sound of shattering crockery. Her limbs numb with fright, Margaret peered inside the cottage. A chair lay overturned to the left of the door. Sharp shards covered the floor. A man, back to the door, ran his hands over the stones framing the hearth. His head was crowned in black curls.

"Mr. Ellsworth?" Margaret whispered, her heart sinking. She had harbored a hope that he was innocent, yet here he stood, atlas clutched in his hand, searching the cottage. Margaret stepped back, and a board creaked. She froze.

The man whipped around, searching for the sound's source. His eyes widened as they met Margaret's. "What are you—" Margaret took another step back at the fury in Mr. Ellsworth's expression. Then his face softened into a friendly expression, which arrested her movement.

"Miss Dashwood!" Mr. Ellsworth stepped forward. "What a splendid surprise!" He swept toward her and opened the door all the way. After a deep bow, he took her hand and laid a kiss upon it. Margaret swayed, suddenly dizzy. She gazed at Mr. Ellsworth in wonder, unable to find her voice. "You must sit, Miss Dashwood. Your journey has exhausted you." Still silent, she nodded, though she did not know why. She had so many questions, but she could not find the words to ask them.

Mr. Ellsworth led her to the shabby sofa, its cushions threadbare and emanating a disagreeable odor. All gentleness, he helped her sit. Margaret's mind spun as she struggled to understand what was happening. Mr. Ellsworth sat next to her, still clutching her hand. He favored her with a brilliant smile, which seemed to cut through the fog of Margaret's mind. Why had she been so worried? Here was her Mr. Ellsworth, gazing at her with such love! Everyone had been wrong. She chastised herself for doubting him. Embarrassed, Margaret tore her eyes from his, but they landed instead on the book in his hand. Her father's atlas. A doubt asserted itself in her mind.

Margaret took a deep breath and found her voice. "Mr. Ellsworth, I do not understand what you are doing here."

"I am searching for an item for my collection," he replied. "What brings you here, Miss Dashwood?" He spoke in a light tone.

"I—I was searching for you."

"How pleased I am that you have found me! Tell me, Miss Dashwood, how did you manage such a feat?"

Margaret did not want to answer this question, though she knew not why. Nevertheless, her hand found its way into her pocket, and she pulled out the map. "With this."

Mr. Ellsworth examined it. "Remarkable! Your father was a genius, Miss Dashwood."

"You knew my father?"

"Alas, I cannot say yes, although I wish I had known him. No, he and my mother's cousin, a Mr. Bennet, enjoyed a long and friendly correspondence, the fruits of which I happened upon quite by chance. Your father wrote often of his atlas." Again came that dazzling smile. "But I have work to do here, my dear Miss Dashwood, although...." He studied her. "Yes. The perfect solution!"

"I beg your pardon, Mr. Ellsworth?"

"May I be so bold as to request your aid, Miss Dashwood?"

"Of course, Mr. Ellsworth!"

In reply, Mr. Ellsworth brought her hand again to his lips. Margaret could almost hear the reading of the marriage banns. How marvelous that Mr. Ellsworth was also a sorcerer and that he wished her to help him! She could not tear her eyes from his. "What do you seek?"

"A gem. A blue diamond from the court of King Louis the Fourteenth."

"Oh my!"

"Indeed!" Mr. Ellsworth gestured to the cottage's disorder. "I have searched everywhere, but I cannot find it." Margaret nearly wept at the disappointment in his voice.

"I shall find it for you, Mr. Ellsworth. I promise."

Margaret walked to the center of the room. Away from Mr. Ellsworth she shivered, suddenly chilled. She closed her eyes, willing away all other thoughts. "*Que le voile se retire; que la vérité soit révélée!*" When she opened her eyes, they were drawn immediately to a stone in the hearth wall. "There it is, Mr. Ellsworth! Behind that stone."

"Thank you, Miss Dashwood!" he cried as he dashed forward and laid his hand upon the stone. "Give!" With a rasping sound, it slid forward. In the hole left behind sat the most beautiful gem Margaret had ever seen. Mr. Ellsworth cradled it in his hand, staring into its depths. "The last piece. It is remarkable," he whispered, his attention taken fully by the diamond.

The veil of fog lifted from Margaret's mind. She clasped a hand to her mouth to hide her startled gasp. Thoughts and memories came flooding back with startling clarity. Mr. Ellsworth had enchanted her and taken the atlas because he was stealing magical objects. She wanted to sob, but she knew she had to maintain her composure. Perhaps she could determine his plan.

"What will you do with it, Mr. Ellsworth?" Margaret asked, her voice cheerful.

Mr. Ellsworth lifted his gaze from the diamond and considered Margaret with narrowed eyes. Had his glance always been so cold? She forced herself to remain calm. "I shall use it in a spell," he said at length.

"Oh? What spell is that, Mr. Ellsworth?"

Mr. Ellsworth raised an eyebrow. "You are a curious young lady, Miss Dashwood."

"I am always fascinated by new spells." Margaret

cringed at her reply, afraid that Mr. Ellsworth would suspect her.

His laugh sent a chill through Margaret. "You will play an important part in this one."

"I will? How?"

"With your blood." Mr. Ellsworth smiled, and the veil began to settle once again over Margaret's thoughts.

Horrified, she struggled to keep her mind clear. "No!" she cried, all her energy given to repelling Mr. Ellsworth's control. Mr. Ellsworth fell backward and caught himself on the mantel. Margaret reeled, startled by her spell's strength.

Mr. Ellsworth recovered his composure quickly. "No more of that, Miss Dashwood. We have work to do elsewhere!" Golden light burst from his fingers, heading straight toward her. Margaret leapt to the side, and the light hit the wall, scorching it.

"Protect me!" The strong arms of her spell encircled Margaret. She searched the room for a weapon. "Move there, please!" A chair sailed into Mr. Ellsworth, knocking him to the floor and trapping him. Margaret held out her hand. "Come to me!" The atlas flew from the mantel.

"Stop!" Mr. Ellsworth commanded from under the chair. The atlas hovered in the air between them. He pushed the chair aside. "Here!" Mr. Ellsworth's voice boomed, and the atlas obeyed. The blue diamond in Mr. Ellsworth's other hand pulsed with light. At the same time, the protective arms dropped from Margaret. "That is enough, Miss Dashwood." He waved his hand, and Margaret dropped to the floor, unable to move or to speak. Mr. Ellsworth tucked the diamond into his pocket and knelt at her side. He opened the atlas. "Fold Rouen—"

"Miss Dashwood!" Mr. Barrington burst into the room and pushed Mr. Ellsworth away from Margaret. Behind them Lady Isabelle raised her hands. But before she could speak, Mr. Ellsworth had disappeared.

Slowly feeling returned to Margaret's limbs, though they remained heavy. Movement seemed almost impossible.

Lady Isabelle took Margaret's hand. "Mademoiselle Dashwood, you are safe now. We shall take you home to Barbary Hall."

Margaret allowed Mr. Barrington to help her to her feet, clinging to his arm for support. Mr. Barrington exchanged a worried glance with Lady Isabelle.

"The journey may be difficult," She took Margaret's other arm. "Monsieur Barrington."

Mr. Barrington cleared his throat. "Fold Rouen into Barbary Hall." Immediately a great force pressed into Margaret's body, stealing her breath. She clung to Mr. Barrington and Lady Isabelle, certain that she would not survive the journey. Then it was over; they reached Barbary Hall. Margaret collapsed, too exhausted and heartbroken to stir.

"Miss Dashwood!" Mr. Barrington knelt by her. "Miss Dashwood!"

She longed to slide into a dream, but the desperation in Mr. Barrington's voice stirred her to speak. "I am well enough," she whispered. She could not open her eyes.

"Get her to the sofa!" Mrs. Bristlethwaite directed. "Lucy, tonic!" Worry pinched her voice. Other voices filled the room, but Margaret could not understand them. Strong arms lifted her, and set her gently upon the sofa. Mr. Barrington sat next to her, an arm supporting her. Someone held a cup to her lips.

"You must drink, Miss Dashwood," said Mr. Barrington softly. Margaret sipped at the tonic, coughing a little at the burning in her throat. "That is right, Miss Dashwood, slowly." Margaret took another drink. Her exhaustion began to ebb, and she could hold herself upright. She opened her eyes.

The coven's concerned faces surrounded Margaret. She took a deep breath and finished the tonic. Relief settled across everyone's countenance. Mr. James offered her a scone. Margaret took it, but could not bring herself to eat.

"What possessed you—" Miss Cottlebury began.

"Not now, Agnes," scolded Mrs. Bristlethwaite. "Miss Dashwood has suffered enough for her foolishness."

"I am sorry," Margaret said. "I must have caused you so much distress." She brought her hands to her face and sobbed.

"It was a foolish thing to do, Margaret, but as we have you safe among us again, we need not belabor the point," Mrs. Bristlethwaite replied. "We owe Lucy our gratitude for your safe return. She modified a spell for locating lost household items in order to find you." Mrs. Bristlethwaite brimmed with pride.

"An extraordinary spell," Sir Berwin agreed. No one remarked upon his change of heart.

"I do not know how to thank you enough, Lucy. You saved my life. And you, Mr. Barrington, Lady Isabelle." Tears flowed from her eyes. "Mr. Ellsworth...." She paused, her throat tightening. "Mr. Ellsworth was about to take me with him."

"He was? Why?" Lady Jane's outrage rang through

the room.

Margaret swallowed. "Because he found the last item he needed, and he was going to use my blood for a spell."

"*Mon Dieu!*" cried Lady Isabelle.

"The beast!" exclaimed Miss Cottlebury.

Mr. Barrington tightened his grip on Margaret's hand. "What was the spell, Miss Dashwood?"

Margaret shook her head. "He would not tell me. I tried to pretend that I was still in his power—"

"What do you mean?" Mrs. Bristlethwaite demanded.

"He used a spell to cloud my mind when I arrived at the cottage, but after he found the blue diamond, I was able to free myself. I do not understand how."

"He turned his attention elsewhere, I warrant," suggested Sir Berwin.

"Yes, and when he tried to use that spell again, I resisted." Murmurs of approval met Margaret's statement, and she forged onward. "But I thought I could learn more about his intentions, so I pretended still to be in his thrall. He did not believe me. I only learned that he planned to use my blood." She looked at the faces of her friends. "I suppose he only told me because he thought that I would not be able to report it to you." Margaret shuddered.

"You demonstrated extraordinary fortitude, Miss Dashwood," said Mr. Barrington.

"Here, here!" agreed Sir Berwin.

"But I did not retrieve the atlas!" Margaret protested. "And Mr. Ellsworth took the map—the one we found in my father's diaries. We cannot find him now." Her sobs began anew.

"I can find the atlas, Miss Dashwood," said Lucy

quietly. "The same way that I found you."

"That is right, Miss Dashwood. Lucy will help us." Sir Berwin beamed at the maid.

Mrs. Bristlethwaite fixed him with a look, but said nothing. "Margaret, you need not worry yourself about anything. Lucy, help Miss Dashwood to her room. I shall be up shortly."

"Come along, Miss Dashwood." Lucy's touch on her arm was gentle. The coven's whispers followed them up the stairs. Lucy led Margaret into her room, easing her into the chair by the hearth. Margaret struggled for composure as Lucy whispered the words of a fire spell. Flames jumped about the logs, crackling and filling the room with warmth. Margaret sank into the chair, exhausted.

"Miss Dashwood, may I be of any assistance?" Lucy ventured.

Margaret shook her head, inconsolable. She could find nothing romantic or sublime in her pain. Where was the rapture of heartache that she had read about in poems? She chided herself for her childish beliefs as the storm of sobbing ebbed. Lucy wrapped a blanket around Margaret's shoulders. "What a fool I am," Margaret whispered.

"I beg your pardon, Miss Dashwood?"

"I am a fool, Lucy."

"You must not say that, Miss Dashwood."

"No, my dear, you must not." Mrs. Bristlethwaite stood in the doorway. "Lucy, I shall take over from here." Lucy curtsied, and with a compassionate look at Margaret left the chamber. Mrs. Bristlethwaite came to Margaret's side and with some difficulty on the stool at Margaret's feet, taking Margaret's cold hands in her own warm ones. "You had no way of knowing what he was, my dear."

"But if I had listened even for a moment—he gave us hints: his collection, his unexplained and sudden absences, his fascination with my father's books. He must also have seen the enchantment on the atlas and pretended not to. How could I be so silly?"

Mrs. Bristlethwaite tucked a curl behind Margaret's ear. "He fooled the entire coven—all older and, one would think, wiser than you."

"Not Miss Cottlebury. At least not at first."

"Miss Cottlebury dislikes everyone she meets." Mrs. Bristlethwaite chuckled. "Remember how rude she was to you?" Margaret nodded tearfully. "You must not blame yourself, my dear."

"But—but I should have known. I looked into his eyes—" Her voice caught as she remembered the coldness of his blue eyes. She shivered. "I loved him, and I thought he loved me, too," she said through the tightness in her throat.

Mrs. Bristlethwaite gently lifted Margaret's chin until their eyes met. "You cannot chastise yourself for the choices your heart makes." She kissed Margaret on the forehead. "I know how terrible you feel. But I promise that this is not a permanent condition." Mrs. Bristlethwaite stood. "You need a bit of rest and then some company, my dear. So I suggest you dry your eyes and wash your face. Then join us downstairs. I imagine Mr. Barrington might well wear a hole in the hearthrug in the meanwhile." With a wink, she left Margaret alone.

Margaret stared at the fire and cried until she had spent all her tears. She must have dozed for a while, for when she awoke, the clock had advanced by three quarters of an hour. Margaret did as Mrs.

Bristlethwaite suggested, drying her eyes and splashing a little water on her tear-stained face. Then she took a deep breath and headed to the drawing room.

"Miss Dashwood!" said Mr. Barrington. "I am happy that you have joined us. I—I have taken the liberty of removing a few volumes of poetry from the library. If you would allow me, I should like to read to you."

"That is very kind of you, Mr. Barrington. I would like that very much."

They took the chairs by the hearth. Mr. Barrington held up two volumes and smiled. Margaret avoided the Cowper and pointed instead to the Shakespeare. "A sonnet or two would be perfect, Mr. Barrington."

"A superb choice, Miss Dashwood," offered Lady Jane from across the room.

Mr. Barrington opened the book and cleared his throat before beginning. Margaret was surprised by the sonorous quality of Mr. Barrington's voice as he read. And while he demonstrated less taste than one about whom she would no longer think, he offered an innocence she found appealing.

"Oh, Miss Dashwood," Mr. Barrington said, looking up from the book. "I am sorry."

Margaret wiped away her tears. "No, Mr. Barrington, you are not to blame. Please, continue reading. It soothes me."

"I am not much of a reader," Mr. Barrington said.

"On the contrary. You read with honest feeling, Mr. Barrington. One cannot ask for anything more."

CHAPTER XX

"I have an idea about Ellsworth's intentions," announced Miss Cottlebury. She strode into the breakfast parlor and dropped a stack of books on the table, spilling tea and rattling cutlery. Impervious to the others' grumbling, Miss Cottlebury pulled a piece of paper from the stack. Brandishing it, she continued. "Thanks to Miss Dashwood, I was able to cobble together a few possibilities."

"What do you mean, Agnes?" Mrs. Bristlethwaite said.

Miss Cottlebury returned Mrs. Bristlethwaite's gaze. "Magic of the darkest kind." Silence met her statement as the coven members exchanged glances ranging from worried to confused.

"Are you certain?" Mrs. Bristlethwaite breathed.

Miss Cottlebury waved the question away with an impatient gesture. "I cannot be certain. But I have made a list of all the magical items we suspect Ellsworth to have. All of them contain a great deal of power." She looked at Margaret. "Remember the Orb of Loch Leven?" Margaret, recalling the garnet crystal's irresistible pull, nodded. "Then I searched Mrs. Bristlethwaite's books for references to these objects. I found bits and pieces, but nothing that would help us envision Ellsworth's purpose. Until...." She handed a book to Mrs. Bristlethwaite. "Page one hundred and twenty-five."

The rest of the coven watched Mrs. Bristlethwaite, breath held. Margaret longed to ask what Miss Cottlebury meant, but remained silent.

"How is it possible?" Mrs. Bristlethwaite muttered.

"The vessel of a god, the stone of a king, and the blood of a sorcerer, all placed within a ring of endless power."

"I am afraid I am not following, Miss Cottlebury," said Mr. Barrington.

"Oh for goodness' sake. All of the objects he has collected can form the Ring of Endless Power when placed in a circle. He planned to use Miss Dashwood's blood, and he has the Urn of Osiris and the King's Diamond." Miss Cottlebury gestured to the book in front of Mrs. Bristlethwaite. "It is all right there."

Lady Isabelle pulled the book to her, read a few lines, and clasped a hand to her chest. "*Le Diamant du Roi!*" Her voice trembled.

"What does that signify, Lady Isabelle?" asked Sir Berwin.

"It belonged to *Le Roi-Soleil*," she began. "Louis *Quatorze*. It is a gem of exceptional power, but it disappeared after he died."

"And I found it for Mr. Ellsworth," Margaret said, appalled. "The blue diamond."

"Never mind, Margaret. What is done is done."

Mrs. Bristlethwaite turned back to Miss Cottlebury. "Please sit, Agnes, and explain to the others what you mean."

Miss Cottlebury took a seat and accepted a cup of tea from Lady Jane. "Thank you," she said after a sip. "I had rather a long night in the library, but they were hours well spent. I found an account of a spell used to summon...." She consulted her notes. "'A darkness that seethes with power, tempting sorcerers with promises of glory.'" She paused. "Yes, well, we know that story, do we not?" Lady Isabelle patted Miss Cottlebury's hand. "At any rate," Miss Cottlebury continued. "This darkness does not have material form. But Mr. Ellsworth now has everything he needs to give the darkness a shape and allow it to walk in our world."

Margaret looked at the others, whose faces mirrored her horror. "But why?" she said. "Why would anyone do such a thing?"

"I cannot answer that," Miss Cottlebury replied. "But I do not think his reasons matter. We must stop him."

"How do we know he has not already succeeded?" Lady Jane asked.

"He no longer has the blood of a sorcerer—unless he uses his own." Miss Cottlebury shuddered. "But according to what I have read, he would not live to complete his spell."

Margaret inhaled sharply, understanding the full meaning of Miss Cottlebury's statement. Mr. Ellsworth had meant to kill her in order to work his spell. Until this moment she had not fully comprehended the extent of her peril. She clasped her hands to still their shaking. No one spoke as the clock ticked away on the mantel.

"Lady Isabelle," Mr. James said into the stillness. "Could you pass me another bun?"

Despite the horror of her realization, a giggle bubbled up in Margaret. She did her best to tamp it down, considering it most inappropriate given the circumstances. But next to her, Mrs. Bristlethwaite chuckled, causing Lady Isabelle to laugh Soon the coven roared with hilarity, while Mr. James sat calmly eating his bun, his countenance a study in contentment.

The laughter settled, and Mrs. Bristlethwaite wiped her eyes. "A little mirth goes a long way toward lightening the fear, does it not? And we need the memory of such lightness to carry with us into battle." She pulled the bell to summon the servants.

"When?" Sir Berwin asked.

"Tomorrow morning," Mrs. Bristlethwaite replied. Margaret's stomach dropped at the thought of facing Mr. Ellsworth again. But she drew a deep breath and lifted her chin. She would not give in to her dread.

Lucy arrived and curtsied to Mrs. Bristlethwaite. "How can I help you, Madam?"

"Thank you for coming so quickly. Gather whatever you need for performing your lost items spell and meet us in the drawing room in half an hour," said Mrs. Bristlethwaite.

"Of course, Madam," Lucy replied.

"Thank you, Lucy." Mrs. Bristlethwaite stood. "Mr. James, could I have a word?"

"But I have not finished breaking my fast," he protested.

"I will send for something from the kitchen."

Mr. James brightened. "Perfect."

"We shall reassemble in an hour to provide Lucy with whatever assistance she needs." Mrs. Bristlethwaite swept from the room, Mr. James in her wake.

Margaret's head swam. A battle tomorrow? How did it happen so quickly?

"Miss Dashwood, are you well?" Mr. Barrington asked.

Margaret looked up. "I—I am merely—"

"I understand your trepidation, Mademoiselle Dashwood," said Lady Isabelle. "We are all frightened. But we shall support each other, *n'est-ce pas?*"

"Of course!" cried Sir Berwin, jumping to his feet. "Not to worry, my dear. You are in good hands." He patted Margaret on her shoulder and then turned to his wife. "Shall we? Perhaps we might be of use to Lucy," he said.

Lady Jane fixed him with a look of incredulity. "What has prompted this change of heart?" she demanded.

Sir Berwin pursed his lips and gazed out the window. "It is one thing to locate a missing stocking in a household. But to find a person somewhere in the world—that is impressive work. I do not think that I could have accomplished it." He paused, still not meeting anyone's eyes. "We might have lost Miss Dashwood had Lucy not intervened. My concerns about everyone staying in their proper places seem rather petty after that, do they not?"

Lady Jane laid a loving kiss on her husband's cheek. "You never cease to surprise me, my dear." With a broad grin, Sir Berwin offered her his arm. "We shall see you later," Lady Jane said as they hurried from the room.

"Monsieur Barrington, I think a turn in the garden would do Mademoiselle Dashwood some good," suggested Lady Isabelle.

"Pardon? Oh, yes," Mr. Barrington said. "That is, would you care to walk with me, Miss Dashwood?"

"I would like that, Mr. Barrington."

"Excellent. Lady Isabelle?"

"*Non, merci, mon ami.* I am content here."

Mr. Barrington pulled out Margaret's chair and offered his arm. Lady Isabelle smiled at Margaret as, blushing, she took Mr. Barrington's arm and allowed him to lead her to the garden.

Outside the morning was fine, and they strolled for some time in silence. Margaret appreciated Mr. Barrington's company, but she was also glad for the absence of conversation. The air was cool, with just a hint of the spring's coming warmth.

"The daffodils have started to bloom," said Mr. Barrington at length, pointing to the cheerful blossoms lining the path. "I am always a little relieved when they return. Although the seasons turn one after the other no matter what we do, I like bearing witness to spring's arrival."

"What a beautiful thing to say, Mr. Barrington."

"I find the most joy in small things, Miss Dashwood. The first appearance of a flower in the spring. The tiny green buds on that tree. The things that we may not notice in service of something grander."

Margaret looked down. "You must think me a very silly girl, Mr. Barrington."

"Oh, no, not at all, Miss Dashwood! I—I meant

nothing—"

"It is true, Mr. Barrington. I have always cherished grand ideas about beauty and love. But now all that I held dear appears rather frivolous. Until I saw the truth about Mr. Ellsworth, I fear I played a role in an elaborate drama."

"Miss Dashwood, I admire your dedication to the idea that beauty and poetry are important. The world can be such a stark place if one does not notice the beauty. I suppose we simply approach the same notion from different sides." He turned toward her. "I consider you a remarkable young woman, Miss Dashwood."

"Thank you, Mr. Barrington. You speak so kindly."

"I speak what I feel, Miss Dashwood."

Margaret regarded Mr. Barrington. How had she never noticed the softness of his eyes? Mr. Barrington returned her gaze.

A footstep nearby drew their attention; Jenkins appeared. "Mrs. Bristlethwaite has sent for you. The coven has assembled in the drawing room."

"Thank you, Jenkins. We shall be right there," replied Mr. Barrington.

"Very good, sir." Jenkins bowed and slipped away.

"I hope we have another chance to walk together, Miss Dashwood. After everything has settled."

"As do I, Mr. Barrington."

Mr. Barrington presented his arm. "We must hurry now. Lucy's magic is not to be missed!"

"Margaret, Barrington!" Mrs. Bristlethwaite's eyes twinkled at the pair of them as they entered the drawing room. "We are all assembled. Lucy, you may proceed."

Lucy, a small pouch in her hand, stood in front of the table on which was spread a map of England held down by a candle at each corner. Lucy closed her eyes and whispered to herself. Margaret strained to hear, but could not make out the incantation. Across the table from her, Sir Berwin watched Lucy with interest.

With a deep breath, Lucy opened her eyes and cast a handful of herbs from her pouch onto the table. They scattered across the map and sat, motionless. Margaret thought the spell had failed until the herbs drew themselves into a small circle in the area of the map marked "Yorkshire." In unison the coven leaned forward. Suddenly, the circle exploded, sending herbs everywhere. Margaret brushed them out of her hair. Mr. Barrington picked them from his eyebrows.

"What happened?" Mrs. Bristlethwaite asked.

"I do not know." Lucy appeared bewildered. "That was my grandmother's strongest spell." She looked at Mrs. Bristlethwaite. "Shall I try again?"

"Absolutely."

Margaret held her breath as the maid tried a second time to cast the spell. The herbs again formed a circle. Margaret made note of the location, near a little village in the Yorkshire Dales. This time the circle of herbs began to smoke, and then they burst into flame. Next to Margaret Mr. Barrington muttered an incantation, and the fire was suppressed.

"Did anyone notice the location?" Mrs. Bristlethwaite asked.

"The Yorkshire Dales, near Hawes," Margaret replied.

"What do you suppose caused the fire?" asked Lady Jane.

"I imagine the estate has several protection spells

guarding it," said Miss Cottlebury. "Well done, Lucy," she added.

"Here, here," enthused Sir Berwin.

"Indeed, Lucy. Thank you for your help. Go and have a cup of tea," Mrs. Bristlethwaite said. Lucy favored Mrs. Bristlethwaite with a look of gratitude before leaving. "Agnes," Mrs. Bristlethwaite continued. "You must rest this afternoon. No, I shall entertain no arguments. You have done enough for now. I expect to see you refreshed at dinner." Miss Cottlebury, knowing defeat, grumbled her way out of the room. "I suggest the rest of you prepare as best you can. I shall be in the library should anyone care to join me. We shall discuss our plans for battle over dinner."

With that, the coven adjourned. Margaret returned to her chamber, desiring to work in private. Though she did not care to dwell on what had transpired in the French cottage, she wished to know more about the spells she had cast in English. The power of them had astonished her. Had that power been born of her fear? But then she remembered casting the spell to locate the missing atlas. She had used English then, too, as she did when she and Mrs. Bristlethwaite returned from Dartmoor. Could the strength she experienced in France have come from using her native language?

"Perhaps it was merely a coincidence," she murmured to herself. "But I may as well try."

Margaret moved the small table near the hearth to the center of her room and then placed a vase upon it. Putting all her attention on the vase, she said, "Move here, please." She leapt out of the way just in time as the vase careened across the room, smashing into the hearth and shattering. Margaret stood, staring at the shards for several moments, catching her breath with difficulty. The surge of power she had felt nearly knocked her from her feet. She steadied herself on the back of a chair. Clearly there had been no coincidence.

"Reassemble," she said, waving her hand at the ruined vase. The pieces flew from the hearth and reformed before the vase settled, intact, on the table. Margaret smiled. Gone was her need to create pretty spells. She would much rather have more effective ones, especially in the battle she knew was coming.

Dinner was a quieter affair than usual, as each member of the coven was lost in his or her own thoughts. Only Mr. James seemed unaffected by the looming battle; he ate with his usual gusto and exclaimed over Mrs. Crawford's culinary delicacies.

"We should discuss our plans for tomorrow," said Sir Berwin, setting his fork on his plate.

"We leave at dawn," said Mrs. Bristlethwaite. "After breaking our fast," she added, anticipating Mr. James's concern. "To minimize the difficulty, we should leave from the garden. I do not wish to risk any breach in the protection spell around Barbary Hall. I suggest we arrive at some distance from Ellsworth's manor so that we do not announce ourselves."

"I agree," said Mr. Barrington.

"Do you have any idea what might be protecting his manor?" Lady Jane asked.

Mrs. Bristlethwaite shook her head. "Nothing concrete. But given the reaction during Lucy's spell, I believe the protections are quite potent. We may encounter fire spells or a magical guardian or two."

Murmurs went round the table. Margaret shivered.

"Mr. James will lead the attack," Mrs. Bristlethwaite continued.

Margaret was astonished both at this announcement and at the mumbled agreement from the rest of the coven. Mr. James, to all appearances oblivious to the discussion, reached across the table for another serving of pudding.

"We will have to proceed slowly," said Sir Berwin, "as we have no idea what we face."

"Naturally," agreed Mrs. Bristlethwaite. Both of them fixed Miss Cottlebury with a stern look.

"Oh for goodness' sake. Do you require a promise from me that I shall not rush into the battle?"

"That might go some way toward reassuring us, Agnes," said Mrs. Bristlethwaite.

"Then I promise!" Miss Cottlebury grimaced.

"Thank you, Agnes. We need you fit should we encounter any magical beasts." Mrs. Bristlethwaite patted Miss Cottlebury's hand.

"That you do."

"Mr. Barrington, you and Miss Dashwood will work together," instructed Mrs. Bristlethwaite. "Do not fret, Margaret. I know you would acquit yourself well in battle. But I would like you and Mr. Barrington to find the Urn of Osiris and the King's Diamond. If the rest of us fail to stop Ellsworth, at least he will not be able to perform his dreadful spell without those items." Margaret nodded, her mind too full of what was to come to respond.

After dinner they retired to the drawing room. Margaret could not settle herself to any occupation.

She tried reading, but her thoughts turned too often to subjects she wished to avoid. Then she paced by the windows, but that activity only heightened her agitation. Finally, she sat at the *pianoforte*, touched a few keys, and then played, the music weaving a calming spell over the room's inhabitants.

"Thank you, Miss Dashwood." Mr. Barrington's voice was soft.

Margaret looked up. "Whatever for, Mr. Barrington?"

"For playing so beautifully." He gestured toward the others. "Everyone seems soothed by the music." He pulled a chair closer. "The prospect of battle frightens all of us."

"But everyone appears so much calmer than I do," Margaret said.

Mr. Barrington smiled. "We have more experience at hiding our emotions."

"Are you frightened, Mr. Barrington?"

"Of course I am." He paused, his face darkening. "I have seen too much fighting, though not as much as the others."

Margaret winced at the heaviness of Mr. Barrington's voice. Without thinking, she reached for his hand. Mr. Barrington regarded her, surprised. But he did not pull his hand away.

The clock on the mantel chimed. "We should go to bed," announced Mrs. Bristlethwaite. "Try to sleep. We need all of our strength tomorrow."

CHAPTER XXI

After a night of tossing in her bed, Margaret joined the others just before dawn. Despite Mrs. Bristlethwaite's exhortations, it was clear that few members of the coven had slept well, except perhaps for Mr. James. They broke their fasts in silence, the darkness heavy around them.

As the sun's first rays crept into the breakfast parlor, Mrs. Bristlethwaite rose. "It is time." Margaret's teacup rattled as she set it in the saucer. Terror gripped her. Mr. Barrington helped her out of her chair and offered his arm. Margaret, grateful for his chivalry, accepted it. In silence, the coven followed Mrs. Bristlethwaite to the garden.

She led them to a raised area in the garden's center. Still silent, they formed a circle and clasped hands. Margaret stood between Mr. Barrington and Lady Isabelle. Though their faces revealed no emotion, the coven's commitment surged through the magical binding of their joined hands. Mrs. Bristlethwaite nodded.

"Fold Barbary Hall into the Yorkshire Dales!" the coven cried in unison. Margaret braced herself for a painful journey, but the coven's strength carried them easily through the Fold. They arrived in the misty dales, still clutching hands. Margaret did not even waver in her place. She gazed around at the green hills dotted with sheep and stone. No manor loomed nearby.

"Which way should we go?" asked Lady Isabelle. No one replied, but Mr. James closed his eyes and turned slowly in place.

"What—" Margaret began.

"*Regardez*," Lady Isabelle whispered.

Mr. James continued his slow, smooth revolution. Then he stopped suddenly, and his eyes flew open. "There," he said, pointing. Without waiting for the others, Mr. James set off at a brisk trot.

"Shall we?" Mrs. Bristlethwaite asked.

The coven filed through the early morning stillness, their breath making little white puffs on the cold air. Margaret wished she understood how Mr. James knew where to go, but she held her tongue. As the coven entered a quiet woodland, a sudden prickling in Margaret's skin shocked her. She glanced at Mr. Barrington with alarm. He held a finger to his lips, but took her arm. A heavy, unnatural silence hung over the land, and magic charged the air.

Ahead of her, Mr. James pointed again. Margaret could see nothing but a small clearing ringed by ancient trees.

"Are you certain this is the correct direction?" Lady Jane asked.

"There are no signs of habitation for miles around," said Sir Berwin, a hint of anxiety in his voice.

"Stay back," Mr. James commanded. He stepped forward and raised his arms. "Illuminate!" The depth of his tone startled Margaret. The air in front of Mr. James began to glow. "Destroy the barrier!" Lightning lashed the shimmering barricade. Thunder crashed above the coven. A great crack rent the air, and Margaret gasped as the glow abated.

"The first protection spell is down," announced Mr. James. He reached into his pocket and pulled out a bun, taking a large bite and chewing thoughtfully before slipping it away.

"Well done, James!" boomed Sir Berwin.

"Indeed, *mon ami*," agreed Lady Isabelle.

The others echoed their sentiments. Margaret drew an easy breath, enjoying a slight respite from the trepidation that had plagued her since the previous night.

"Mr. James, I believe we are ready to resume our trek," said Mrs. Bristlethwaite.

Mr. James strode forward, the others in tow. They picked their way through the copse alert for any signs of danger. Margaret thought she spied a field between two ash trees several yards ahead.

"Look," she began. But a powerful wind interrupted her. Margaret leaned into the fierce gale, struggling to remain on her feet. Her bonnet was pulled free, and her hair flew in wisps around her face. Mr. Barrington grasped Margaret's hand and shouted something. A gust, heavy with leaves, whipped his words away. A few yards ahead, a thick branch broke and fell, knocking Sir Berwin to the ground.

"Berwin!" cried Lady Jane through the roaring

wind. She labored to reach him.

"Cease at once!" thundered Mr. James. Everything stilled. Margaret nearly fell over. Only Mr. Barrington's steady hand kept her upright. Mrs. Bristlethwaite rushed to Lady Jane.

"He is insensible," said Lady Jane. "But he is alive."

Mrs. Bristlethwaite's face relaxed, and a relieved sigh rippled through the coven.

"I must stay with him. He may not survive a Folding," said Lady Jane.

"Of course," said Mrs. Bristlethwaite. "Mr. James—is there anything you can do?"

Mr. James circled Sir Berwin and Lady Jane, muttering words Margaret could not hear. When he returned to his starting point, he raised his arms and then brought them down with a flourish. "That should keep you safe until we finish."

"Thank you, Mr. James." Lady Jane's voice was muffled. "Good luck, everyone."

"We will return for you," promised Mrs. Bristlethwaite. She turned to the rest of the coven. "Shall we proceed?"

Mr. James led them out of the trees and into a meadow, hands raised as though he made his way through a dark room, showing no signs of fatigue despite the enormous spells he had just worked.

"How is he managing this magic?" Margaret whispered to Mr. Barrington. "He seems tireless."

"He maintains his strength."

Margaret gave Mr. Barrington a quizzical look.

"Mr. James's love of food comes not from gluttony but necessity," he explained.

"Oh!" said Margaret. Before she could speak

further, however, a tremendous shock rumbled through the earth, knocking everyone off balance. Margaret tumbled a few feet before managing to catch herself. The earth continued to shake, and Margaret clung to the ground, her stomach heaving.

"Miss Dashwood," shouted Mr. Barrington. "Move!" Margaret looked up and saw the earth splitting in front of her with an appalling noise. Just in time, she rolled out of the way. Margaret watched in horror as the crack widened near Lady Isabelle, who tried in vain to escape its progress. With a cry, Lady Isabelle disappeared. Just as abruptly as it started, the shaking stopped.

"No!" screamed Mr. James. He ran to the spot where Lady Isabelle had fallen and threw himself to the ground. Margaret, nearest to him, rushed to pull him back from the deep crevice. She peered over the edge. Lady Isabelle's crumpled form lay at the bottom. Her blue eyes stared lifelessly back up at them.

"Mr. James," Margaret cried. "You must come away from here." Margaret tugged on his arm, but he would not move.

"Please, James." Mr. Barrington took Mr. James's other arm and helped him up. Mr. James appeared stunned. "We will return for her," Mr. Barrington murmured.

Mr. James dried his eyes on his sleeve. A steely gleam replaced his tears, shocking Margaret. She would never have believed him capable of such ferocity.

Dazed, their diminishing band continued walking. Still no sign of the manor house appeared. Margaret scanned the tense faces of her fellows, wishing she could perform some spell that would alleviate their grief. She tried to banish the memory of Lady Isabelle's lifeless form, but it refused to disappear.

No one spoke as they trudged over the wet green earth. Mrs. Bristlethwaite cast frequent concerned glances at Mr. James, who kept his eyes on the horizon and betrayed no emotion. He set a difficult pace, and Margaret soon grew breathless. But she hurried along, determined to do her part to avenge Lady Isabelle.

When the coven finally stopped to rest, Margaret sank gratefully to the ground. Mrs. Bristlethwaite and Miss Cottlebury found seats on a couple of large stones, while Mr. Barrington sat beside Margaret. Mr. James remained standing, searching the area for any signs of the manor.

"He must have hidden it from view," Mrs. Bristlethwaite ventured into the silence.

"But we are close." Mr. James pointed to a spot several yards away.

Margaret followed the direction of Mr. James's arm. Certain that he was correct, she stood and fixed her gaze on the spot. "Show us the truth!" she said. A surge of power passed through her, just as it had in her chamber the day before. The air in front of the coven wavered and something shimmered into view. Ellsworth Hall.

"Well done, Miss Dashwood," said Mr. Barrington.

Although gratified by her success, Margaret could not look upon the Hall without mortification. She had wished to be its mistress, but remembering that desire brought her only shame. Her thoughts were interrupted by a sound growing steadily louder. Hoof beats. Margaret scanned the landscape for their source. Horror seized her as two monstrous creatures larger than any animals Margaret had ever seen raced toward the coven. Their hooves made sparks against the ground. Flames shot from their nostrils. They were equine in shape, with wild red eyes and manes of fire.

"What are those?" Margaret cried.

"Blazing Coursers," Miss Cottlebury replied. "Run, Miss Dashwood!"

"But—"

"Go!"

Mr. Barrington grabbed Margaret's hand and pulled her with him, Mrs. Bristlethwaite just ahead of them.

Behind them Miss Cottlebury's voice joined Mr. James's, already raised in incantation. A scream brought Margaret to a stop. She turned and gasped. Miss Cottlebury and Mr. James were battling the ferocious beasts. But where had they gotten those swords? Margaret stepped closer. The swords sparkled in the sunlight. They were made of ice! With each stroke that the two sorcerers landed, a hiss of steam rose from the animals, yet somehow the swords did not melt. Margaret stood, amazed.

The monster that Mr. James fought shot a huge flame from its nostrils, but Mr. James jumped nimbly to the side. The fire scorched the earth. When the animal reared up in anger, Mr. James plunged his ice sword into its soft belly. With a screech that echoed across the land, the Courser fell to the ground, the ice sword a puddle next to the smoking carcass. Mr. James turned to help Miss Cottlebury, who still waged a furious battle.

The Courser she faced also belched flames, but

Miss Cottlebury did not move quickly enough. The fire scorched her arm, and she dropped her sword. "Blast!" She bent to retrieve the icy blade. But the beast jumped between Miss Cottlebury and her sword, pawing the ground. Mr. James shouted at the Courser, which turned and trotted towards the slight sorcerer. Without thinking, Margaret raced forward.

"Miss Dashwood, no!" shouted Mr. Barrington.

"Margaret, you must not!" exclaimed Mrs. Bristlethwaite.

Margaret ignored their protests and grasped the sword, wincing as the cold stung her skin. "Leave him alone!" she shouted.

The Courser swung its broad head around. Then it stalked toward Margaret. She shivered despite the heat coming from the enormous fiery steed. "You must leave us! We are too powerful for you!" Margaret gripped her sword, steeling herself against the beast's fury. It raked her with its red eyes and then charged. Margaret leapt to the side at the last moment. The angry Courser skidded to a stop and faced her, stomping the ground. Margaret gritted her teeth. "You do not frighten me," she said. The Courser reared, and Margaret raced forward, thrusting the ice sword into its middle. The creature shrieked as it fell backward, crashing to the ground, its entrails steaming.

Trembling, Margaret dropped to her knees and stared at her hands. Her bright red palms stung with the cold. Mr. Barrington knelt by her and took her hands in his, rubbing them to warm them. Their eyes met.

"That was a foolish thing to do, Miss Dashwood."

"I know," Margaret replied.

Mr. Barrington smiled. "But you did it well."

Margaret returned his smile. Mr. James handed her a biscuit.

A few yards away, Mrs. Bristlethwaite tended to Miss Cottlebury.

"Smart of you to bring Lucy's grandmother's burn cream, Mrs. Bristlethwaite," said Miss Cottlebury, her face clenched against the pain. As the salve began to work, she relaxed.

"Agnes, you must go join Lady Jane and Sir Berwin. I will not have you sustain further injury," said Mrs. Bristlethwaite. Miss Cottlebury started to argue, but then she simply nodded and allowed Mrs. Bristlethwaite to pull her to her feet.

"Make sure you exact retribution for this," Miss Cottlebury said to Margaret, indicating her burn. "And for Lady Isabelle."

Margaret wiped the sweat from her brow and nodded.

Once Miss Cottlebury had disappeared from sight, the rest of the Devonshire Coven continued toward the house, alert for any danger. They crossed the sweeping lawns without incident; Margaret was not sure whether to be relieved or terrified. Finally Mr. James, Margaret, Mrs. Bristlethwaite, and Mr. Barrington reached the entry. Breathing heavily, they paused on the path that led to the front door.

"What do you suppose we shall find inside?" Mr. Barrington asked.

Mrs. Bristlethwaite pressed her handkerchief to her forehead. "More of the same, I imagine," she replied. Margaret trembled.

"What are we waiting for?" Mr. James stepped forward. "Open!" he shouted. The door ripped from its frame and hurtled over their heads, stirring the air as it passed. Margaret clasped her hands to her chest, panting.

"Was that strictly necessary, Mr. James?" Mrs. Bristlethwaite asked.

Without answering, Mr. James entered the manor. Margaret, Mrs. Bristlethwaite, and Mr. Barrington followed him into the cool silence of Ellsworth Hall. Their footsteps echoed off the marble of the entryway. The silence unnerved Margaret, as did the emptiness. Should there not be servants scurrying about? Surely someone had heard the door being torn from its hinges!

"Eugenia," said Mr. James quietly.

"What is it?"

He pointed. Mounted on the wall opposite the door was a large wooden staff.

"But I thought he had failed to acquire that," said Mrs. Bristlethwaite.

"I did. At first. But I returned, and Mr. Sadik proved much more amenable," Mr. Ellsworth said from the wide staircase behind them. He hissed several strange words, and a surge of light erupted in the hallway.

Mr. Barrington pulled Margaret to the ground as the light shot past them, radiating heat.

Mrs. Bristlethwaite whirled and sent a globe of golden light toward Mr. Ellsworth, which he deflected easily. Mr. James pulled the Staff of Adalet off the wall. He weighed it in his hands. Then he stalked toward Mr. Ellsworth, grimacing.

"Put that down!" ordered Mr. Ellsworth. He swept his hand toward Mr. James.

The Staff wavered in Mr. James's hands, but he

clung to it as he continued to advance. Mr. Ellsworth snarled, and Margaret recoiled at his transformation.

"Margaret, Barrington, run!" Mrs. Bristlethwaite commanded.

Mr. Barrington took Margaret's hand. Margaret resisted, unwilling to leave Mr. James and Mrs. Bristlethwaite to fight alone.

"Miss Dashwood, please!"

At the entreaty in his voice, Margaret allowed herself to be pulled away. They raced down the long, wide corridor, battle sounds echoing after them. Mr. Barrington paused in the doorway of a salon. Margaret glanced into the room. "Reveal!" Mr. Barrington said. He shook his head. "Nothing here. Come, we must keep searching."

A terrible crash sounded from the front hall. Margaret turned to go back.

"No, Miss Dashwood!"

"We cannot leave them!"

"We must." Mr. Barrington's face softened. "They can take care of themselves, Miss Dashwood. I promise. No sorcerer knows more about battle than Mr. James. But their efforts will come to nothing if we do not find the stolen items. We must keep searching."

Margaret glanced over her shoulder and then looked back at Mr. Barrington. "Then we had better hurry."

They found themselves next in a formal dining room. An enormous oak table dominated the room. Again Mr. Barrington commanded the room to divulge its secrets. Again they were disappointed. Another crash sounded from the front hall, but Margaret followed Mr. Barrington to the next room, an impressive library, where their search proved once more fruitless.

At the end of the corridor they came to a narrow staircase. Margaret struggled for breath as they hurried to the next floor. They paused on the landing, long enough to draw a few deep breaths, before resuming their search. But as room after room disappointed them, Margaret's frustration mounted. She had no idea how Mrs. Bristlethwaite and Mr. James fared, and Margaret worried that she and Mr. Barrington would never find the magical objects in time.

Nevertheless, Mr. Barrington led her onward into the last room in the hallway. They stopped on the threshold, aghast at the sight that met them. At least two dozen different objects formed a large circle, in the center of which stood the Urn of Osiris.

"Where is the King's Diamond?" Margaret said.

"I imagine it is inside the urn, which awaits only a sorcerer's blood. I think Miss Cottlebury was correct." Mr. Barrington strode forward, but at the edge of the circle he stopped.

"What is it, Mr. Barrington?"

"A barricade of some sort."

Margaret reached forward, but quickly withdrew her hand. "Show me!" she commanded. A shimmering haze of fire appeared in the air around the circle. Both Margaret and Mr. Barrington took a few startled paces backward.

"There is an awful elegance to Ellworth's spell," observed Mr. Barrington.

"Thank you, I suppose."

Margaret and Mr. Barrington spun around. Mr. Barrington stepped in front of Margaret and held up his hands. A statuette that had been careening toward them stopped mid-air and then shot toward Mr. Ellsworth. He stooped just before it struck the wall and shattered. Margaret glanced up as Mr. Barrington sent a ball of fire at Mr. Ellsworth, who, with a word and a gesture, turned it to ice. The glittering sphere dropped to the floor and rolled to Mr. Ellsworth's feet. He sneered at Mr. Barrington. "I would have thought you had more to offer, Barrington."

Mr. Barrington leapt aside as a stream of golden light flowed toward him. He caught his balance and then fixed his eyes on the circle. "Collapse!" he shouted.

The air around the magical objects softened. Mr. Barrington had destroyed the protection spell. Margaret dashed toward the urn, but Mr. Ellsworth roared, "No!" He made a slashing gesture, and Margaret hurtled toward the far wall.

"Miss Dashwood!" cried Mr. Barrington from the other side of the room. Just before Margaret hit the wall, something cushioned her. She slumped to the ground, winded but otherwise unscathed. Mr. Ellsworth repeated the slashing motion, and Mr. Barrington brought his hand to his cheek. Blood poured from it.

Margaret's only thought was to help Mr. Barrington. She scanned the room for a weapon. Two long swords were mounted over the hearth, their steel glinting in the daylight. "Come here!" Margaret insisted, hand extended. She caught the sword easily. The hilt felt familiar to her grasp. Without knowing why, she faced Mr. Ellsworth and swung with all her might, cutting the air in front of her. Mr. Ellsworth clutched at his side and backed away from Mr.

Barrington.

Margaret advanced on Mr. Ellsworth, swinging the sword side to side. But Mr. Ellsworth held up his hand, and the sword stopped. He uttered more strange words and clenched his hand into a fist. The sword was ripped from her grip and flew to the other side of the room.

"I am impressed, Miss Dashwood. The Sword of Calder tells few people its secrets. Alas, now it will no longer obey you. Nothing in this room will obey you."

Mr. Barrington stepped forward. "Bind," he began.

But Mr. Ellsworth swung toward him, hand raised. "Enough!" he bellowed, and Mr. Barrington crumpled to the floor.

"Mr. Barrington!" Margaret cried, but he lay unconscious at her feet. Mr. Ellsworth took her by the arm.

"Now, Miss Dashwood, I would like to get on with my spell."

"What—what will you do to me?" Margaret asked.

"I will drain much of your blood into the urn. It will not hurt. You will merely fall asleep." He glanced down. "I could use Mr. Barrington's blood, of course. But I think yours would be more *poetic*. Do you not agree?"

Horrified, Margaret struggled with all her might, but she could not free herself from Mr. Ellsworth's grip. He dragged her into the circle and pulled her down next to the urn. In her terror Margaret suddenly longed for her father. He would stop Mr. Ellsworth, if only he were still alive.

"There is no one here to help you, Miss Dashwood. Stop resisting, or I shall have to hurt you."

"But I am not alone, Mr. Ellsworth." Margaret's voice trembled. She closed her eyes. "Guards!" she shouted.

Mr. Ellsworth's frightened gasp told Margaret that she had succeeded. She opened her eyes. Two familiar ghostly figures flanked Mr. Ellsworth, whose countenance tightened in terror. "No, no you cannot do this! Do you have any idea what—?"

"Take him," Margaret said with a steady voice.

The Guards crossed their axes, one in front of Mr. Ellsworth and the other behind. With a slight bow of the head to Margaret, they faded away, bringing Mr. Ellsworth with them. The faint echo of Mr. Ellsworth's frightened cries hung on the air, chilling Margaret to the bone. Suddenly she felt the weight of all that had happened and collapsed onto the floor next to Mr. Barrington. But a new thought burned her. *The atlas!* Had she lost it forever? She looked to the spot where Mr. Ellsworth had stood, and her heart leapt. Something small sat on the carpet. Unable to stand, Margaret crawled toward it. With a cry of relief, she hugged the atlas to her chest.

CHAPTER XXII

"*M*iss Dashwood?"

Margaret looked up. Mr. Barrington was struggling to sit. She hurried to his side and helped him. "How do you feel, Mr. Barrington?" Margaret hid her alarm. His face was pale. Blood stained his shirt and coat.

Mr. Barrington managed a grin, which turned into a grimace. "Not particularly well, but I shall survive." He glanced around, puzzled. "Where—?"

"I called the Ghostly Guard. They took Mr. Ellsworth, although I know not where."

Mr. Barrington fixed her with an astonished gaze. "You summoned the Ghostly Guard?"

"Yes. Did I make a mistake?"

"Oh, no, Miss Dashwood! Quite the opposite— you have done something remarkable. Calling the Ghostly Guard is no simple feat! It requires strength and skill."

"Oh, I see." Margaret blushed.

"And the atlas?" Mr. Barrington asked.

Margaret held it up.

"Well done, Miss Dashwood!" Again Mr. Barrington winced when he smiled. The cut on his face still bled a little. Margaret touched her handkerchief to it gently. Mr. Barrington remained still.

"Lucy will know how to fix this."

"Never mind. A battle scar never did anyone harm."

Their eyes met. "I am glad that you survived the battle, Mr. Barrington."

"And I, you. But you have a cut on your forehead, Miss Dashwood." Margaret touched her face. When she pulled her fingers away, they were covered in blood.

"Goodness," she said.

Gingerly, Mr. Barrington reached into his pocket for his handkerchief, which he applied with gentleness. "I suspect Lucy will set you to rights as well. We should find the others and return to Barbary Hall." He came to one knee and made his careful way to standing. Then he assisted Margaret to her feet. They started out of the room, but at the threshold, Margaret hesitated.

"What is it, Miss Dashwood?"

She gestured toward the circle of magical objects. "We should not leave the Urn of Osiris and the King's Diamond. We may as well carry as many of these as we can."

"A splendid idea, Miss Dashwood."

Margaret tucked the atlas into her coat pocket and then began collecting items. She handed the urn and blue diamond to Mr. Barrington. They managed to retrieve a good number of the objects, though they had to leave larger pieces behind.

"We can return soon," Mr. Barrington said.

Margaret followed him into the hall and then shut the door. "Lock," she said. With a click, the door obeyed. "The rest of the objects will be safe until we return." She turned to Mr. Barrington. "You do not look well. Lean on me—I can support you." Mr. Barrington hesitated. "Please, Mr. Barrington." With a sigh, he leaned against Margaret, who wrapped her arm around his waist. She did not mind bearing some of his weight.

They made slow progress down the hall, stopping once for Mr. Barrington to catch his breath. Margaret hid her concern and urged him onward—the quicker they could return to Barbary Hall, the sooner he would receive the tonic.

They found Mrs. Bristlethwaite at the end of the hall, crumpled against the wall. "Mrs. Bristlethwaite!" Margaret cried. Stomach clenched with dread, she helped Mr. Barrington to the wall. He leaned against it as Margaret hurried to Mrs. Bristlethwaite's side. She took the older woman's hand in hers. It was warm. Next Margaret put her cheek close to Mrs. Bristlethwaite's mouth. Her breath brushed softly against Margaret's cheek. "She is still alive,' Margaret said, her voice catching.

Mr. Barrington's face reflected Margaret's relief. "Of course she is," he said.

"What should we do? I do not think we can carry her."

"For Heaven's sake, Margaret, I do not need to be carried." Mr. Barrington and Margaret jumped. Mrs. Bristlethwaite squeezed Margaret's hand. "Did you get the atlas?" Her voice held an edge of worry.

"I did," Margaret replied.

"Thank goodness!"

"How are you feeling, Mrs. Bristlethwaite?" asked Mr. Barrington.

Mrs. Bristlethwaite considered him. "Probably no worse than you." She touched her head. "I just have a little bump. Ellsworth hit me with something that felt like a solid piece of wood." Despite her reassurances, Mrs. Bristlethwaite required several more minutes of rest before she could sit upright and even more before she could walk, her hand on Margaret's unburdened shoulder.

The three of them limped toward the main staircase, Margaret supporting the other two valiantly. They made their way downstairs, stopping often to rest. The arm holding Mr. Barrington began to ache, but Margaret soldiered on, unwilling to let go.

They had just managed to get down to the entry when Miss Cottlebury rushed in. "There you are! Oh, thank goodness," she said, tears staining her cheeks. "I thought—I thought—"

Mrs. Bristlethwaite let go of Margaret's shoulder and hobbled to Miss Cottlebury. "I wondered how long your patience would last." She laid her hand on Miss Cottlebury's shoulder. "We are fine, Agnes. Just a bit bumped and scratched."

"And frozen," Mr. Barrington added softly.

The three women turned. Mr. James stood near the wall, arm extended, a thick coat of ice surrounding him.

"He will need thawing. Are you up to it, Agnes?" asked Mrs. Bristlethwaite.

"With a little aid," replied Miss Cottlebury. "Miss Dashwood, I need your assistance."

"Of course!" Margaret helped Mr. Barrington to sit

on the stairs and then joined Miss Cottlebury.

"The incantation is simply 'Thaw!' But we must concentrate on melting the ice without burning Mr. James."

After the trials of the day, Margaret welcomed this sort of difficulty. She took Miss Cottlebury's hand, amazed at its strength, and said, "Thaw." Slowly the ice encasing Mr. James began to melt until he stood there, wet and shivering.

Mr. Barrington removed his coat. "Here, Miss Dashwood."

"Thank you," Margaret said. She wrapped the coat around Mr. James's quaking shoulders. It engulfed the small man.

"Lucy has her work cut out for her," Mr. Barrington remarked.

"A—a c—c—cup of tea and a b—bun would be nice; do you not think so, Miss D—Dashwood?" said Mr. James through chattering teeth.

"I do think so, Mr. James."

"That will do, James," said Miss Cottlebury, but her tone was light. She took Mr. James's arm. "We have to collect the others and go home."

The band of wounded warriors left Ellsworth Hall. "We shall have to come back, you know, to see that each item returns to its rightful home," said Mrs. Bristlethwaite as they crossed the wide sweep of lawn outside the manor house.

"Miss Dashwood has anticipated that necessity," said Mr. Barrington. "And we have already retrieved several of the items."

"Well done, Margaret!"

"She also thought to secure the remaining objects with a lock spell." Admiration filled Mr. Barrington's voice.

"Your father would be so proud," said Miss Cottlebury. "Did you find the atlas?"

"I did."

"What happened to Ellsworth?" Miss Cottlebury asked.

By the time Margaret had finished her tale, the small group had arrived at the rift in the earth. Mr. James dropped to the ground at its edge. His shoulders began to shake, and Margaret knelt next to him, taking his hand.

"She was a wonderful friend," said Mr. James through his sobs. "I shall miss her terribly."

Margaret said nothing, but her eyes blurred with tears.

"We cannot leave her here," he whispered.

"Margaret, stay with Mr. James. With Miss Cottlebury's assistance, Mr. Barrington and I will collect Sir Berwin and Lady Jane. Then we shall all return to Barbary Hall. The *entire* coven."

While the others limped away, Margaret remained behind with Mr. James, who cried quietly. Margaret felt dreadful. She had admired Lady Isabelle, and she could not help but believe that she was responsible for her death.

"I am sorry, Mr. James," Margaret whispered.

Mr. James fixed her with his enormous blue eyes. "Whatever for, Miss Dashwood?"

Through her tight throat Margaret managed to say, "I believe Lady Isabelle would still be alive if it were not for my folly."

"Oh, my dear girl! Lady Isabelle—like the rest of us—entered this battle of her own will. The fault lies squarely with Mr. Ellsworth, who is being more than adequately punished, I imagine. No, Miss Dashwood, you are not to blame." He patted her hand and then turned his gaze back to the hole in the ground.

It was a solemn group that returned to the safety of Barbary Hall with the atlas's aid. They staggered inside, and Mrs. Bristlethwaite rang for Lucy and Jenkins, who arrived in the drawing room almost immediately.

"Lucy, we shall need tonic for everyone. And please bring the Purple Stone of Dawlish."

Mr. Barrington began to protest, but Miss Cottlebury interrupted. "No, we must use it to restore ourselves. We have a grueling task ahead, Mr. Barrington. The sooner we finish restoring everything Ellsworth stole, the better off the world will be."

Mr. Barrington assented. Lucy curtseyed before leaving to retrieve the tonic and amethyst.

"Jenkins, please see that Lady Isabelle's remains are given the proper care. And I need you to make the arrangements for her funeral. We have letters to write and travel to organize," instructed Mrs. Bristlethwaite. "She would have wanted to be buried on her family's estate, and I intend to fulfill those wishes."

"I will help you, Jenkins," said Mr. James, his small face somber.

"Very good, Madam. Sir, if you would come with me," said Jenkins. Mr. James cradled Lady Isabelle's limp form in his arms as he followed Jenkins from the room.

Margaret saw Mr. Barrington settled onto the sofa close to the fire and then helped Mrs. Bristlethwaite to a large chair. When Lucy returned, Margaret administered the tonic and the amethyst while Lucy saw to the more serious wounds. Staying busy kept thoughts about all that had passed at bay. After the injured coven members had received care and been assisted to their chambers, Margaret stood by the drawing room window. Despite her crushing fatigue, she was afraid to go to her bed. She did not wish to close her eyes only to remember Lady Isabelle broken at the bottom of the chasm or the expression on Mr. Ellsworth's face when the Ghostly Guard trapped him in their crossed axes. She pulled on her pelisse and went out to the garden. The pouring rain did not deter her.

She reached the small bower where she and Mr. Ellsworth had spent a happy morning and could no longer contain her tears. So deep was her misery that she did not hear Mr. Barrington's approach; indeed, she had no idea anyone was near until he sat beside her on the bench.

"Miss Dashwood," said Mr. Barrington, placing a gentle hand on her arm. "You must rest. You are exhausted."

"But I cannot rest, Mr. Barrington," she said, giving voice to her thoughts. "Whenever I stop moving, I remember every detail. I am to blame for all of this," she gestured toward the house. "For your wounds, for those of Mr. James, Miss Cottlebury, and Sir Berwin, and for Lady Isabelle's death. I am to blame for everything." Her voice dissolved back into sobs.

"No, Miss Dashwood, you must not think so. Every member of the coven knew the risk involved in this battle. Not one of us holds you accountable for any part of it."

"Mr. James said the same."

"He is correct." Mr. Barrington studied her. "Why do you think you are to blame, Miss Dashwood?"

"Because—because I allowed myself to be deceived. I thought Mr. Ellsworth loved me, and I played a silly part in an invented romance." Margaret blushed furiously. "But he never did. He just wanted to get to the atlas, and I let him."

"Among many other things, he was a fool, Miss Dashwood. A fool who did not see your worth." Mr. Barrington paused, looking down at his feet. "I hope—I hope you will forget him soon. There are others more inclined to see you for what you are."

"And what is that, Mr. Barrington?" Margaret held her breath.

"A talented sorceress with a good heart."

Tears spilled out of Margaret's eyes at his kind words. "Thank you, Mr. Barrington," she whispered. Mr. Barrington brushed a tear from her cheek and smiled. His face was still pale. "Mr. Barrington, you should not be outside in this weather!"

"Neither should you, Miss Dashwood," Mr. Barrington replied, standing. "Come, we should both go inside."

Margaret stood and took his arm. Together they went into Barbary Hall, Margaret's heart a little lighter.

CHAPTER XXIII

A few days after the coven returned from Lady Isabelle's funeral, Margaret arrived in the breakfast parlor and found Mr. James alone at the table stirring his porridge, an absent expression on his face.

Margaret took the seat across from him. "Mr. James?"

"Oh, Miss Dashwood. Good morning." His voice was flat and soft.

Margaret watched him, nonplussed by his disinterest in his food. "Would you like a bun?"

Mr. James shook his head. "No, I have enough here." He set his spoon down and pushed back his chair. "But I think I shall...." His voice trailed away. He stood staring out the window before turning abruptly and striding from the room.

Margaret watched him go, sadness mingling with regret. Despite everyone's assurances otherwise, she still laid some measure of blame for Mr. James's devastation at her own feet. Had it not been for her folly, perhaps—she arrested the thought. With a sigh,

Margaret poured a cup of tea and set a bun on her plate.

"Good morning, Margaret," said Mrs. Bristlethwaite. She took Mr. James's abandoned seat, pushed aside the half-eaten porridge, and inspected Margaret's countenance. "Your forehead shows no sign of a scar. Lucy's healing skills have grown quite impressive!" Mrs. Bristlethwaite poured a cup of tea.

Margaret touched her forehead and then dropped her hand. She picked at the bun without much interest, aware of Mrs. Bristlethwaite's keen attention.

"What is it, my dear?" Mrs. Bristlethwaite said at length.

"Mr. James." Margaret indicated the porridge. "He has not eaten much since—since Yorkshire."

"My dear, he suffered a dreadful loss. He will no doubt grieve for some time before he returns to himself. In the meanwhile, we have work to do, which is the best salve for a broken heart."

Margaret knew that Mrs. Bristlethwaite spoke the truth but wished that it were not so. She sipped her tea and took a proper bite of the bun. It went a little way toward restoring her.

"I have been meaning to speak with you, Margaret, but have not had the opportunity until now, with all the arrangements and then the journey to France."

"Oh?" Margaret replied.

"Your use of English incantations did not escape my notice. What prompted your change of heart?"

Margaret looked at the room's small fireplace, reminded of the hearthstones in the French cottage. "When I faced Mr. Ellsworth in France, I was too terrified to remember any French words. Out of desperation, I shouted a spell in English. It was the most powerful spell I had ever worked. At the time I wondered if that power might simply have come from my fear. But later I remembered having a similar experience on two other occasions. So I tried casting another spell in English in my chamber. The results astonished me." Margaret paused, unsure whether or not to continue. At the kindness in Mrs. Bristlethwaite's eyes, she decided to tell the truth. "I chose potency over poetry."

"A wise choice, my dear. There are some sorcerers who believe that simplicity results in the strongest magic. I count myself among them."

Margaret fixed Mrs. Bristlethwaite with a searching gaze. "Why did you not attempt to dissuade me from my practice?"

Mrs. Bristlethwaite set her teacup in its saucer. "From long experience I have learned that people discover certain truths best on their own."

"What if I had not reached this conclusion?"

"An excellent question, Margaret!" Mrs. Bristlethwaite chuckled. "On occasion, I have been known to push someone toward a new discovery."

Jenkins appeared at Margaret's side. "A letter has arrived for you, Miss Dashwood."

"Thank you, Jenkins," Margaret replied, taking the letter. She turned it over and saw her mother's handwriting. "Will you excuse me, Mrs. Bristlethwaite?"

"Of course, my dear."

As the morning was fine, Margaret brought the letter to the garden. Eager to learn her family's news, she settled herself on a bench bathed in spring sunlight. She pulled her shawl a little closer against the cool breeze and began reading.

Dearest Margaret,

I hope my letter finds you well and still enjoying your visit with Mrs. Bristlethwaite.

In answer to your questions: we look forward to the baby's arrival in the next few weeks. Yes, Marianne still complains about remaining in bed, but she manages to entertain herself with books, just as she did when she was a girl. Colonel Brandon remains devoted to her and does whatever he can to help her pass the time in comfort. Her children also cheer her immeasurably.

Marianne bade me thank you again for the gift of dried flowers. She keeps it about herself always and claims that it brings spring indoors. She longs to return to the peace of Delaford, but must content herself a while longer in London.

You have not mentioned dear Mr. Ellsworth in your latest letters; am I to assume a lovers' quarrel has occurred? Worry not, my dear. I have no doubt of his affection for you.

Margaret shook her head. She would have to tell her mother something about Mr. Ellsworth. For the time being, she put that sad business out of her mind.

Alas, my dear, Marianne has summoned me, and I must hurry along. I look forward to your next letter.

With great affection,

Mama

Margaret smiled, her heart filled with affection for her mother and sisters. She would write letters to everyone that afternoon.

A shadow fell over her bench, and Margaret looked up. "Miss Dashwood? I am not disturbing you, am I?"

"Not at all, Mr. Barrington." Margaret moved aside. "Please, join me!"

Mr. Barrington accepted her invitation. He indicated the letter on Margaret's lap. "Good news, I hope?"

"A letter from my mother. Everyone is well, although my sister Marianne has had enough of being bound to her bed. I expect a letter announcing my new niece or nephew soon."

"That would be good news, indeed!"

They sat in companionable silence, enjoying the sunshine and birdsong. Margaret noticed that Mr. Barrington's wound had all but healed. She could tell that in certain light a scar would be visible, but otherwise he retained no marks from their battle with Ellsworth.

At length, Mr. Barrington turned toward Margaret. "There is no scar," he said, running a gentle finger over Margaret's forehead. Their eyes met, and Mr. Barrington withdrew his hand. "I apologize, Miss Dashwood. I should not have presumed."

In answer, Margaret laid a gentle hand over his cheek. "Lucy has nearly erased yours, but I know that it is there."

Mr. Barrington grasped her hand, holding it in place. "Do you mind?" he whispered.

Margaret shook her head. "Nothing can mar a countenance so dear to me," she replied with feeling. Then she blushed and looked down.

"I am glad, Miss Dashwood." Mr. Barrington drew her hand away from his cheek and kissed it.

Another moment passed before Mr. Barrington stood. "As much as I would prefer to remain here indefinitely, I have been charged with delivering you to the drawing room. Will you accompany me, Miss Dashwood?"

"Of course, Mr. Barrington." Margaret took his proffered arm. "Nothing would give me more pleasure."

Margaret was surprised to find the entire coven gathered in the drawing room. Under Lucy's skillful care, everyone's battle wounds had mended, but Margaret suspected that they bore deeper scars that would take longer to heal.

Mrs. Bristlethwaite rose and held out her arms. "Margaret, we have decided, unanimously, to invite you to become a full member of the Devonshire Coven."

Stunned by this pronouncement, Margaret brought her hands to her mouth.

"But—but it has not yet been a year," she spluttered.

Mrs. Bristlethwaite raised an eyebrow. "Do you wish to wait?"

"Oh, no! Not at all!"

"Good. Then we may proceed." Mrs. Bristlethwaite opened a wooden chest that rested on a table near the window. She drew out a large, ancient book and laid it on the table. "Miss Dashwood, come here, and we shall perform the ceremony of membership." Margaret joined Mrs. Bristlethwaite. The book was open to a page containing several signatures and dates with room for one more. "Miss Margaret Dashwood, you have demonstrated fortitude, resourcefulness, and impressive power in the service of the coven, but before you inscribe your name into the Book of the Devonshire Coven, you must take the vows. Are you prepared to do so now?"

Margaret gave an enthusiastic nod. "Oh yes!" Several of the coven members laughed good-heartedly.

"Very good. Miss Margaret Dashwood, will you swear to abide by the code of the coven, to practice magic only for the good of your fellow beings, to put life and friendship before power, and to defend your sisters and brothers in magic?"

"I do!"

"Then to seal your dedication to our causes, you may inscribe your name in the Book." Mrs. Bristlethwaite handed Margaret an elaborate quill pen with which Margaret signed her name, happiness attending every stroke. When she finished, everyone cheered.

Mr. Barrington smiled at Margaret. "Welcome to the Devonshire Coven!"

The others voiced their agreement.

"Lady Isabelle would have been so pleased," said Mr. James quietly.

"Thank you, Mr. James," Margaret replied, touched by the sentiment.

Sir Berwin cleared his throat, interrupting the chatter.

"Yes, Sir Berwin?" Mrs. Bristlethwaite said.

"I do not mean to infringe upon Miss Dashwood's celebration, but I wish to raise another item of business."

"By all means, Sir Berwin."

He cast a shy glance around the room. "I would like to invite Lucy to enter into an apprenticeship with us."

Stunned silence met his request. Lucy, who had been laying out the tea, froze, her eyes wide.

"Indeed?" Mrs. Bristlethwaite said at length.

"Yes," Sir Berwin replied stoutly. Next to him Lady Jane smiled.

"I suppose we may as well put this to a vote—unless anyone wishes to discuss this item of business further?" When no one replied, Mrs. Bristlethwaite continued, a little nonplussed. "Well, then, who agrees with Sir Berwin?"

Everyone raised a hand.

"Does anyone disagree?" Mrs. Bristlethwaite looked at Miss Cottlebury, who made no motion. "Lucy, do you accept the offer of an apprenticeship—contingent, of course, upon your successful completion of a trial?"

Lucy drew a breath. "I would be proud to accept." She blushed at the cheers that met her statement.

"Excellent!" Mrs. Bristlethwaite said. "Of course, we must maintain the utmost secrecy. No need for the Sorcerer's Council to get wind of our activities."

"Indeed," said Sir Berwin to general agreement.

"At our next meeting, we shall determine a suitable task. Margaret, I think you will enjoy helping us to decide!" Mrs. Bristlethwaite invited the coven to take their seats, adding an extra wave for Lucy. Margaret took her place at the table, beaming with pride. "In the meanwhile," Mrs. Bristlethwaite continued, "I think we should attend to the other matter at hand, namely that it is time to return the stolen items to their rightful places."

"And then tea?" whispered Mr. James.

Mrs. Bristlethwaite's eyes shone. "Yes, Mr. James. And then tea."

FIN

ACKNOWLEDGMENTS

Despite the hours spent alone in front of a computer, no writer can claim sole credit for any written work. My debts extend across centuries and over oceans. Jane Austen supplied my heroine in her pre-teen form, Norland Park, and the delightfully nasty Fanny Dashwood. J.K. Rowling's Harry Potter books still kindle my imagination and inspire the magic of my Regency series. Emma Thompson's splendid adaptation of *Sense and Sensibility* gave me a Margaret fascinated with world travel and infatuated with an atlas. To these marvelous women, I extend my gratitude.

Several people closer to home provided invaluable feedback and support. As always, I am grateful to my writing partner and sister-in-spirit Emily June Street, who carefully shepherded Margaret through several drafts with her usual astute suggestions for revision and gentle reminders that some darlings have to be released. Christine Kam-Lynch, always a stalwart supporter, applied her keen eye for detail to a later draft, giving generous advice and pointing out errors and inconsistencies. Jessica Grey offered encouragement from afar. Julien Modéran and Caroline Kostecki provided beautiful French translations for Margaret's spells. Any linguistic errors are purely mine. Throughout the writing of this book, my husband Dave Peticolas offered a willing ear as I brainstormed ideas at the dinner table. He also suggested two key plot changes that gave Margaret a much more satisfying shape. For that and a world of other reasons, I thank him.

ABOUT THE AUTHOR

Beth Deitchman wrote her first book in third grade. Since then she has also had short-lived but very entertaining careers as a dancer, a university lecturer, and an actor. These days she writes and teaches Pilates in Northern California where she lives with her husband Dave and dog Ralphie.

Follow @beth_deitchman on Twitter
www.bethdeitchman.com
www.luminouscreaturespress.com

Read more Regency Magic in Mary Bennet and the Bloomsbury Coven from LCP!